Gin Palace Girl

Gracie HART

Gin Palace Girl

1

Ebury Press, an imprint of Ebury Publishing,
20 Vauxhall Bridge Road,
London SW1V 2SA

Ebury Press is part of the Penguin Random House group of companies
whose addresses can be found at global.penguinrandomhouse.com
Copyright © Gracie Hart 2021

Gracie Hart has asserted her right to be identified as the author of this Work in accordance with the Copyright, Designs and Patents Act 1988

This novel is a work of fiction. Names and characters are the product of the author's imagination and any resemblance to actual persons, living or dead, is entirely coincidental

First published by Ebury Press in 2021

www.penguin.co.uk

A CIP catalogue record for this book is available from the British Library

ISBN 9781529104134

Typeset in 12/15.5 pt Times LT Std
by Integra Software Services Pvt. Ltd, Pondicherry

Printed and bound in Great Britain by Clays Ltd, Elcograf S.p.A.

The authorised representative in the EEA is Penguin Random House Ireland, Morrison Chambers, 32 Nassau Street, Dublin D02 YH68.

Penguin Random House is committed to a sustainable future for our business, our readers and our planet. This book is made from Forest Stewardship Council® certified paper.

To Zoe, our lovely daughter-in-law.

Chapter 1

Twenty-five-year-old Mary swept away the lonely tear that was running down her cheek as she watched the handful of dirt and soil scatter on the top of her foster mother's coffin. The distant memory of doing the same at her birth mother's funeral flooded back as she looked down on Nell's coffin. She had so much to thank Nell for. After her mother Eve's untimely death, Nell had rescued her from a life in the workhouse orphanage. Together, Nell and Eve had seen hard times and good times when they had lived in the yard of the Mucky Duck and through it all they had been the best of friends until Eve's death. Now, after Nell dying of pneumonia, Mary had neither mother and she felt lost. She stood back and said a quiet prayer before turning and smiling at Toby, whom she regarded as her best friend and brother.

'Well, at least she is in peace now,' Toby whispered, before holding his breath as the cough that had plagued him most of his life came over him. Toby took Mary's hand, gripping it tightly as they looked down into the grave and then across at Robert Jones, who looked stern, dressed in his long black coat, his hard bowler hat tucked under his arm. He, too, was showing his respect for the death of the woman he had loved in his own way and had lived with for twenty-one years. He'd never got around to actually marrying Nell, but to the force he worked for and the rest of the outside world, they were known as a married couple, to keep up appearances. He turned to scowl at the gravediggers who hovered like jackals at a kill as the day's light ebbed.

Toby echoed Robert's thoughts. 'Pity he never lived up to his promise of marrying Nell. I don't know what he'll do now he's lost the second woman he loved,' Toby said quietly as he looked at the father he was no longer close to because Robert had changed so much over the years as his position and responsibility in society grew. He caught his breath as a bout of coughing struck him.

'No, I can't think either,' Mary said. 'In fact, now Nell has gone, I think it's time for me to go my own way. I've not been keen on the looks that he's been giving me of late. Remember, he's no relation of mine and he owes me nothing, and I've caught him looking at me the way a foster father shouldn't look at his daughter. I even caught him spying on me as I bathed in front of the kitchen fire the other evening – I saw his reflection in the mirror as he hid behind the kitchen door. I shouldn't really tell this to you; after all, it's the last thing that you want to hear about your father.' Mary shook her head and then went silent as Robert walked around the grave's edge and joined them.

'That's her gone, then. She was a grand woman, was Nell. I'm going to miss her, but she couldn't have carried on living the way she was.' Robert Jones looked at Toby and Mary and then put his bowler on his head. 'I'm away for a gill with some of my colleagues; I'll be back later this evening, so keep the door unbolted because I'll be late if I know this lot.' He looked at a group of men who were waiting for him to join them and then stared at Mary. 'Leave me something out for my supper; I'll need something to soak the ale up before I go to bed.'

'Aye, I will, Father,' Mary said softly, looking down at her feet so as not to look into the steely grey eyes of the man who, of late, she was beginning to fear.

'And you,' he said to Toby, 'make sure the horse is fed and that there's enough coal in the bucket to keep me warm when I return. I want nowt with having to see to jobs that you two can do. It's no good having a dog and barking yourself.' He gave Toby and Mary a backward glance as he walked away to his group of friends, who slapped him on his back and gave him their condolences once again as they walked away from the graveside.

'He's changed since Nell took ill,' Toby said. 'I know he's the head of the local constabulary and that he does a good job for the people of Leeds, but he's no longer the kind man that he once was. He was all right when he first brought Nell to live with us, after the death of my mother – and, despite his reservations about you coming to live with us, he was a good father to us both. However, of late he seems to have decided he could have done a lot better for himself and has grown ashamed of me, you and Nell.' Toby reached for Mary's hand. 'I thought that at least he would have had a funeral tea for her, but instead he's drowning his sorrows in the Bluebell with his cronies.'

Mary shook her head. 'I know it's hard for you, but I think he expected you to follow in his shoes; instead, you love your horses and have no wish to be of importance. Don't worry, Toby, let him be – he's best left alone in the mood he's been in of late. He did his job and brought us both up and I think, with Nell gone, it's time we moved out and let him get on with his own life. I've not said anything to you before now, but I've been and looked at a place in Riley's Court the other day – I can just about afford the rent because I thought it best if I moved out, things being like they are,' Mary said, seeing the shock on Toby's face.

'You'd leave me alone with him? He might be my father, but there's not a day goes by that we don't argue; you or, bless her, Nell, always acted as the buffer between us.' Toby's face dropped. 'I'd be out on my arse as soon as you left. He's told me often enough that it was time for me to be finding a woman of my own and settling down. Which is all right for him to say on the money he brings home, but I earn next to nowt in the livery stables. Besides, nobody will have me; I'm not exactly reliable with these dodgy lungs of mine and I'm not that fussed about taking a wife. I don't want the responsibility,' Toby moaned as they stepped out of the churchyard and onto the busy streets of Leeds.

'I'd not leave you behind if you don't want me to; you can come with me, as long as you pay half the rent and do a few odd jobs around the place. We'd have to lie to the neighbours, perhaps, and tell them that we're true sister and brother, else they'd think I was just living with you and I'm not having that. The place I've looked at does have two bedrooms, but there is one drawback: it backs onto the railway line, so it's noisy.'

Mary hadn't really wanted to leave Toby behind but, at the same time, she was beginning to need a life of her own. With Nell dead, she thought it was the right time to strike out on her own in life because the last thing she wanted was to be stuck at home, looking after a man she no longer trusted. She'd made a small living doing mending and sewing for those who were not so skilled in that area. However, now she had found the place in Riley's Court and had been cheeky enough to ask the bar manager at Laithwaites, in the centre of Leeds, for a place of work if one came available. She'd no intention of keeping house for Robert, to be there at his beck and call like Nell had been, and that, she knew, would be what happened if she did not make a move now. And it could even be worse than that: Robert Jones had never been a truly loving father to her and now, having caught him looking at her in a certain way, she knew that she would no longer be safe from his advances, living under the same roof as him.

'If you'll have me, I'll come with you. I do love my father, but I sometimes think he doesn't feel the same way about me.

I know he's fed us and clothed us over the years and I know we are both grateful for that. I might be his son, but I just know he's not got the time of day for me, that he thinks I'm a failure. So, aye, I'll join you in your new venture. No one will know different that we're not related through blood – and if the neighbours do think different, then let them talk. We know that we are just as close as sister and brother but nothing more – it'll be their dirty minds that have it any other way.' Toby grinned and winked at Mary. 'Can't we do better than Riley's Court if I'm to help with the rent? That place fair shakes when trains go past and there's some rum folk live there.'

'It's all right, the cottage will soon be made clean and tidy; there's even a table and chairs in the kitchen and two beds left from the previous tenant. There's an outside privy that the four houses share – and granted the curtains twitched in the houses next door when I looked around it, but that's just what we would have done if we were to have new neighbours. One old lass even came out and asked all about me, but she seemed all right. She only wanted to know if I was single or married and was more concerned that I hadn't a brood of children than anything else. She didn't want the noise of them in the yard, despite her house backing onto the railway line,' Mary said and laughed.

'She'll be the nosy one, then, the one everyone moans about. We'll have to keep her sweet.' Toby sighed as they made their way down the busy paved street to the wharf and the warehouses of the Leeds-to-Liverpool canal, to the square-set house that stood on its own and was home to them and had seen them live happily, with Nell to care for them, until her death.

Mary unlocked the front door and entered the hallway, taking her shawl from her shoulders and stopping for just a moment as she looked at the hat hanging up on the coat stand – Nell's flamboyant hat. She sighed and felt tears come to her eyes as she looked at the blue ribbon that had been tied at an angle so jauntily when Nell had been well enough to venture into Leeds for shopping. Now she was gone and, even though the house still smelt of her and every room had a memory of her in it, the house down by the wharf was no longer their home and they both knew it.

'I'll bring some coal in and feed and water Buster, else I'll get a tongue-lashing off Father.' Toby hung his cap on the hallstand and looked around the gloomy house. 'Lord knows what time he'll get back – or in what state. He doesn't have much to say for himself until he gets the worse for a drink and then he's hard to shut up. I don't know how my mother and Nell put up with him all these years, him and all his cronies from the police force.'

Toby walked off down the central passage and out of the back door, leaving Mary standing alone. She closed her eyes and tilted her head back, thinking of the previous days when Nell had lain upstairs dying. She owed everything to the kind woman that had taken her in when her own mother had died in her arms and Nell had been true to her promise of always being there for guidance and love, but now Mary knew she was on her own once more, albeit older and wiser – but even at her age she still craved a mother's love. Working-class girls were invariably married with children on their knees while she had kept herself from loving any man and now she just craved the love and kind words of her mother. She dropped her head and sighed, making her way into the kitchen, where she looked at the range and the fire that needed to be coaxed back into life again, the embers nearly out. She scrunched the newspaper that she had read the previous day into a ball, pushing it into the dying coals along with some dry kindling sticks from the hearth. Next, as the flames rose, she added lumps of coal and watched as the fire came to life. She lifted the blackened kettle from off the trivet and shook it to see how much water it held and then, knowing that it was nearly empty, went out into the yard where the water pump stood and filled it full.

She could smell the hay that Toby was feeding the horse in the stable as she pumped the water from out of the well and it reminded her of summers when she, Toby and Nell had walked down by the River Aire and watched the farmers in their fields making ready for the winter months to come. Now, most of the land around had been claimed for houses and factories, for Leeds was growing with every day that went by, gobbling up the outlying farmland with industry, all in the name of progress. The rich seemed to be growing richer, while ordinary, everyday folk only just managed; she'd noticed that more and more, even though living under the roof of Robert Jones meant that she never went without. It was strange times.

'Here, give us that here,' Toby called as he walked out from the stable and across the yard, brushing the remnants of hay from his jacket. 'That's the hoss fed, so I'll get the coal in and then that's me done for the evening.' He took the filled kettle from Mary's hands and opened the back door for her. 'What's for supper, our lass? Don't tell me I've to finish that brawn that you've been feeding us for the last day or two – anything but that!'

'No, I'll fry some bacon and eggs once the fire gets going a bit. I can make Robert a sandwich to come back into; he likes cold bacon and a fried egg and that'll line his stomach after a night on the pop.' Mary took the filled kettle and placed it on the hook above the fire to boil.

'Aye, he'll need something to sober him up and we're best away to our beds before he comes back home, else I might say something to him about Nell not having a funeral tea – and it'll only cause a row.' Toby lifted the brass coal scuttle up from the hearthside and looked at Mary. 'I keep thinking that he could have spent a bit of brass on a tea for her, it's only right.'

'I know, but he didn't and there's nowt we can do about it.' Mary reached for the flitch of bacon that was hanging from the kitchen ceiling and cut into the cured, fatty roll with her long sharp knife before placing it in the well-used frying pan. 'Just keep your head down and your mouth shut until we definitely have the house in Riley's Court. I'll go and see about it tomorrow and pay the deposit, then we can move in, come Friday. And maybe by then I'll have got myself better work than taking in sewing and mending as I do at present. I only started sewing and mending so that I could nurse Nell and keep house.'

'Nay, not Friday! You know what they say, "Friday flit, short sit!" Make it Saturday or even Sunday. And what's this better work you're on about?' Toby looked at Mary; she'd been keeping a lot of things to herself of late, it would seem.

'I'm after a job at Whitelock's. Lord knows if I'll get it and I don't even know if I'll fit into the position of barmaid, but I can but try. After all, that's what my birth mother did at one time, so it should come easy. I've not been blessed with her voice, else I'd have loved to have starred in the music hall like her and I know I take a bit of sewing in at the moment but I'm fed up of mending other people's clothes.' Mary grinned as she placed the pan with the bacon on the now-glowing fire.

'Never! What do you want to do that for? And at Whitelock's. You'd be better keep doing other folks' washing than serving all the drunks in Leeds that go there.' Toby shook his head in disbelief.

'It might be, but I think I've got a good chance of being taken on there. The owner himself I know to be a right good man. He sometimes talks to me when I go up the market. He was telling me that he's renovating the place and will be in need of staff shortly. Anyway, it's a way out of here and that's what I need, what we *both* need if we are to leave here and Robert Jones. You know and I know it's only a matter of time before he throws us both out, especially if he finds another woman to replace Nell. Beggars can't be choosers, Toby, and I have a feeling that I'll fit in well there now it's had some money spent on it. I need something more than doing folks mending and keeping house.' Mary looked at a crestfallen Toby.

'I think you're wrong in giving everything up to go behind a bar and serve any Tom, Dick and Harry. You're following in your mother's footsteps – and think how that ended.' Toby looked at the bacon and egg put in front of him and shook his head.

'Unlike my mother, I'm wise to the city's ways. Nell brought me up to recognise wrong'uns and to keep my wits about me. I'll be fine, Toby. You know me, enough cheek for the devil himself and more besides. Now stop worrying, eat your supper and let's have an hour or two's peace before we get out of Robert's way. I aim to get to bed and bolt my bedroom door before he returns. Now Nell's dead, who knows what's going through his head? I really don't trust him.'

'He wouldn't be so daft as to force himself on you, would he? He'll have gone to one of his haunts like he's been doing when Nell was dying. He thinks himself a just and good man but he's still got his old traits of liking a loose woman. Nell, however, was sometimes thankful of that, I'm sure – it gave her a bit of peace.' Toby blushed, talking to Mary about his stepmother and Robert's sex life was not comfortable for him.

'I don't know what he'll do, but I'm taking no chances. I also know, no matter what, I'm leaving. He thinks nothing of me; it was only because of Nell he put up with me. You make sure you lock your door and all, else he might pick a fight with you over your work if he's been thinking about it.' Mary sat down next to Toby and started to eat her bacon and egg.

'He hates my guts, I'm his only son and he hasn't got the time of day for me.' Toby bowed his head.

'Hey, stop feeling sorry for yourself. Tomorrow the house in Riley's Court will be secured by me and we'll leave your father to do as he likes. He need no longer look at us. He can go around town as head of the constabulary, a respectable man to those who don't truly know him, and he'll soon find himself a new housekeeper who will fulfil all his needs.' Mary said her words with a trace of bitterness, because although Robert Jones had been good enough to take her and Nell into his home, it had not been without a price being paid by all. His word, both in the town of Leeds and in his own home, was law – and woe betide any of them who ever stepped out of line. It was time for her and Toby to break free from his grip and tomorrow she would see to that, come hell or high water.

Mary lay in her bed, hearing Robert downstairs knock a chair in the kitchen over before staggering upstairs to bed. It was as she suspected, he'd drowned his sorrows with one too many gills and now he was finding it hard to climb the stairs. She held her breath as she heard him breathing heavily at her bedroom door and swearing as he tried the handle only to find the door locked. She hardly dared move while she listened to him swear again and then reconsider his actions as he stumbled along the corridor to his bedroom. Tomorrow could not come soon enough; even if the house in Riley's Court was next to the gates of hell, she was going to rent it and take the job at the famous Whitelock's Ale House. She was never going to replace Nell as Robert Jones's private prostitute in all but name.

Chapter 2

Mary stood on the flagged floor of the small two-up, two-down and looked around her. Toby was right, Riley's Court *was* squalid. It was a long way from the house that they had been living in down by the wharf but at least, in this one, they would not be living under the same roof as Robert Jones. She looked out of the dust-covered windows where spiders had made their home and sighed. It was a big step for her to take, but it had to be done.

She watched as the yard outside was suddenly filled with black and grey smoke that wisped down from the steam engine that she could hear trundling down the track behind the small terraced houses that had been narrowly saved from demolition when the now-busy railway had been built. She would have to secure a job at Whitelock's if she was to pay the rent that she had signed for and not be evicted within the first few weeks of her tenancy. She breathed in the coal-filled fumes of the steam engine and watched as smuts floated down behind the owner of her new home. Old

George Summerfield, the landlord, put the sixpence into his worn leather purse and passed her the key to number two Riley's Court; his mittened hands were as filthy as his craggy, dirty face and he grinned as she looked at him with doubt in her eyes.

'It's a grand little place and you'll soon make it home. I should have charged you more, but I'm not a greedy man, I just need enough to make myself comfortable in my old age.' He smiled again, showing his rotten teeth, and pulled his old ragged coat around him. He was dressed like a scarecrow but everyone knew he was richer by far than his appearance would have people believe.

'I suppose I will; a fire in the hearth and some curtains up in the window will make all the difference.' Mary looked at the old man and watched as he grinned before looking around him for a sign of his other tenants in the small square that he owned.

'Bloody old Tess is not to be seen and she owes me last month's rent so I'll away and knock on her door; she'd better not think she can live for nothing in these most precious properties. I can soon find somebody else to fill them, so I can do without her sort. I'll be wasting my time, though, for she'll not answer and I'll have to send one of my boys round and demand it from her, as usual.' George shook his head. 'She's an old bugger; she knows she can't get away with it but she has to be threatened with eviction nearly every month before I get any brass out of her.' He turned and looked at Mary. 'Don't you be taking lessons from her, for I'll not be as sympathetic with a lass your age – it's only because she's on her last legs that I put up with her.'

'I won't. You'll have no problem getting your rent from me and my brother, Mr Summerfield; we'll make sure we pay on time.' Mary watched him walk across the cobbled yard and knock on the door of the neighbour she knew to be in. As when she had looked at her new home, the off-white lace curtains had moved as Tess had watched for George Summerfield. Now Mary turned her back on him and smiled as she heard him swearing and shouting threats at his absent tenant before shuffling out of the yard. She couldn't help but admire the old woman who made her landlord wait for his rent – if her cottage was like Mary's it was really only worth half the sum he was charging, but just like her, beggars could not be choosers, and as long as it was dry and clean, that was all that mattered, she thought, trying to convince herself as she stood in the one room that served as both kitchen and living space and looked around her.

The kitchen hearth needed blackleading and the stone-flagged floor needed a good scrub and then there were the two bedrooms upstairs to tackle; both really needed a coating of limewash to freshen and clean them before they were lived in. She couldn't help but think that Toby would be disappointed with his new home, but for now, it was all they could afford and he'd have to appreciate that. Mary climbed the uncarpeted stairs to the two bedrooms and looked out of the front bedroom window. She smiled as she watched the door of Tess's cottage open and the old woman come out and check that her landlord had gone, keeping her front door open for the late summer's light to fill her rooms. She picked up her cat that was wanting her attention and trundled back into her home.

In the back of Mary's mind were memories of living in a similar yard, with her long-deceased mother; they'd had no money, but what they did have was love for one another. She could just remember her mother's soft features, remember, too, the minute that Nell had pulled her away from her dead mother's side to her new life with Toby and Robert Jones. How her heart had ached – and now she felt the same as she had then, vulnerable and lost, but she knew, as she wiped a tear away, that she had to make her own life and feeling sorry for herself would do no good. She sniffed and breathed in hard and looked at the key in her hand. It was time to put the next part of her plan into action; there was no time for sorrow if she was to make the best of her life – and standing there blubbing didn't pay the bills, so she would have to just get on with it and figure out when was the best time to move into her new home – hopefully, without confrontation from Robert Jones. But first, it was a walk into the centre of Leeds to persuade the manager of Whitelock's that she needed a full-time job . . .

As she set off, Mary wished yet again that she had been blessed with her mother's voice, for she would have loved to appear at the music hall as her mother had. But before her music hall success, Eve Reynolds had worked as a barmaid and Mary was going to pay no heed to Nell's warning words when she was alive about the men who would take advantage of her and the long hours on her feet. It was her life now so she would do what was needed to get by – and the refurbished Whitelock's was going to be just the place to learn the trade. She walked up through the busy market street of Briggate, chin fixed firmly and her head set on the job in hand. She was in her best dress and her green hat with its jaunty feathers was perched on her thick dark hair at an angle, but still she felt her heart beat fast as she stood at the entrance of the ginnel leading down to Whitelock's Ale House, where two workmen balanced a new sign for the well-established public inn.

So, it was changing its name as well as its appearance, Mary thought, as she saw a modern scripted sign bearing the name Whitelock's Luncheon Bar on it. The sign was just the beginning, she discovered, as she entered into the low-set room. The old bar that she had seen from gazing through the windows in the past had been replaced with a smooth cream and brown marble counter that was decorated on its side with flowered tiles in green, cream and brown, interspersed with brown columns, and behind the bar was row upon row of bottles of spirits that shone and beckoned the drinker, while huge etched-glass mirrors reflected the clientele. The only thing remaining from the alehouse that had once served Turk's Head Yard until the Whitelock family had taken it over was a solitary window with the old Turk's Head engraved on the glass panes on it.

Mary gasped as she looked around her; this was going to be one of the poshest eating and drinking places that there had ever been in Leeds and she only hoped that she would be lucky enough to convince the owner, John Whitelock, to take her on as a member of staff. Beer was now the working man's preferred drink because it was by far the cheaper way to get drunk and forget your sorrows than gin and whisky and he'd need plenty of staff to keep his empire running. Combined with serving food, the new Whitelock's was going to be no ordinary public house, she thought, as she noted the elegant chairs and polished tables for people to dine at. The place was immaculate.

'What do you think? It's cost the family a pretty penny, but I think it's worth it.' John Whitelock stood back and admired the latest designs that made his bar look the height of fashion and desirability.

'I've never seen anything quite like it. It's magnificent.' Mary looked around, awestruck.

'It's cost a pretty bob or two and my family thinks I'm partly mad, but I've told them that we will make our money back if I have my way.' He grinned and then looked serious, hoping that he'd be proved right. 'Now, what brings you here? Are you still after employment with me? I'm not the best of bosses but everyone says I'm fair and, as you can see, we expect to be serving quite a few folk when those doors are properly opened. It'll not just be anybody that I let in, though.' He looked the lass up and down; he'd spoken to her on many occasions when she visited the market in Briggate and knew her to be the adopted daughter of Robert Jones, the respected, if disliked, police inspector. If she worked for

Whitelock's, John would have the law in his back pocket and she was certainly bonny enough to be seen behind his bar. Besides, he needed lasses like her if he was to expand his plans even more. This would be a luncheon club for the well-to-do, if he had his way, not a beer-swilling den of iniquity and he wanted his staff to reflect that.

'I would like to, if you would have me, sir? We have just buried my foster mother and I have decided that I need to seek permanent employment and become independent. I've walked here from a cottage that I've rented in Riley's Court because I no longer want my foster father to feel that he is obliged to look after my well-being. After all, he is no blood relation of mine.' Mary spoke openly, not realising that she was being considered because of her relationship with Robert Jones.

'Oh, I see … But you'll still be regarded as his family, I presume?' John quizzed her.

'I don't know, sir, I would hope so.' Mary smiled, shrewdly realising that John Whitelock would like to count Robert Jones as a friend rather than an enemy, like any alehouse owner in the growing town of Leeds.

'Then, I'll find you a place in my establishment. We'll discuss your position and wages when you start with me on Monday. I have to see to the drayman shortly and I've got a delivery of glasses from the Yorkshire Glass company scheduled, so you'll have to excuse me – I haven't the time today to see to a slip of a lass. Come back on Monday at seven o'clock in the morning and I'll put you about your job.'

He turned away from Mary; perhaps he should not have taken her on if she had fallen out of favour with Robert Jones, but there was something about her . . . she had a spark to her as well as the looks, so she'd be all right serving his customers behind the bar or, if she wasn't up to that, she could always be replaced.

Mary couldn't help but smile as she left Whitelock's; she'd got a job, a new home and she was about to break free of Robert Jones and, with Toby, make her own way in the world. The next thing that they would have to do would be confront Robert and tell him that they were leaving him and their home along the wharf. Would he be angry or would he be glad to see the back of them? He'd be losing his housemaid and cleaner but that's all, and Toby and he had not been seeing eye-to-eye for a long time, both jostling for position in the three-bedroomed house that they called home and in which both she and Toby had felt like unwelcome guests of late. She would be glad to leave, no matter that the small cottage in Riley's Court was little more than a hovel; she'd soon have it looking homely – and it would be wonderful to work in the newly refurbished Whitelock's, meeting and serving the drinkers there. Life was grand and she would embrace what it threw at her, be it good or bad.

'Bloody hell, Mary, you haven't wasted any time! A new home and a fresh job – now all we've got to do is tell our so-called father.' Toby leant back next to the stoneware sink in the kitchen where he had just washed his face and hands before sitting down to eat the evening meal which Mary had prepared for them, plating one up for later for the absent Robert Jones. The smell of carbolic soap surrounded Toby, eradicating the smell of horses that always accompanied him, as Mary put his supper on the table.

'Well, I told you what I was about last night. Now I've gone and done it. So, are you coming with me or are you staying here? Because, knowing you, you'll have changed your mind in the cold light of day and I'll have rented a house that I can't afford on my own.' Mary sat next to Toby and looked at him, waiting for a reply.

'I'm coming with you. You're not leaving me here on my own. Now, when are we flitting, that's the question, and do we tell the old bastard or not?' Toby picked up his knife and fork and started to eat his mutton stew.

'I was thinking of leaving on Saturday, seeing you were so against leaving tomorrow. So we will have to tell your father. Besides, there are one or two things that I want to take with me. I know I came with nothing, but over the years, since leaving school, I've worked as you know sewing and mending for the more respectable ladies of Leeds. I've bought one or two bits for the house, as you have. We could do with taking our own mattresses and there isn't much furniture in the cottage at Riley Court – a table and two chairs is all.'

Toby looked serious.

'So we're leaving a perfectly good home for a place that has nothing? Do you think we're doing right? I know you don't trust my father, but he has given you a home for over twenty years. And I'm not like you, I can put up with him despite the odd gruff word.' Toby looked around him; he was comfortable in his home although he knew it was only a matter of time before another woman would come on the scene, perhaps with her own children, and that would be when he'd be thrown out of the family nest.

'You just don't want to confront him, Toby! Well, I'll tell him when he comes in, and at least if he throws us out tonight, we have somewhere to go, even if we have no beds.' Mary held her thoughts back as she looked at her foster brother; sometimes Toby was weak and she knew he was intimidated by his father's position and reputation in Leeds. But ordinary people didn't really know Robert Jones – and if they knew his love of women and betting, they wouldn't hold him in such high esteem. She looked up through the kitchen window and saw the man they were speaking of coming down the path and quickly put her finger to her lips. 'Say nothing until he's had his supper, I'll pick my moment,' Mary whispered as the front door opened and Robert entered the hallway before putting his head around the kitchen doorway.

'I see you two are eating me out of house and home. I just hope that you've left plenty for me after the day that I've had.' Robert hung his long coat up on the coat stand at the bottom of the stairs and balanced his bowler hat on the hat peg before entering the kitchen and sitting across the other side of the table from Toby. 'I've been busy all day, trying to get to the bottom of a fella being stabbed by another in the Globe Yard. Oh, it's a sordid spot! It wants knocking down and the Globe Inn with it, both only attract the worst of society.' He sighed and looked across at Mary. 'Well, get my supper, lass, I'm waiting!'

Mary got up, leaving her own supper partly eaten, and went to the side oven to get his. 'Mind, the plate is hot and I've put you some cabbage and potatoes on because I didn't know how long you were going to be.' Mary watched as Robert scowled at his plate.

'You should know by now I don't eat cabbage. You're not anywhere as good as my first wife at cooking – she knew how to look after me.' Despite complaining, Robert set about the supper with a will and, although he had moaned about the well-boiled cabbage, he ate that too before sitting back in his chair and commenting about the silence around the table when all had eaten their fill. 'You're both quiet tonight. You always had plenty to say when Nell was alive.'

'Nowt to talk about for nowt's happened; I've been at work in the stables all day and I don't know what our Mary's been up to,' Toby quickly replied and then glanced at Mary, who said nothing but cleared the places off the table.

'Aye, well, happen you'll talk more tomorrow night for I'm going to be gone this weekend. Me and some of the lads are going to the York Races. We're getting tickets for the new stand they erected a couple of years ago and we'll have a flutter on a horse or two, so you'll be shot of me for a day or two.' Robert sat back and glanced at them, trying to catch the mood.

'That'll be good for you. It's a good job I've ironed all your shirts and starched your collars this morning. Do you want me to pack them for you?' Mary looked across at him and said nothing more.

'Aye, you can do that and then I'm away to my bed. We are catching the six o'clock train from the station in the morning – there's nothing like getting an early start and a few whiskies down your neck before the racing starts. They'll be better than the old nags that you look after, lad; these are thoroughbreds, not old clapped-out hacks.' Robert slapped Toby's back as he got up from the table and sat next to the kitchen fire.

'I'll go and see to your packing, and then I'll come down and wash the pots up.' Mary glanced at Toby as she left the table and knew that he wouldn't dare tell Robert that they were about to leave the unhappy home.

'Aye, I'll be up there myself in a minute and put what I think I may want in my case. I'll take that small leather one with my initials on it, which will do just the job.' Robert watched as Mary left them and went up the stairs.

Mary made her way up the stairs to what had been Nell's and Robert's bedroom. She glanced at the picture of Nell on the dressing table and smiled sadly. She missed her and this was no longer a home without her there. She reached up to the top of the wardrobe and lifted down the small tan-coloured case, with the initials R. B. J. etched into it, and then picked up the matching leather case filled with shirt collars from the dressing table along with a collection of shirt collar studs, which Robert would need to look respectable.

She then walked to the window and reached for the shirts that hung there on the curtain rail and were airing on coat hangers in the warmth of the spring sunlight.

'They'd better be ironed well and fold them right an' all. I don't want any creases,' Robert said as he walked into the bedroom and stood close to her, looking her up and down. 'When I get back from York, me you are going to have to sit down and talk and come to an understanding, now that Nell has left us.' He sniggered.

Mary looked at him and felt her stomach churn; she knew damn well what he meant and she was not about to be a party to it.

'Nell stayed with me because she liked her life here but there were certain things I expected her to do for me. After all, I rescued her from a life of hell and it was only right that she did what she did for me. Your mother was nearly in the same situation, so you should know what I'm asking of you. It's only right that you see to my other needs.' Robert moved closer and ran his hand down Mary's cheek.

'You can think again! I'll iron, clean and cook for you but I'll not be yours to bed,' Mary said as she threw the ironed shirts onto the bed alongside the suitcase, not caring whether they were creased or not as she quickly stepped aside from the leering Robert as he tried to grab her arm.

'You'll see sense once you realise that nobody cares a jot about you. You little fool, I'll bed you when I want, or else out on the streets you go, along with that surly son of mine!' He yelled at her as she made for the bedroom door.

'Pack your case yourself and don't you ever touch me again, else I'll tell everyone in that precious force of yours just what a bastard you are!' Mary stood in the doorway and glared at him.

'And you think that they would believe the daughter of a harlot who was nothing more than a gin soak over *my* word? You'll come around to my ways else it will be the worse for you, my girl!' Robert yelled as Mary slammed his bedroom door behind her and went downstairs to Toby, who looked worried at the shouting.

'Tomorrow, when he's at York, we take what is ours and we leave. And I hope the devil takes his soul!' Mary said as she stood, full of anger, in the kitchen that had once been a warming home for her, but no longer. How dare he speak about her mother like that? She might have sung on the stage but she had never worked the streets; and as for Nell, she had been kindness itself, albeit a prostitute before she came to live with Robert.

Mary didn't even bother getting out of bed or putting breakfast in front of Robert Jones and heard him shout 'Lazy bastards!' as a parting comment before the back door slammed and he went to catch his train for the hard day of drinking and betting that he was to enjoy at York racecourse. She turned over and looked at the bedroom wall. She'd lived in this house for almost as long as she could remember but had never felt as if she truly belonged. Nell had done her best in trying to mother her, but she had only been a substitute for real maternal love. It really was time to leave with her own home and new place of work.

'Are you awake, Mary?' Toby knocked gently on her bedroom door and listened for a reply.

'Aye, I'm awake. Give me five minutes and I'll be up and dressed and make breakfast and then let's be out of this place,' Mary replied in a quiet voice. It was a big step for Toby to take and she knew his stomach would be churning, just like hers, at the thought of Robert coming home to find the note they planned to leave him and some of the contents of the house missing.

'I'll go and saddle Buster and get him ready to pull the cart while you see to breakfast. Don't make a lot, I don't feel like eating this morning. I'm frightened that my father will come back just as we're moving out and catch us. He'll probably be glad to see the back of us, but he'll still kick up a fuss.' Toby leaned on Mary's closed bedroom door and heard her bed springs move as she got out of bed and dressed and washed in the cold water from the jug and bowl on her washstand.

'All right, I'll be down in a minute.' Mary dried her face and stood for a second, thinking that she'd not have the luxury of her comfortable bedroom and the security that living with Robert Jones brought. Likewise, she wouldn't have the worry of his now lecherous ways towards her. It was definitely time to leave, she thought as she watched Toby bring the well-ridden Buster out into the yard and start to put him into his harness. She looked around at her unmade bed and quickly bundled her bedding into a pile and placed it on the bedroom floor; she was tempted to take her brass bed with her as well but thought better of it. They mustn't take too much – but Robert could afford to have one or two household pieces go missing and she'd leave him a note and offer to pay for them once she and Toby had got settled and she was earning better money. She was just thankful that she would not be here when he came back from his weekend at York Races because his mood would depend on whether he had won or lost money and how much he and his cronies had drunk. Yes, time to go and make her own way in the world and try and forget her past, the past that Robert reminded her of on a daily basis.

'Lord, Mary, you can't take any more, else he'll have us put in the nick!' Toby looked at the cart loaded with bedding, pots, and clothes.

With her hands on her hips, Mary looked at the precariously balanced load and scowled at Toby. 'Most of it's mine or yours and we need the mattresses unless you want to sleep on the springs of the iron bedstead tonight. Besides, I'm leaving him this note. And although I've not told him where we're going, I've said in my note that we'll pay for the stuff that isn't ours once we're settled.' Mary looked at the handwritten note and folded it, stepping back into the kitchen and leaving it on the table for Robert to find on his return. She then pulled the back door behind her and locked it, putting the key through the letterbox before turning to look at Toby. 'There, that's that done; once you've returned Buster and the cart we'll have washed our hands of your father.'

'You know, I owe him a lot, perhaps we shouldn't leave him like this . . .' Toby took Buster's reins off and watched as Mary climbed up onto the cart.

'Toby, he takes every penny you earn and he expects me to be his skivvy *and* now his whore if he gets his way. Neither of us owes him anything, he's been paid and more besides for our upbringing and he's never shown either of us much love. If it hadn't been for Nell our lives would have been completely miserable. Now, come on and get up here; let's get this load moved and then you can return the horse and cart before nightfall.'

Toby climbed up beside her and cracked the reins over Buster's haunches and the horse pulled the cart out of the cobbled backyard with a sharp jerk, making Mary worry that the pile behind her might fall off as they trundled along the busy streets of Leeds to their new home at Riley's Court. Once there, Toby looked up at the railway viaduct that spanned the yard and shook his head. 'Lord, Mary, what have you brought us to?'

'It'll be fine, Toby, it's our home now. A proper home where we will be there for one another and not feel beholden to anyone,' Mary said and hoped that she was right.

'It's a shithole – but I suppose it's *our* shithole. We'll make do, won't we?' Toby said and sighed.

'Of course we will – together, as usual, we'll take on the world,' Mary said with defiance as she climbed down from the cart and prayed that she had the strength to prove that she was right.

Robert Jones alighted from the train with his latest conquest, picked up from his weekend at York Races, on his arm. She was funny and entertaining, dressed immaculately, and she hung on his every word as he left his police colleagues behind on the station platform. All of them were jealous of the man who was well past his prime but had managed to pick up such a charming woman. He walked with a smile on his face but inside he was worried that once she realised that he had a ready-made family she would no longer be interested in the man who had wined and dined her all weekend. His heart sank as he walked down by the wharf and then on to his well-built house, hoping upon hope that Mary and Toby would keep their mouths closed when he introduced the exotic Dulcie.

He tried the door but, unusually, found it locked and fumbled in his back pocket to find the key as he smiled at his replacement for Nell. Turning the key, he walked into his usually warm and welcoming kitchen, but now the fire was not lit, nor were the gas lamps, and there was no smell of food being prepared. He turned and smiled at Dulcie and asked her to take a seat while he lit the fire and turned the gas lights on as the daylight dimmed and night encroached on the house on the canal bank. He scowled as he realised that the previous day's ashes had not been cleared from the grate and that there was no sign of either Mary or Toby.

'You keep your house lovely and tidy, honey.' Dulcie crossed her legs and looked around the immaculate kitchen with its well-stocked shelves and the Welsh dresser with its blue and white pottery that stood against the longest wall of the kitchen. She sat back and watched as Robert stood back from the fire and watched as the flames started to leap and catch hold of the coal and kindling sticks which he had hurriedly laid. 'You must have had a good maid because everything is immaculate.'

'Yes, yes, I do, and she should have been here to see to the house on my return,' Robert replied quickly and smiled.

'There's a note here, darling, on the table; perhaps she's left it for you to explain why she's not here.' Dulcie fingered the note and was tempted to read it but Robert quickly took it out of her hands.

'It *is* from my maid, Mary – she says that her mother has been taken ill and she's had to go and nurse her. Bugger!' Robert screwed Mary's note up and threw it on the fire. So, she and Toby had deserted him, the ungrateful buggers. After all the money he had spent on raising them, they had shown their true colours and had left him and taken some of his possessions by the sound of it.

'Are you all right, my love? You look worried.' Dulcie rose from her seat and ran her hand around the back of Robert's shoulders, then whispered, 'Never mind; that means we are alone, with time to ourselves, and there is so much I know that we can do to pass the time . . .' She kissed his neck and smiled.

Robert responded by grabbing her around the waist and kissing her passionately. What did it matter that the two ingrates had left him? They'd only have been in his way now that he'd got a new plaything. He was well rid, he thought, as he hastily unbuttoned his trousers and sought to satisfy his new love.

'There, I told you we'd soon have it looking like a home.' Mary stood with a well-worn brush in her hand and looked around the small living space that was to serve as their kitchen and living room. 'I'll polish the flagstones tomorrow with some lavender polish once I return from my first day at Whitelock's. However, for now, I'm done in! I'm going to have to put my feet up just for a few minutes.'

'Here, I'll take the kettle and fill it up at the pump and make us a brew. I'm ready for a sit-down and all. It's been a hard Sunday, Mary. We don't usually do a lot on the Sabbath except enjoy the day and I'm going to be jiggered tomorrow at work.' Toby picked the kettle up but then coughed and spluttered, trying to catch his breath.

'That cough of yours is getting worse, Toby. Go and get something for it at the apothecaries tomorrow.' Mary frowned with concern, noticing how pale he looked.

'It's the dust from the hay that I feed the horses. It gets stuck on my lungs – it's nothing, really,' he said to Mary, making light of things.

*

'Now then, lad, have you two just moved in?' Tess Butterfield looked at the dark-haired lad who was filling his kettle from the communal water pump in Riley's Court and decided she needed to know a bit about the couple that were to be her new neighbours.

'Aye, which we have. It's been a fair weekend, moving everything and cleaning the place, like, but Mary's nearly got it all spick and span.' Toby stood with the filled kettle in his hand and looked at the old woman.

'Husband and wife, are you? Although I've not seen any children. Maybe some are on the way, eh?' Tess quizzed.

'No, no, no, we're not wed.' Toby shook his head.

'Living over the brush then, are you?' Tess grinned and showed her rotten teeth.

'No, it's not like that, we're sort of brother and sister,' Toby protested.

'Well, you're either brother or sister or not, there's no sort of about it.' Tess grinned again.

'You could say we are stepbrother and sister, but there's nowt going on between us.' Toby was getting annoyed with the nosy old woman.

'Aye, and I've heard that one before and all. Whatever you are, it doesn't matter; you're part of the court now. We've all to get on, no matter what.' She looked hard at Toby. 'I'm Tess Butterfield and I've been widowed for over ten years now. My old man drowned in the cut after having one too many, the selfish bugger, and now I'm dependent on my own ways and means.'

'I'm Toby Jones and my sister is Mary. I work for the livery stable on Swan Street and Mary is to start her new job at Whitelock's Luncheon Bar tomorrow. We are here because my stepmother died recently and we decided not to live with my father after her death.' Toby started to walk away, trying to avoid any further interrogation from the old woman.

'Aye, your sister told me all of that. I was just checking, like! A bad lot was he, your father? You're best on your own if he was like that. You'll be all right now; we all look after one another here.' Tess turned and started to walk back to her home; she'd found out what she needed so now she could go and rest her eyes and have a sleep for an hour or two.

'No, my father wasn't that bad, but we just didn't see eye to eye,' Toby said as she walked away.

'He'd only be doing what he thought was right for you. You young'uns never appreciate the love and time that your parents give you. Anyway, you're here now and I hope that you are happy, both you and your sister.' Tess closed the door behind her.

'I've met Tess; she's not frightened to say what she thinks, is she?' Toby placed the kettle on the hook above the fire and waited for it to boil.

'No, she certainly says what she thinks, does that one. I bet she quizzed you as to how we're related – I had a feeling that she didn't believe me when I told her.' Mary grinned.

'Aye, and she told me that my father would only be doing right by us when I told her we didn't get on with him. Little does she know what it was like to live with him!' Toby sighed.

'That's it, she doesn't know, so stop fretting; he can soon find us if he wants us back. After all, he knows Leeds like the back of his hand. Now, I've made your bate box up for work tomorrow and there's cheese and bread for our supper. Tomorrow, on my way to Whitelock's, I'll stop by the market and fill these empty kitchen shelves so it will soon feel like home.' Mary stood with her hands on her hips and smiled. 'Cheer up, Toby, I'll have a game of rummy with you if you want before we go to bed.'

'No, I'll have my supper and then I might go for a walk out. I need to clear my head before I settle down for the night.' Toby hoped that Mary would not want to join him and he said nothing more as a plate of bread and cheese was placed in front of him and the tea brewed.

'I'll start to shorten these curtains I pinched out of the drawer back home; they'll do just the job for in here with an inch or two taken off them. It might take me a night or two but when they're up, that will stop old nosy Tess looking in of an evening. Not that there will anything interesting to look at in this house.' Mary folded the rich green curtains on the table and looked across at Toby. 'Are you all right, Toby? You do want to live here? It's different for me, Robert isn't my father but I know somewhere deep down you love him – you've got to, he's your father.'

'No, I'm all right. It just feels strange and I keep thinking about our mothers; we never really got to know them, either of us, yet they loved us so much.' Toby hung his head.

'Aye, and so did Nell, but they're all gone now. Time to put the past behind us and look to the future.' Mary held out her hand and gripped Toby's firmly. 'We'll be fine, Toby.'

He lifted his head up and smiled; they probably would be, but he needed to make things right with his father first and that's where he was about to go on his walk later.

Toby went through the garden gate at the house that used to be his home. He tried the front door and found it bolted but he knew his father was at home because the oil lamps were lit in every window and smoke was rising from the chimney. He knocked hard and shouted, 'Anybody at home?' His stomach churned as he heard the sound of footsteps coming to the door and the bolt being pulled back. He'd rehearsed what he was going to say a hundred times on his way back to his old home but now he found himself standing like a mute when the door was opened.

'Yes, what do you want?' Dulcie, in all her finery, stood and looked him up and down, waiting for a reply.

'I-I want to see my father. I'm Toby and I'd like to come in, please.' Toby felt awkward, standing on the steps of his own home, cap in hand and asking permission to see his father. He heard Robert shout through from the kitchen, 'Who is it?'

'He says he's your son and that he wants to see you,' Dulcie yelled back.

'Tell the bastard I have no son and not to bother knocking on this door again!' Robert yelled and then came and stood in the hallway, bare-chested and with his braces down around his waist. He glared at Toby and didn't say anything more.

'You heard the man.' Dulcie turned and looked at Toby. 'Now bugger off and leave us to it – we're busy.' She closed the door on Toby's face and then laughed loudly for him to hear as she ran back into Robert's arms.

Toby stood motionless on the doorstep and then put his cap back on his head. So that was how it was; he was disowned and Nell had soon been replaced. Mary had been right, it *had* been time to move out and make their own way in the world.

Chapter 3

The world was changing for Mary; she was running her own house and seeing to the needs of Toby and now she was running as fast as she could up through the streets of Leeds to her first morning at her job. She swore under her breath as a horse, with its heavy load of coal, shied right in front of her, the wagon driver swearing and pulling on the reins of the protesting beast, making it more scared and problematic as Mary veered out of the way and ran down the alleyway to the white-fronted inn with its new, modern look.

John Whitelock was standing in the doorway. 'Is this the time I can expect you every morning? You're late, by a good five minutes. That's not a good sign; the first morning in a brand-new job and you can't be bothered to get yourself out of bed?' He looked at his watch's face and then fastened the gold case on it and put it back in his waistcoat pocket; the gold Albert chain to which it was attached hung across his chest, securing it.

'I'm sorry, Mr Whitelock, but we only moved house on Saturday and I had to see to my brother and I didn't realise how long everything takes, so the time slipped away from me,' Mary said apologetically.

'Aye, well, you can stop your excuses; the lasses in the kitchen could do with your help right now and then Lizzie, who helps run the bar, will be here by eleven and she'll put you through your paces. You can make up your time, I'll see to that.' He turned and yelled at a lass who was setting the tables out with white embroidered tablecloths and the best of plated Sheffield silver, all engraved on the handles with a cartouche showing the initials JW. 'Nancy, show Mary here to the kitchens; tell Cook to find her some work until Lizzie comes in to show her what to do.'

'Yes, Mr Whitelock.' Nancy bobbed a curtsey and stopped laying her tables. She frowned at Mary as she led her to behind the bar and into the hub of the Whitelock's world, the kitchen.

'His bark is worse than his bite,' she said. 'He's a good boss really. And he's so proud of what the new Whitelock's looks like.' Nancy turned slightly as she led Mary into the kitchen. 'I'm Nancy; I set the tables and clean the silver and sweep the floors and generally make things tidy.'

Mary smiled and followed her into the kitchen where two other girls and a plump woman, who Mary realised instantly was in charge of the kitchen, were busy.

'Cook, this is our new girl, Mary. Mr Whitelock says you've got to find something for her to do until Lizzie comes.'

The two other girls kept their heads down as the cook, Mrs Trotter, came and inspected the new arrival.

'He does, does he? If he'd listened to me in the first place, he'd have got someone to work full-time in the kitchen. It's all very well him having this fancy new menu, but he's not the one cooking it. And then he sets a bit of a class on behind the bar as if to spite me.' Mrs Trotter wiped her hands on her apron and looked Mary up and down. 'You can help Fanny peel the potatoes and mind you peel 'em thin and don't take half the skin off them. Fanny, give her a knife and let her get on with them and then you can do the carrots.'

A young lass of around fourteen looked up at Mary from the sink she was standing at and passed her a knife, nodding to a sack full of potatoes that stood on the scrubbed kitchen floor. 'We need all those peeling and boiling before we start serving at eleven. Put them in the pans over there and then Mrs Trotter will take them as she needs them. We used to just serve them boiled, but seemingly we've got to cook them some fancy way nowadays, baked in cream and cheese with that stinking French garlic that Prudence is peeling with the onions.'

Mary looked at the sack of potatoes and then at the flushed faces of all the girls in the kitchen. Pans of stew were cooking, fresh oysters were waiting to be cleaned and there were enough vegetables and meat to feed an army being prepared. Mrs Trotter was piping elaborate designs on a cake that Mary had never seen the likes of before, as well as keeping her eye on a huge pan of custard that was coming nicely to the boil on the top of the range. The kitchen was working at full steam and Mary could feel nothing but sympathy for the woman who was running it all, seeing how much pressure she was under. She picked up her knife and started to peel her way through the sack of potatoes and no sooner had she filled one pan full than Mrs Trotter took them from under her nose. It was a thankless task, she thought, as the kitchen got warmer with the heat from the ovens and the air filled with deliciousness.

'Aye up, the bloody penguins are here!' Mrs Trotter looked up from what she was doing and put her hands on her hips and nodded at the two waiters who had come into the kitchen. Up until that day they had been dressed in normal clothing, but from now on they had been told to wear black sharp suits with a white starched shirt and bow ties.

'Hold your noise, we feel daft enough,' said one of the waiters.

'Well, I hope that all these changes are going to be worth it. I don't know what John Whitelock's going to do if nobody comes and eats at this spot,' Mrs Trotter said before going to check her oven.

'It's worth it, all right. He's got a queue waiting outside already. Lizzie could hardly get past 'em,' one of the waiters said.

'Oh lord, we have so much more to do and now you'll have to bugger off and leave us!' Madge Trotter sighed and looked at Mary. 'I suppose you'd better go through to the bar and help her, seeing that's what he's taken you on for.

Go on, bugger off, we'll finish them off, you've not many left now anyway.'

Mary was glad to get out of the kitchen and she smiled at the waiters as she passed them.

'Who are you, then?' one asked as she brushed past him. He gave her a glance up and down and nudged his mate.

'I'm Mary, Mary Reynolds,' she replied.

'I'm Frank and this is George. You must be the new lass that's to help Lizzie?'

'That's right, glad to meet you both,' Mary replied, leaving the chaos of the kitchen behind her for the organised bar and restaurant. Frank, she could tell, was the outspoken cheeky one, but both men, she had noticed, were quite handsome.

Mary stopped in her tracks and smiled at a beautiful blonde-haired woman who was busy at work behind the newly fitted bar.

'Now, you must be Mary? I'm Lizzie and I've been working behind this bar for the last two years, for my sins. Or, should I say, the *old* bar, because I don't know if Leeds is quite ready for this posher affair? Although by the looks of the folk waiting outside I think Mr Whitelock might just have made the right decision. There are some fairly posh folks out there, so let's hope that we don't disappoint. Now, have you any done bar work before or am I to learn you everything from scratch?' When Mary said that she had never worked in a bar before, Lizzie shook her head slightly. 'Well, the main thing is to remember to smile and agree with the customer whether you know that they're in the wrong or not. If they get too pushy, like a lot of them do after one or two too many, ask Mr Whitelock or get the two jokers that you've just met to suggest that they perhaps should refrain from another refreshment. That soon brings them to their senses. Now, let me tell you about the drinks …' Lizzie looked around and saw the look on Mary's face. 'Don't worry, a week into doing this job and you'll know everything off by heart.' Lizzie knew that she had no option but to encourage the novice in her job. John Whitelock had made it clear that he wanted her to work for him, knowing that she was the step-daughter of Robert Jones, a man to be humoured if he was to keep a good business in Leeds.

'I don't think I will – just look at all the bottles and casks! I don't know my whisky from my brandy. I'm beginning to think I'm not the right person for this job.' Mary sighed.

'The fellas that come in here usually like the beer and we've three types: a pale ale, a bitter and a stout. All you've to do is pour it from the jugs that are kept under here and smile. It's that easy. And then, if their womenfolk or them want a tot of something stronger, like gin or brandy, there's a measure to make sure you don't give them short. Just watch me for a while and you'll soon get the hang of it.

Most of the time you've just got to smile, no matter what, and listen to some of them moan and tell you their worries. You'll soon get to know who drinks what and who to flirt with and who not to. Although Mr Whitelock says that we have to rise above any dirty talk and act like ladies now that

Whitelock's is going up in the world. That's why he's taken you on, I think; seemingly you've caught his eye.' Lizzie smiled at Mary. 'He thinks you'll be good for this place.'

'Oh lord, I really don't want to disappoint him and I know he's given me a chance without him knowing me that well . . .' Mary looked down at her dress and hoped that she'd met her new boss's expectations.

'He's never wrong; he's got a shrewd eye and he'll expect you to work hard, so don't you worry. He'll soon say something if he thinks you're not fitting into his scheme of things. Anyway, get ready, because here comes George in his new get-up – and doesn't he think himself the one, strutting about and putting his nose up in the air!' Lizzie whispered to Mary as George came through the kitchen doors with a white napkin over his arm and glanced quickly at the girls before going towards the locked doors. The customers were jostling and beginning to lose patience as he pulled the brass bolts of the heavy wooden doors back, opening them wide and making them welcome as they rushed to be the first customers over the new threshold.

Mary and Lizzie watched the customers' faces and listened to their comments as they looked around the new, fashionable décor and realised that the common drinking hole had gone upmarket and was now a respectable luncheon club.

Frank came out of the kitchen and, along with George, enquired who was expecting to eat in the restaurant and then guided them to the pristine tables, pulling chairs out for them to sit on and then giving them a menu card to read. Others just stood at the bar and looked around them before turning to Lizzie and Mary to order their drinks.

'Bloody hell, Lizzie, it's too posh for me now! Old pillock Whitelock must have some brass to do this to a mucky drinking hole in the middle of Leeds. He'll not want the likes of me now.' A scruffy man dressed in his work clothes leaned up against the spotless bar and looked at Mary. 'And he's got himself a new barmaid that looks the part.' The old fella grinned at Mary and then shook his head. 'I'd have a gill, but I think I'm out of place with this swanky lot. I'll go to the Bluebell from here on – I know my place in life and it's not here any more by the sound of some of these toffs that are being served and seen to.'

'Oh, you're welcome to stay, Bill; we still need our regulars. A pint of bitter, is it?' Lizzie smiled and tried to reassure one of her oldest customers that he was still welcome. 'Mary will serve you. She's brand new to the job so have this one on the house.' Lizzie winked at Mary and urged her to get the old man a pint of bitter.

Mary reached for the large, embossed jug behind her and bent down to the barrels filled with ale and slowly opened the tap on the one that had Tetley's Best Bitter written on it, watching the jug fill up with brown frothing ale.

'Hold the jug at an angle, Mary, then it doesn't froth too much, and do the same when you pour Bill his pint.' Lizzie watched her new worker and coaxed her as she pulled Bill a pint and placed it, with a smile on her face, in front of him.

'Well, I suppose it would be rude to leave it,' Bill said and winked at Mary. 'And I have got a new bonny face to look at. I've never yet turned down owt that's free.'

Mary watched as he drank the first pint that she had ever pulled and felt a sense of satisfaction as he wiped the top of his lip free from the froth and smiled at her. She had no time to feel smug, however, as people were queuing at the bar and Frank and George were waiting there with trays demanding drinks orders, which she had to give priority to. By the end of the lunchtime rush she realised that she would be earning every penny paid to her as she leaned back and watched Nancy clearing the tables and refreshing the pristine white tablecloths and cutlery.

'You did well today, Mary, I hardly had to show you anything and the customers have taken to you. I think Mr Whitelock has made the right decision to go posh – more upmarket – we have taken twice the money that we usually do at dinner time, although some of our usual locals soon decided we were no longer for them. I noticed Bill left after he'd supped his free pint.' Lizzie sighed and untied her apron from around her waist. 'That's the last customer for now, so let's go and grab ourselves something to eat before the doors open again – that is, if Cook has anything left. The new menu seemed to be popular and a lot of the great and good of Leeds were in here today – and that will have suited Mr Whitelock.'

'You'll have to tell me who is who; I hardly knew anybody that I served today. I recognised the Mayor only because

Mr Whitelock was making a fuss of him and his wife was demanding attention from George and Frank. She ordered a bottle of wine and George struggled opening it, so she gave him a really dirty look.'

'Yes, she's been in here before and she thinks the world revolves around her. You'll get used to her sort. All in all, I think we've had a successful first lunch and word can only spread if folk have enjoyed themselves. Come on, let's get something to eat and rest your feet for a while.' Lizzie nodded her head towards the kitchen door as George pulled the bolt shut on the last customer of the afternoon.

Back in the kitchen, all the staff were sitting around the scrubbed table looking shattered.

'Bloody hell, we've served some folk today!' George sat back in his chair and lit a cigarette.

'You think you've had it bad? Try cooking for them all and then having to make you lot something. My legs are bloody killing me.' Mrs Trotter rested her ample frame in her usual position at the head of the table after placing a huge pork pie in front of them. 'Fanny, leave those mucky pots and come and join us for dinner. I'm glad I made it last night for us all,' she said as she divided the pie up and watched as quiet young Fanny joined them at the table. 'There's plenty of pickles and there are some rock buns for pudding. Them out there might like their fancy food, but you can keep it plain and simple for us lot. Me, cooking with garlic, the stinking stuff? My mother will be turning in her grave. I don't know why they all think it's so posh, it's stunk my kitchen out all morning. There's nowt wrong with the good old onion.' Mrs Trotter shook her head as she moaned about the new dishes that she had been forced to cook for the more refined diners of Leeds.

'So, Mary, what do you think of the great Whitelock's? Do you think you can put up with us all?' Frank reached for a slice of pie then opened a jar of pickled onions and passed it to Mary for her to help herself.

'I didn't think it would be this busy, but I've enjoyed it so far.' Mary looked at Frank; he had the cheekiest grin she had ever seen on a man and he looked so handsome in his waiter's suit.

'Just you wait until later this evening. Thank the good Lord that we are only open until ten, else we would all be dropping down dead, worked off our feet,' George commented quietly as he stubbed his cigarette out and reached for a piece of the pie. 'Old Whitelock certainly gets his money's worth out of us.'

'Just you be careful what you're saying,' Mrs Trotter snapped and scowled at George. 'He's been in and out of this kitchen and restaurant all morning. And you can thank him for what you are eating, because he doesn't charge you for it. He's a good man with a good business head on him.'

'If you say so,' George mumbled and the kitchen table went quiet as all the staff took some time to themselves before the next rush.

*

The evening service was just as busy as the morning's and Mary found her feet hurting and her head buzzing as she served gin, beer and any of the other drinks that were proving popular with the citizens of Leeds. Some of her customers treated her with disdain and others were polite to her as she tried to do her best on her first day as a barmaid. Lizzie was a godsend to her, telling her how to pour and mix her drinks, pointing out the people who would expect to be recognised the next time they returned. Whitelock's was the busiest place she had ever seen and George was right – you certainly did earn all of your pay. Sitting on one of the velvet-covered chairs at the bar, with the gaslights turned low and the last of the customers gone, she untied one of her boots and rubbed her aching foot.

'You need to come in something flatter tomorrow, else your feet will be crippling you by the end of the week.' Frank stood next to her and looked at Mary as she quickly replaced her boot and stood up to make her way home.

'I think you're right, but I like my boots with a bit of heel on them. I'm not that tall and I prefer wearing them this high.' Mary looked at him as he watched her pull her skirts down around her ankles.

'It's your choice,' Frank sighed. 'Comfort or pride, or, as my mother says, pride comes before a fall, probably literally in your case.'

Mary reached for her shawl from behind the chair and put it around her shoulders, ignoring him.

'Are you walking home alone? Where is home, by the way?' Frank asked casually.

'We've just moved into Riley's Court, so it isn't that far to walk on my own.' Mary looked back at Frank as she made for the door with him following her.

'We! Are you wed then?' He asked with interest as he stood behind the closed doors at the end of the alley that led to Whitelock's.

'No, I live with my brother and he'll be waiting for me. Hopefully, he'll have remembered to leave me something for my supper, but knowing Toby, he'll have scoffed all the stew that I put out for him to warm once he'd returned from the stables.' Mary stood for a second in the dim gaslight and looked at Frank. Was he going to ask to walk her home? She hardly knew him at all and she'd have to say no to the offer if he did.

'Oh, your brother. Then I'll let you be off to him. I live in the opposite direction, up Hyde Park, and my mother will be waiting for me. See you tomorrow, Mary – and wear flat shoes in the morning.' Frank walked off but glanced back at the new lass in his life; she was a bonny one, but not very talkative. Give her time, though, and she'd soon be asking him to walk her home. He'd play it slow for now, but she'd take to him, they always did, the lasses that worked behind the bar, and there had been a lot …

Mary walked home down the cobbled streets. Courting couples were making love in the shadows and prostitutes were plying for trade as the many drinkers came out of the busy pubs and inns while respectable couples walked arm in arm, ignoring the darker side of their home town. It reminded her of her foster mother's previous life, for Nell had once made her living working the streets. Nell had always told her that her birth mother had never lowered herself to those depths, that she had pride and should be remembered for that.

Mary shook her head as a woman yelled at a man for payment for his entertainment. She walked quickly to the safety of Riley's Court and was grateful to see that Toby had placed an oil lamp in the window to welcome her home. As she walked into the yard, a goods train rattled by and billowed smoke down into the yard from the embankment above, sparks of hot ash lighting the night sky up like fireworks. Toby was right: it *was* a shithole they lived in, but they wouldn't be there for long if she had her way; she'd work hard, earn good money and then they could move to somewhere better. No, she would not always live in the small cottage dominated by the noisy railway above it. She had plans for a better life for her and her brother and nobody was going to stop her.

Chapter 4

'You've got a smile on your face this morning. It can't have been all hard work at Whitelock's yesterday.' Toby grinned across the breakfast table as he pulled his jerkin on before eating the porridge that had been placed in front of him. 'You looked jiggered when you first stepped in last night, but I suppose it is your first real job outside of the home, you'll get used to it eventually. Taking sewing in I bet seems a doddle compared to serving folk all day.'

'You can hold your noise when it comes to taking in washing. You're right, I do have a smile on my face because I know more what I'm doing today and I've taken Frank's advice and I'm wearing my old flat shoes so my legs and feet shouldn't hurt as much tonight. Now, there's some cooked meat in the pantry along with some bread and I've put a milk pudding in the side oven to slowly cook with the heat from the fire while we're both out at work. You'll not starve if you can be bothered to get up from off your backside.' Mary shook her head as

Toby had a coughing fit and she watched as he pulled a handkerchief from his jacket pocket and spat into it.

'This bloody cough – I'm fed up with it,' he said quietly as he looked at the contents brought up from his lungs and quickly put the handkerchief back into his pocket before Mary saw what was on it. 'Who's this Frank that you've mentioned? You haven't gone and got yourself a fella already, have you?' Toby looked across at his sister while she hurriedly ate her porridge and noticed her cheeks blush.

'No, I have not! He's just one of the waiters that I talked to yesterday. There's Frank and George, the waiters, then there's Mrs Trotter, the cook, and two or three others help in the kitchen while I help Lizzie Lambert at the bar. She's ever so bonny, Toby, you want to come and meet her; she turns many a man's head.'

'I want nowt with a woman, they only let you down. I'd rather sleep with my horses than a woman,' Toby said as she took his empty dish to the stone sink to be washed. A first love who had cheated on him in his early twenties had made Toby wary of women and had made him decide not to trust any woman ever again other than Mary and his mother.

'Talking of sleeping with horses, I think it's time you had a bath, Toby, you really don't smell right sweet at the present!' Mary don't really like having to tell her brother that he had an odour problem – but he had!

'Hmm, I'll strip off and dip myself in the horse trough before I come home tonight. I'll take this bar of carbolic soap with me. Will that do for you? After all, you can't have a brother that smells of honest man's toil now you're working for the likes of John Whitelock, can you?' Toby picked up the bar of red soap from next to the sink and put it in his jacket pocket.

'Don't be daft, we'll put the kettle on to boil a time or two this Sunday evening and fill the tin bath that's hanging up outside in the yard. You'll be fit to bury, bathing in a horse trough. That cough of yours is bad enough without tempting fate. When I get paid, you can get yourself to the doctor and see what he has to say about it.' Mary went and put her hand on Toby's sleeve and looked at him with sympathy.

'It's alright, it's only a cough. It's the dust off the hay, like I keep telling you,' Toby said defensively.

'Well, we'll see what a doctor has to say about it and never mind the expense.' Mary was not going to let her concern for her brother's health rest so easily; she had heard him nearly every night, coughing and spluttering, and his health, she was sure, was worsening.

'I'm going to work; I'll see you when you come back home. Don't be led on by any of them fellas that you work with. Remember, they're only ten-a-penny waiters – you can do better than that.' Toby looked at his foster sister whom he loved but only in a brotherly way. They had grown up together and he now felt responsible for her. But for how long he would be able to be there to support her he didn't know because the consumption that he knew he was suffering from was wreaking havoc with his body and was getting worse. Soon he would have to tell Mary that it was more than the hay dust that was irritating his lungs and that his life on earth was soon going to be shortened.

'Stop worrying about me, Toby. I'm going to pick myself a millionaire from the ones that come and dine at Whitelock's. A millionaire who has a stable, so that you can look after his horses!' Mary shouted as he left the house.

'Aye, and I'm off to see the man in the moon,' Toby replied before making his way out of the yard to his work.

Mary smiled at John Whitelock as he wished her good morning; he wasn't looking at his timepiece this morning, she'd made sure of that.

'Lizzie tells me you handled your job well yesterday and I'm glad that you did – you fit in well behind my bar. Folk don't want to see a miserable face when they are out to enjoy themselves.' He looked at her. 'Remember to smile, no matter what's thrown at you. You can rant and carry on behind the customer's back once they've spent their money, because you'll need to sometimes. There are some right cases come and go through these doors and the more money they have, the worse their manners, I sometimes think.' John Whitelock was a tough northerner who had made his money through sheer hard work and he despised those born with a silver spoon in their mouth and no manners.

'I will, Mr Whitelock. My foster mother always said it costs nowt to be pleasant and a smile always makes folk feel better.' Mary walked into the bar area, she still was in awe of the decoration there and the pristine splendour of the tables that were being laid out again by Nancy, who scuttled about like a busy mouse and hardly spoke.

Mary watched as Mr Whitelock made his way into the kitchen, leaving her standing behind the bar waiting for Lizzie. She made herself busy by polishing some glasses that had been left to dry from the previous evening and then decided to try and hold a conversation with Nancy.

'So, do you live in Leeds, Nancy?' Mary asked as she watched the girl polish each piece of silver with a cleaning cloth before laying it, just so, on the table.

'I do, I live with my family,' Nancy answered without stopping in her work.

'I live with my brother; we've just set up home together and this is my first job serving behind a bar. I enjoyed it yesterday, but Lord, I was tired when I got home.' Mary sighed and tried to make eye contact with the busy maid.

'The devil makes work for idle hands, that's what I was told. You'd be better finding something to do with your time than gossiping to me. I've no time for tittle-tattle,' Nancy said in a sharp rebuke, leaving Mary feeling awkward. She was relieved to see Frank, already dressed in his waiter's suit, enter the restaurant and behind him, Lizzie; at least they would talk to her.

'Decided you'd come back for another dose then, this morning? You looked knackered last night.' Frank grinned and didn't even acknowledge Nancy as he swanned in, in front of Lizzie.

'I was tired, but I'd enjoyed my day, all thanks to Lizzie here – she was a marvellous teacher.' Mary smiled at them both as Lizzie took off her shawl and gave it to Frank to hang up, then walked through behind the bar and joined her new recruit.

'You learned quickly – and just as well, because I've been talking to my beau and he's nearly ready for us to move on in our lives. It'll probably be April when we leave – we were thinking of moving to Carlisle or perhaps York – if the job he has planned pays off. I should think that if Mr Whitelock thinks that you're good enough for my job he'll be offering you my position.' Lizzie grinned and then turned to look at Nancy as she muttered under her breath.

'You're leaving?' Mary gasped. 'Thank heavens you're not going until April, that gives me three months to learn everything if I'm to impress.'

'You'll be all right, lass – unlike some, you have the gab. That, and the looks, is all that's needed. It's no good being able to do your job but not be able to communicate, like some we know …' Frank whispered the last few words quietly and nodded his head in Nancy's direction. 'I'll go and get my orders and see what Cook is brewing up this morning, I thought she was going to explode by the end of lunchtime serving yesterday. *She's* having to get used to the new menu, so everyone is learning something new.' He winked at Mary and went whistling into the kitchen.

'I have every faith in you,' Lizzie said. 'Mr Whitelock decided to take you on, knowing that you'd fit the part with your looks and attitude towards people.' Lizzie smiled and began to check that there was enough beer and spirits in the bar for the day.

'Some of us weren't good enough for the job, or so we were told,' Nancy said in a loud voice for both girls to hear.

'Oh, Nancy, you know you wouldn't have liked it. You like to keep yourself to yourself and if anybody flirted with you, you'd run a mile,' Lizzie said with a softness in her voice.

'It would have been nice to have had the chance, that's all I'm saying. Now, I'll never get a look in because *she'll* be staying, I know.' Nancy spat on her cleaning cloth and gave one of the silver spoons an extra violent rub as she made her feelings abundantly clear to Lizzie and Mary.

'I might not; I might decide that here's not the place for me. I'm sorry if you think I've taken your place, Nancy, but please don't hold it against me.' Mary went over to Nancy and looked at her.

'I'll see,' the girl said, stopping for a second to look up at Mary and then carrying on with her job.

'Mary, let her be, she'll come around. Won't you, Nancy? Once she's got to know you.' Lizzie sighed and looked towards the doors. 'Here comes George and it's a good job as well because the queue's beginning to form outside already; looks like we're going to be in for another busy day and that we really are offering the best dining experience in Leeds!'

Mary patted Nancy's hand; she could understand her disappointment at not getting the job she had set her heart on, but at the same time, it wasn't her fault that John Whitelock had not seen fit to offer her it. The truth was that Nancy was rather plain in her looks and her attitude towards people was somewhat lacking – but, Mary thought, happen if she had been supported that could have been turned around. Mary decided to go out of her way to befriend Nancy, whether she liked it or not.

'Bloody hell, Lizzie, have you seen who's in the queue today?' George came in through the doors and swept his dark hair back. 'It's only Thomas Winfield who owns nearly half of Leeds! Wait until Mr Whitelock sees him, he'll not believe his eyes. Make sure he gets served first if he comes to the bar. I'll open the doors now, Mary, so can you tell Frank to get his arse in here right away? Nancy, stop faffing about and go and tell Mr Whitelock that Thomas Winfield is dining with us – he'll need to greet him.' George looked flustered as he pulled his jacket down and straightened his bow tie before opening the doors for the public to come in and be seated. Mary dutifully went into the kitchen to get Frank, who was busy chatting up Prudence, who had turned a deep shade of crimson with the suggestions he was whispering in her ear.

'George says hurry up and come through quickly because there's somebody called Thomas Winfield waiting to be served and he seems to think he's to be made a fuss of,' Mary said and looked around at the amazed faces in astonishment.

'What's he doing here? I didn't think he'd have time for anything. After all, he's building that bloody big monstrosity at the end of the Headrow,' Mrs Trotter gasped and then went quiet as Nancy, followed by John Whitelock, rushed out of his office and through the kitchen.

'Whatever Thomas Winfield wants, you see that he gets it. We need folk like him dining here!' John shouted. 'Now, get a move on, all of you.'

Thomas Winfield looked around at the newly opened Whitelock's; it was certainly causing a stir within the community of Leeds and now he could see why. It was not your ordinary drinking place any more. In fact, he'd even go so far as to say that the interior was definitely decadent in style. Whether it was going to cause him trouble in the shape of being a rival to his plans for the grand hotel that he was building was another matter, he thought, smiling as John Whitelock bustled forward with his head waiter behind him.

'Ah, John! I thought that I'd come and see for myself this place that I'm hearing so much about. I must say you've surprised me – it is beautifully decorated, the tiles and suchlike must have cost you a small fortune.' Thomas picked up the menu and started to read what was on offer as John stood by the side of the table, looking hot and bothered.

'They did cost quite a bit, but it's proved its worth, importing the best from Italy; folk comment on them every time they walk in here. Anyway, it's good to see that you're joining us for luncheon today. Frank here will see to your needs so just you take your time looking at the menu and perhaps, in the meantime, a drink would not go amiss?' John urged Frank to take Thomas's drink order and was taken aback when all he asked for was a glass of water and asked Frank to wait for his choice of food.

'How's the new building coming along? I hear that it's to be a hotel. Do you think that's wise? There are plenty of hostelries and hotels in Leeds as it is, do you not think?' John said and waited for a reaction from Thomas.

'Aye, there are plenty of hotels, but not like the one that I'm planning. You've got to move with the times, much like you are doing, John. Our good Queen is getting old; she'll not be on the throne for much longer and there's a new mood about. Folk are no longer happy just sitting and drinking, as you well know, and Leeds needs a new look for the breath of new life that will be blown through it. You've spent some brass on this old place to give folk some decadence in their lives. Well, I aim to do just the same, but on a grander scale.' Thomas looked up at John, whose face told him exactly what he was thinking. 'Don't worry, I'll not tread on your toes; my place will be different from this. Although I must admit I admire your new bar girl. She's a bonny bit of work and I'll be needing quite a few girls like her.'

'Aye, well, you can take your eyes off her. She'll be staying just where she is. You must find your own lasses like we all have to,' John grunted. 'Can Frank here get you anything as well as the water, or have you just come to get ideas?' John's manner had changed; if Thomas Winfield wasn't going to spend any money with him, he could at least free up the table.

'Stop worrying, you old fool, and yes, your lad can get me some lunch. I'll have the turbot in Dutch sauce followed by the fillet of beef with fried potatoes and peas – but send your new lass over to me with my glass of water and let's see as if she speaks as elegant as she looks.'

Frank wrote the luncheon order down quickly and waited for John to tell him to send Mary with the drink. Instead, John just nodded in her direction and couldn't be bothered to speak as he left Winfield smiling at the worry that he had given him.

'Here, Mary, Thomas Winfield wants you to serve him with a glass of water. You've taken his fancy and Mr Whitelock isn't happy with him, but he'll not dare say anything to him, so you keep Winfield as a friend, not an enemy, in our work,' Frank whispered over the bar to Mary and glanced back at the man who could request almost anything anywhere he visited in Leeds.

'What does he want with me serving him? Doesn't he know that I'm new in my job?' Mary took one of the better cut-crystal glasses from beneath the bar and filled a matching water jug with water before putting it on a serving tray to take to the honoured guest.

'It seems he's taken a fancy to you.' Frank shrugged his shoulders. 'Anyway, he's given the old man a good order – he's ordered the dearest things on the menu to eat. I hope he doesn't think he's getting them for nowt, though, else Mr

Whitelock will *not* be suited.' He gave Winfield a backward glance and winked at Mary as he hurriedly took the request through to the kitchen.

'Your water, sir.' Mary curtsied and placed the jug and glass in front of Thomas Winfield as he sat back in his chair and looked at her. 'Will that be all, sir?' She felt uneasy as his eyes looked her up and down and a smile came to his lips.

'It is for now, my dear. Tell me, what's your name? Have you been working long for John Whitelock?' Thomas poured himself a drink and looked intently at Mary as she replied.

'I'm Mary Reynolds, sir, and this is my second day working for Mr Whitelock,' she answered politely, only just daring to look at the handsome bearded and moustached man who she knew to be one of the wealthiest men in Leeds.

'Well, Mary, I thank you for the water and I hope that you enjoy working for Mr Whitelock. I'm sure that with your looks and manners you will be valued by him.'

'Thank you, sir.' Mary smiled and curtsied once again before turning her back on him and going back to the bar and Lizzie, who was being rushed off her feet with orders from drinkers as well as from Frank and George.

'What did he want with you, then?' Lizzie whispered.

'I don't know. He didn't say much, just looked at me.' Mary looked across at the handsome man everyone was in awe of and, realising he'd been watching her, blushed as she served her next customer and tried not to keep looking at him as she replied to Lizzie.

'Well, he's never looked at me like that in the past. He's obviously taken a fancy to you, as Frank says.' Lizzie grinned. 'It'll keep John Whitelock on his toes when it comes to you if he thinks Thomas Winfield wants you; they're big rivals, you know.'

'Well, he's got nothing to be worried about – I'm happy working here and I aim to stay,' Mary whispered while passing a pint of Tetley's finest over to a man at the bar.

'For the time being, I think,' Lizzie said. 'I have a fancy that Thomas Winfield is not the only one who thinks he's in with a chance when it comes to you. Frank was asking about you as well this morning. Only two days with us and you've men wanting you already!' Lizzie winked. 'Make sure you get one with brass, lass. Brass and a good heart – and I'll tell you now those are hard to come by because I've never found one. My Harry has a good heart and not a penny to his name – but I'll make him do because I love him.' Lizzie smiled and then watched as Mary slipped another glance at Thomas Winfield and noted the smile on both their faces as she served her next customer.

'What are you doing on Friday night, Mary? I just wondered if you'd like to join me in the cheap seats at the music hall?' Frank grinned as he lit a cigarette before heading off into the darkness and his home.

'I hardly know you! Don't you think that I'd be a bit forward if I said yes?' Mary pulled her hat on her head as she answered him, surprised. 'Besides, you were flirting with

Prudence in the kitchen moments ago. Am I second best after being turned down by her?' Mary kept her face straight and thought she'd let Frank, the flirt, know that she'd got his length and would be no pushover.

'No, I only tease Prudence. I've no interest in her really – but you, you're a different matter. Besides, if you've caught Thomas Winfield's eye, you must be classy.' Frank drew on his cigarette and waited for an answer.

'I'm not sure; I hardly know you. Besides, I've no money until I get paid and I've Toby at home; I've hardly seen him since I started working here.' Mary hesitated; she would have really liked to go and see the inside of the music hall where her mother had once sung, but she'd never had a chance in the past.

'Toby? Who the bloody hell is Toby? Have you been leading me on? Have you already got a fella?' Frank sounded disgruntled.

'No, he's my brother, but he's not that well and I feel I'm neglecting him since I started working here. Besides, not once have I led you on, Frank Gibson.' Mary sighed; she was really worried about Toby and the cough that seemed to be getting worse. Perhaps she shouldn't have let him leave home for the smoke and damp of Riley's Court – he might have been better staying at home with his father.

'He'll be right, it's only one evening and I'll pay for you in any case. I can only afford the cheap seats but you can see the stage fine enough. Go on, we can get to know one another better; you don't get a chance when you just work with folk. Old Whitelock doesn't give you time to breathe, let alone make friends.' Frank stood firmly and waited for his answer; he wasn't going to be dissuaded, because from the first time he'd laid eyes on Mary he knew she was a good-looker and he was determined that she would walk out with him.

'I don't know … I hardly know you.' Mary felt awkward, she did hardly know him. For all she knew he could be another Jack the Ripper who, just a few years ago, had been stalking the streets of London.

'I'll behave myself, if that's what you're worrying about. It's only an offer to join me to go to the music hall, nothing else. You can trust me – I'll keep my hands to myself,' Frank said cheekily.

'All right, but just the music hall and then I'll return straight home to Toby and I'll pay you back when I get paid,' Mary insisted.

'Nay, I've got my pride – you don't pay me back. If you're on my arm for the night, then I pay your way. You can pay the next time if you want and if we find that you can bear to be seen with me again.' Frank laughed. 'One night with me might be enough – that's what usually happens with me and women. I can attract them, but I can't keep them.'

'All right, then, I'll look forward to it. Now, I'll have to get home. I'm tired but I'll still have to see to the house and meals for tomorrow. And let's not say anything to anybody we work with, I'd rather keep it to ourselves,' Mary said as she turned to walk home.

'All right, if that's what you want. See you in the morning, Mary. Sleep tight and mind the bugs don't bite!' Frank yelled down the cobbled street at her, then put his hands in his pockets and whistled happily on his way home.

Mary lay in bed and thought about her day. Her feet ached and she'd never worked as hard in her life but she was enjoying every moment. She listened to Toby coughing in the bedroom next to her; he really was much sicker than he was letting on and Mary knew it. Never mind spending any spare money on the frivolities of the music hall, she'd make Toby go to a doctor and get something for the cough. She looked up at the ceiling and closed her eyes as the coughing eased and Toby obviously dosed off to sleep. She, however, found her mind racing with thoughts of the dark, good-looking Thomas Winfield, who had tipped his hat at her and smiled as he had left the restaurant and the cheek of Frank Gibson and the upcoming visit to the music hall. She knew it would not be the first time that she had spent time in the now-famous hall – Nell had told her that she used to be taken to it when her mother was a singer there – but she had lost all memories of that part of her early life; would they all come flooding back when she sat looking at the stage that her mother, the Yorkshire Linnet, once stood on with such pride?

Chapter 5

It was Friday night and the days just hadn't come fast enough for Mary, unlike Toby, who was dubious about letting his foster sister walk out with a lad he had never met.

'You tell him to behave himself, else he'll have me to answer to,' he muttered as he put his head down and ate his supper at the table, while Mary titivated herself and looked at her reflection in the mirror.

'He will! He knows exactly where he stands because I've told him I'll not put up with any nonsense.' Mary smiled at her reflection and turned to look at her brother, who was suffering from another bout of coughing. 'Will you be all right? I'll not be late back – after all, we're both at work in the morning.'

'I'll wait up for you because I won't sleep until I know that you are home safe.' Toby wiped his mouth and looked up at Mary. He'd always been there to protect her when she was a child and now she was a full-grown woman with a mind of her own he was finding it hard to take that she was now the stronger of the two of them.

'You don't have to. Get yourself to bed and don't wait up for me. I'll be fine.' Mary bent down and kissed Toby on the cheek, then checked her straw hat, decorated with cherries and ribbons, as she made for the kitchen door. 'Next week you're going to see the doctor with that cough. You need some medicine.' Mary smiled at the lad she regarded as a brother and nothing more, not realising that Toby's feelings were changing and that secretly he loved her and was quite jealous of her walking out with Frank.

'Aye, you might be right, but never mind that, you just watch yourself tonight.' Toby bowed his head as Mary closed the kitchen door behind her into the night. He sighed and looked into the fire that kept the rundown cottage cheerful. There was no need for Mary to drag him to the doctor; he'd already been and he knew what fate awaited him. However, for now, his worries were for Mary. He only hoped that her head would not be turned by this Frank, who sounded a chancer. Toby wanted better for her. She needed a man with money and, more importantly, someone who would love her and take care of her – not a lad who was only a waiter in a bar. He'd loved Mary all his life and, as he picked up the poker and stirred the dying coals, he prayed that she would take care and not be led astray.

'I feel sick! My stomach is churning, I'm so excited,' Mary said and giggled as she and Frank made their way towards the open stage doors, nudging up the queue along the White Swan Yard with the rest of people waiting to be seated in the music hall.

'Aye, I can't wait, especially now I know Marie Lloyd is singing tonight – she's my favourite. George will be jealous, he's a big follower of hers and what with you on my arm and her singing to me, he'll not talk to me for the next month or two.' Frank grinned to himself, thinking that he'd been wise to make the first move on Mary because George had commented favourably on the new bar girl.

'You haven't said anything to him, have you?' Mary asked as she was urged to keep up with the crowd that was slowly moving into the hall.

'No. Me tell George about what I get up to? I don't think so!' Frank unhooked his arm from Mary's and put his hands in his pockets.

'You have, haven't you? I can tell that you have! I told you I wanted to keep our evening quiet, I didn't want everybody to think that I was easily led on my first week at work. I should have known that you wouldn't keep your mouth shut.' Mary glared at Frank.

'If I hadn't have said I was going to walk out with you, he was going to ask and I wasn't going to have that. I caught your eye first. Besides, he's always the one that catches the girls' eyes. I think even Lizzie is secretly sweet on him,' Frank stated as he paid for thcir tickets at the box office and took Mary's arm again to guide her to the cheap seats instead of the boxes that he could only dream of affording.

'He wanted to ask me out as well? He never said anything. Why didn't he ask me?' Mary stopped in her tracks next to heavy dark red drapes that gave way to the main seating area of the music hall.

'Cos I told him you were my girl and to shut his gob,' Frank said as he pushed her through the curtains into the hall which was packed with people finding their seats, hoping that she would forgive him.

'You did *what*? Let me tell you, Frank Gibson, I'm *nobody's* girl and if you think buying me a ticket to the music hall makes me that, then I'm leaving right away.' People bustled around them as she stood with her hands on her hips, oblivious.

'All right, all right! I'll make it right tomorrow with him, but for now, let's find our seats and enjoy our evening together. I'm sorry, but I didn't want him sniffing around you. He always gets the girls and I never do.' Frank pulled on Mary's arm and showed her to the seats that they were to sit in, right at the back of the hall and where he had hoped to start to court her like a spider caught in his web.

Mary could feel her cheeks were flushed as she made her way to the middle of the row of velvet-covered wooden seats that faced the empty stage and sat down, still fuming, thinking about how presumptuous Frank had been. He'd spoiled her evening and she felt like getting up and leaving, but as she looked around her, the temper that had taken hold of her subsided and she began to calm down.

'I'm sorry, I shouldn't have said anything. I just knew I didn't want to lose the chance to walk out with you.' Frank bowed his head, truly regretting his actions. 'Anyway, we're here now. What do you think? Isn't it wonderful? You can sit back and lose yourself for an hour or two, which is why I come, just to escape the real world.'

'Oh, it's all right. I should be flattered, really. It's just that I don't want people thinking that my head is turned that easy. Now, as you say, let's enjoy the evening together and leave it at friends for the time being.' Mary smiled at the rueful Frank. 'We've certainly got good seats, Frank, we're looking right onto the centre of the stage – and just look up at all these people dressed in their finest. I'd love to be in one of those gilt boxes up there – the view of the stage must be wonderful from them. To think my mother used to sing on this very stage! I just can't believe it.' Mary decided to make the best of the night and forgive the lad who had only tried his best to get her to himself. She was flattered, really, now she had time to calm down.

'Your mother used to sing here? Was she famous? Have I heard of her? Why didn't you tell me earlier?' Frank gasped.

'She was quite famous for a short while, but then she became ill and could no longer sing. She was known as the Yorkshire Linnet and I used to come here when I was very, very small although I can't remember much.' Mary went quiet and could feel tears building up in her eyes. She couldn't remember most of the things around her, but the smell of the greasepaint and expensive cigars being smoked by the gentry in their boxes was bringing memories flooding back to her as she listened to the orchestra warming up in the pit and saw the curtains on the stage beginning to twitch when the acts behind them took quick peeps to see if the hall was full.

'I've heard my father talk about her!' Frank gasped. 'He said she sang like a lark and that she was beautiful, that she sang sad songs that pulled at the heartstrings. In fact, I think my dad was smitten by your mother. Wait until I tell him that I'm walking out with her daughter!'

'Oh, Frank, don't say anything to him, please? My mother died a terrible death and it's best her memory is left in peace.' Mary reached for Frank's hand and squeezed it slightly.

'All right, I've learned. This time I'll keep my big gob shut. I don't want us to fall out again. I must say that you are a bit of a dark horse, Mary Reynolds. But I quite like that …' Frank smiled but couldn't help but wonder what death had befallen Mary's mother as he sat back in his seat, content that he had someone special sitting next to him as the curtains swished open and the evening's entertainment began.

The audience yelled their appreciation as the host announced the acts that were to appear and Mary and Frank clapped and cheered with every act that appeared on the stage. Jugglers, acrobats, clowns, and singers entertaining people and letting them forget their everyday worries. At long last the act that everyone was waiting for was announced, the ever-popular Marie Lloyd. Mary held her breath as she watched Marie Lloyd walk onto the stage dressed in the most beautiful pink dress and a matching hat adorned with roses and birds. She owned the stage as soon as she opened her mouth and she smiled at her audience as they joined in with her singing. She was the star of the show and she knew it; she had more confidence and swagger than ever Mary's mother had, although Mary couldn't know that. Marie Lloyd was born to perform and that was what she was doing as she announced her latest song and blew kisses to her audience as she started singing *The Boy in the Gallery* and Mary was enchanted when it came to the last chorus:

The boy I love is up in the gallery,
The boy I love is looking now at me,
There he is, can't you see, waving his handkerchief,
As merry as a robin that sings on a tree.

As Marie sang, all the men took their handkerchiefs from their pockets and waved them frantically to gain her attention, their wives and sweethearts shaking their heads as she smiled sweetly and blew kisses at the men who adored her. She was the star that Eve Reynolds could have been and Mary felt a tear rolling down her cheek as Frank whistled and shouted Lloyd's name to gain her attention. This was how famous her mother would have been if life hadn't dealt her a hard hand. Mary smiled and wiped her tear away as Frank turned and looked at her, smiling.

'She's absolutely brilliant, isn't she?' Frank enthused.

'Yes, she is. I can see why she's so popular, especially with the men,' Mary said and smiled.

'Just like your mother was, so I've heard my father say. I can't believe you're her daughter. I've fallen on my feet finding you. You will come again, with me, won't you?' Frank asked as Marie Lloyd left the stage to deafening applause.

'I'll see, Frank, but it will be just as friends, for now,' Mary yelled over the second round of applause as Marie Lloyd came and bowed for her loving crowd yet again.

'Yes, as friends, and I'll keep your secret, don't worry. Although I'd be yelling about it if the Yorkshire Linnet was *my* mother.' Frank looked at Mary and wished he knew more about the girl who obviously had many secrets but did not want to share them with him.

'Well, I suppose that's that, time to go home.' Frank looked at the crowds that were now dispersing and wondered whether he should try his luck and ask to walk Mary home, but he was soon told not to.

'Yes, thank you, Frank, for a lovely evening. And there's no need to walk me home, I'm fine on my own and my brother will be waiting for me.' Mary walked out of the music hall with Frank by her side and they stopped and looked at one another awkwardly at the end of the Swan yard. 'I'll see you tomorrow – and remember not to say anything about who my mother was. As far as those at work know, I was brought up by Robert Jones and his wife – which is true – and there's no need to ever mention my mother.' Mary pulled on her gloves and looked up into Frank's eyes.

'No, I'll not say anything and it's nowt to do with folk anyway,' Frank said and put his hands in his pockets. He wanted to kiss Mary but thought better of it; she was so independent and he knew that she would not appreciate his advances.

'Then I'll see you in the morning.' Mary stopped for a second and smiled before turning to walk home down the cobbled gaslit streets with the rest of the dispersing crowds.

Frank watched her go until she was out of sight. Mary was feisty but that was what he liked about her; she was different from the usual barmaids. The fact that she was Robert Jones's foster daughter might have something to do with it – everyone knew him to be a tough copper, but he was also one of the people. After all, he'd married a prostitute and that had been the talk of Leeds for a while. As for Mary's mother, he'd had no idea until now that she was a famous singer, so how had Mary come to be brought up by Robert Jones and what had happened to her father? There was a lot more to be found out about Mary Reynolds and he'd like to be the man who learned it through her friendship.

Frank sat down in the humble home that he shared with his mother and father and pulled off his boots before thanking his mother for a brew of tea that she placed on the table next to him.

'Have you had a good night, lad, with that new bar lass that you were sprucing yourself up for?' His father tapped his pipe empty into the dying ashes of the fire in readiness for retiring to his bed.

'I have, Father, and you'll never guess who her mother was! You've mentioned her name often in the past.' Frank couldn't keep his news to himself.

'Who is she then, lad?' Frank's father asked and looked at his wife, who had fretted all night about her only son walking out with a mystery lass.

Frank beamed with pride. 'She's the daughter of the Yorkshire Linnet – you know, the one you've always talked about singing the Irish songs when you were a young lad like me.' Frank sat back, a look of pride on his face as he drank his mother's lovingly prepared cup of tea.

'Oh, my lord!' his mother gasped.

'By God, tha wants nowt with that 'en.' His father stared at his son. 'Her mother might have been a good singer, but she kept bad company before she died. And her friend, Bonfire Nell, was nothing more than a common prostitute. Nell's the one that brought the girl up after her mother died of consumption, though some said it could have been syphilis. It was the talk of Leeds when she was buried without a penny to her name. You find someone better than that 'en, lad. Common as muck she'll be; you set your sights higher than her.' He stood up and looked at his wife, whose face was fraught with worry. 'She'll be nowt, lad, born in the gutter and that's where she belongs.'

He went to wind the grandfather clock up before both parents went up the stairs to bed, leaving their son thinking about Mary. So, Mary Reynolds was a prostitute's daughter? No wonder she wanted to keep herself to herself – and his father was right, he could do a lot better for himself although she was bonny. There was him thinking she was too good for him, when it was the other way around. Perhaps he should warn George just who they were working with, else he would fall into the same trap as him. She'd probably be carrying her late mother's disease and no man wanted to catch that. From now on he'd give her a wide berth.

Mary looked around her; the people she worked with had been rather quiet and less welcoming this week. She might be imagining things but she could have sworn that the staff in the kitchen were whispering about her when she had entered with an order. Frank had kept his distance as well and any offer of going to the Music Hall again had disappeared. The only one who was treating her normally was Nancy and she was no different in her manners towards everyone.

Mary looked at Lizzie, who looked pale and drawn; even she had not been as talkative of late.

'Are you all right, Lizzie? I'm doing my job well enough for you, I hope?' Mary took her to one side when there was a break in service and asked her outright.

'Yes, of course, you are. In fact, Mr Whitelock was just saying what a good worker you werc; you've impressed him. It's just me, Mary. I've got a lot on my plate at the moment and things are not going to plan.' Lizzie smiled wanly at Mary and tried not to show the worry on her face.

'You're all right, aren't you? I couldn't help but notice that you look a bit white and you're not as talkative as you were when I first started.' Mary thought that if anybody was going to tell her why she felt cold-shouldered, Lizzie would.

'Oh, Mary, I'm sorry. I'm wrapped up in my troubles and have felt so unwell of late. I should have known that you'd pick up on my condition because we work so close.' Lizzie tried to smile.

'Your condition? Do you mean you are . . .?' Mary glanced down at Lizzie's flat stomach.

'Yes, I'm expecting, and it's been a bit of a shock to both of us. It's a good job I'm soon to be married and leaving Leeds, but that doesn't stop me from worrying. My mother says it's my own fault for lifting my skirts and that I should have known better, but that's what you do when you love your man.' Lizzie looked at Mary with tears in her eyes.

'Don't worry, Lizzie, at least you have a good man from what you've told me. He'll not let you down. Now that I know I'll do more behind the bar and look after you. I know it sounds self-centred, but I thought it was me who had done something wrong because everyone seems a little reserved with me at the moment. All except Nancy and she's her usual self.' Mary sighed.

'Thank you, Mary, and it's for the best you learn all my jobs because now I'll be leaving sooner than expected and I think you are just the person for my position, regardless of what other folk think.' Lizzie looked at Mary, hesitant about telling her what she had heard being whispered behind her back.

'What do you mean, "other folk think"? So they *are* talking about me!' Mary gasped.

'I suppose I'm best telling you, now I've told you my secret. Frank has been telling everyone who your mother was and how she lived and died. I don't listen to gossip, but the other ones do – not that any of *them* are squeaky clean.' Lizzie graspd Mary's arm. 'Don't be mad with them; they like to gossip and something else will come along for them to talk about next week so it's best you rise above it.'

'Bloody Frank! He promised me that he wouldn't say anything about my mother. I suspected that he'd think the worst of her if he talked to his father, who'd tell him all the gossip about her. I suppose they think my mother was a prostitute?' Mary said quietly.

Lizzie just nodded and then hung her head low.

'Well, she wasn't, Lizzie. No matter how bad things got she would not sell her body, so you can tell them all that! She was just guilty by association and you can tell them, too, that I'm proud that I was raised by Nell, who once made her living walking the streets. She had a good heart, so they shouldn't judge.' Mary fought back the tears, knowing that no matter where she went, she could not hide her past.

'I'll tell them, Mary. None of them are without their pasts, and they should know not to judge you on your foster mother's lifestyle. Women have always had to do things they didn't want to do to make a living. I just thank the Lord that I've got a good man and that he'll stand by me. You hold your head up high and ignore them all. You do your job well and get my position of bar manager when I've gone because John Whitelock thinks highly of you and that's all that matters; he'll always have the time of day for a good worker.' Lizzie wrapped her arms around Mary and hugged her. 'Come on, lass, show them what you're made of and ignore their wagging tongues. I should have warned you not to have anything to do with Frank. He's his mother's pet, even though he's been caught being light-fingered around the market, so *he's* no need to talk.' Lizzie winked as Frank came through the doors with his nose in the air.

'Mind you don't slip on what's under your nose – it must smell terribly bad, especially if it's come out of your mouth!' Mary shouted at him and scowled. She'd be pleasant with everyone else, but she'd let the backbiting Frank know exactly where he stood with her. He'd not kept his promise and she wasn't about to forgive him this time.

'What do you mean?' Frank looked dismayed at Mary's outburst.

'I know what you've been saying about me. Well, you are wrong, my mother was a good person. She never sold herself to anybody, you snivelling rat, she died of consumption, nothing more.' Mary spat her words at him and then opened the door to the kitchen and yelled through at the staff there. 'I hope you all heard that! My mother was *not* a prostitute, so you can all stop gossiping and avoiding me. I might have lived in a bad area of Leeds when I was little but I rose above it and I will not put up with any rubbish from anyone, especially from a two-faced waiter!'

'Lord, who's rattled your cage?' Frank said and then disappeared back into the kitchen, where he found no sympathy from anyone. They were all in the same position as Mary, just trying to do the best in their lives, and regretted the nasty gossip they'd indulged in.

Chapter 6

Toby sat with his head in his hands; he'd hardly slept all night for coughing and being short of breath and now Mary was lecturing him about his health yet again. Didn't she realise by now that she was wasting her time? That no amount of lecturing and threats of the doctor was going to mend him? Her head had been full of her work of late and she had hardly seen him or had any time for him and his worries, which was perhaps for the best as it would only have given her more concerns if she had realised just how ill he was.

'Right, enough of this delaying; I'm going to go with you this morning and see what Dr Pritchard has to say.' Mary stood with her hands on her hips in her usual bossy stance and looked down at Toby, who was fighting for breath. 'And another thing, you don't go into work tomorrow; we can afford to look after you for a day or two so those horses will have to be looked after by somebody else, just until you shake this cough off.' Mary breathed in deeply and shook her head; her brother looked terrible and every day his cough was getting worse.

'Will you be quiet, our lass? You needn't bother yourself about going to the doctor, Mary, I've already been. I went just before we moved in here and I'm not going back.' Toby sighed and looked up into Mary's eyes and she stared at him in disbelief.

'Why didn't you tell me instead of letting me witter on at you? What did he say? *Is* it the dust from the hay that's getting on your chest? Perhaps you'd be better changing your job.' Mary looked with concern at the foster brother she loved dearly.

Toby shook his head. 'Ah, Mary, I've stopped myself from telling you this in the hope that the doctor was wrong, but I fear he isn't.' He looked up at Mary and sighed. 'I'm dying, our Mary, there's nowt the doctor can do for me. He says I've got consumption.' Toby looked at the shock on Mary's face and said nothing as she flopped like a rag doll into the chair across from him.

'You can't be dying! He must be wrong. You are not *that* ill, surely?' Mary leaned forward and looked at Toby; he'd got to be wrong! She couldn't face life without him. He'd always been there for her, her brother in all but blood. 'You can't have consumption, Toby. My mother died from it and I'll not let it take away somebody I love again,' Mary sobbed

'The doctor's not wrong. Every time I cough now, I cough up blood and have done so for a while and even when I'm just sitting down, I'm fighting badly for a breath of late. My lungs are knackered, Mary.' Toby shook his head again and looked at her with love.

'I don't believe you, the doctor's got to be wrong. We'll get a second opinion.' Mary couldn't believe the news that her brother had just given her.

'You needn't waste your money. Look, I know he's right.' Toby fished a blood-covered rag from out of his pocket. 'This is just what I've coughed up this morning and it's getting worse with each day that goes by. I'm sorry, Mary, I don't want to leave this earth and I don't want to leave you on your own.' Toby dropped his head, dejected and heartbroken; he wasn't ready to face death, he was too young – he'd thought, not so long ago, that he was immortal and that he would live forever.

Tears ran down Mary's face as she dropped down onto her knees and held him close to her. 'You've got to fight it, Toby! I'll be there for you – I'll pack my job in and nurse you better. You can't be leaving me.'

'You'll not pack your job in, for you'll need the money after I've gone. Besides, I don't have long. I've been surviving by taking laudanum of late and I told them at the livery station that yesterday was my last day because I haven't got the strength to manage the tackle and care for the horses any more. I've been struggling for a long time, if I'm honest.' Toby held Mary tight and wanted to sob on her shoulder, but he had to be brave for her sake.

Mary leant back on her heels and, looking into Toby's eyes, wiped her face clear of her tears. 'I'll be strong for you, Toby. I'll nurse you the best I can – and don't you worry about me, you just look after yourself. We've got to be strong, both of us, and I'll go and tell your father that you're ill – he's got a right to know and surely he will care?' Mary breathed in deeply and tried to control her sobs.

'No, you don't tell my father. He hasn't bothered with me while I was alive and I don't want him to bother with me in my death. Besides, the day we left home I went back and he told me to bugger off, so he doesn't care one bit about us. I've enough money saved to bury me and there's money to keep you in the house for a week or two while I kick my clogs and, hopefully, for a while after.' Toby had been thinking about his own mortality for some time and while he hadn't wanted to believe the doctor, he had put plans in place while Mary worked the long hours at Whitelock's. 'You keep your job, Mary; I don't want you moping at my bedside, and you are best being kept busy. Go out there and make the most of your life.'

'I don't know if I want to do that without you by my side. You've always been there for me,' Mary sobbed.

'Now listen, you go and make a life of your own, find a good man, have yourself a family and live each day to the full. My days on this earth are nearly at an end and I know it, but yours are just starting. We can't alter it, but we can learn from it.' Toby held her close to him. 'I love you like my sister, more than I have ever loved anyone in this world. I'll always love you, Mary.'

She looked at him, her heart breaking. She'd faced many things in her life but Toby had always been the true constant in it, the one person she could absolutely rely on being there for her. 'I'll be here for you for as long as you want me to be – and I'll never leave your side in a time of need,' Mary whispered, suddenly frightened of the life by herself that lay in front of her, but she'd have to cope, come what may.

Life was getting more and more difficult for Mary. Now, as she ran down Briggate, she thought of how she was struggling with her job, trying to learn everything Lizzie showed her, but at the same time she'd had no word from John Whitelock about being made head barmaid on Lizzie's departure. And her life at home was breaking her heart. Toby was now bedridden and had been for the last month; he lay, lethargic and fighting for breath, but still insisting that she didn't lose her job because of him. Everyone at Whitelock's had shown sympathy and had covered for her if she had been a minute or two late, especially Lizzie, who had seen her crying and worrying and had done her best to console her when she was at her lowest. She was torn between bettering herself at work and caring for the one person who had always been there for her. She found herself running down the street, her legs not going fast enough to get her home, hoping that Toby was still alive after her day of trying to look as though she hadn't a care in the world to the customers who came into Whitelock's.

Old Tess beckoned from her doorway as Mary ran into the small yard that had become her and Toby's home. 'He sounds in a bad way today, Mary, I've heard him yelling for relief even inside my house. I've been a time or two to his bedside, just to check that he's still in the land of the living but he doesn't recognise me because the laudanum's got a hold of him. I'd prepare yourself for the worst, lass, he's not long for this world. Now, you know where I'm at, lass, and he'll need laying out, which I've done many a time, so you just knock on my door when he's left this earth.'

Mary whispered a quick thank you to the old woman who knew everybody's business but had been a boon to her while Toby had been ill, making sure that he'd been fed and was comfortable while she went to work. She hadn't time to talk to her today, however, and she flew to open the cracked door and shouted upstairs to tell Toby she was home. She threw her shawl down onto the kitchen chair and ran upstairs. At least Toby was still alive – she could hear low moans as she walked along the creaking landing and entered his bedroom.

'I'm here now, Toby, you're no longer alone. I'm here, hold my hand.' Mary pulled a bedroom chair up and sat by the side of her dying brother, grasping his hand tightly as he fought for his breath and moaned in pain. 'I'm sorry, I should have stayed with you today; I knew you were worse this morning, but you insisted that I left you.' She picked up his hand and kissed it as Toby turned his head to look at her.

'I've had the strangest dream, Mary. My mother and Nell were with me and they smiled and said it was good to see me, that soon I'd be free of pain. But I'm so cold, Mary, and it does hurt so much,' Toby gasped and tried to grip her hand tight.

'I'll get the covers from my bed, keep you warm and safe; I'm by your side now.' Mary fought back the tears. Toby was grey in colour and his breathing laboured as she kissed his brow and then went to her room to get her patchwork quilt to put over him. 'There now, let's tuck you in and get you warm,' Mary said as she placed the quilt over her brother, but there was no reply. The heavy breathing had ceased and she realised that his body was at last free of pain and worry; Toby had joined the two mothers who had called him to their world.

'Toby, don't leave me! I can't face this world on my own! Please, please, don't leave me!' Mary sobbed. She clung to his body, not hearing Tess creep upstairs. The old woman stood behind her and gently put a hand on Mary's shoulder.

'Leave him be, lass, he's gone to a better spot than this world. Nowt can hurt him now . . .' She held Mary's shaking, distraught body to her and kissed her.

'He'd waited for my return, Tess, he knew he was dying and he waited to say goodbye,' Mary whimpered and buried her head in the old woman's shoulder.

'Aye, that's what they do, lass; there are more things to this life than we will ever know. You've just to remember he'll always be with you, in your heart or looking down upon you. You just can't see him. Sshh, now, it'll be all right, you've got old Tess to keep an eye on you, and you've got to make the best of each day, take what you want from it and lead a good life. That's what your Toby would have wanted for you. Now, stop your crying and let's get the doctor to say he's passed away and then I'll lay him out for you.'

Tess looked down at the young man who had not had the time on earth he should have been allowed. She'd seen death stalking the streets of Leeds lots of times before and knew it would break his sister's heart for a while and then, hopefully, it would make her a stronger woman. Death of a loved one did that; it made you realise that life was precious and you had to grab it with both hands. 'Now come on, let me make you a brew and then I'll go for the doctor. There's nowt more to be done here now, my love.'

Mary raised her head from the old woman's shoulder and glanced at Toby, who looked at peace in his bed. 'I'm going to miss him so much, Tess, but I'll not let him down. I *will* become someone he would have been proud of because, just like you, he told me to make the most of life and that is what I'll do.'

'That's it, lass, best foot forward and look to the future, never look back at what's been and gone. Now, let's put that kettle on and then we'll see to him and his affairs. Life goes on and no man or woman can ever stop it.' Tess put her arm around the young woman she had grown fond of; she'd be there if she was needed, but somehow she knew Mary had it in her to make it in life on her own.

Chapter 7

Mary stood on the doorstep of the house that she had grown up in, lived in most of her life. She looked down at the step that she and Nell had scrubbed until it was white as a bone and noticed the neglect. She pulled once again on the brass ring pull and waited, stomach-churning, for Robert Jones to answer the door so that she could explain that his son was dead and that he had been buried. She was dressed in a plain chambray dress with a black shawl around her shoulders and a plain black hat to hide her dark hair. She'd not had the money to buy a mourning dress, but had done her best to show her respect for the lad she'd loved as a brother. After she had visited Robert with her news she was going to attend church as it was the custom to do the Sunday after a person's burial and pray that Toby's soul had reached heaven and for any of his sins to have been forgiven.

Her heart fluttered as she heard footsteps coming towards the door. She'd regretted, since the funeral, that she had not informed Robert of his son's death, but she had given her word on Toby's deathbed not to do so and so she had kept her promise. She looked up as the door opened and the man who had brought her up stood in front of her in his vest, his braces hanging around his waist; he looked as if he'd just got out of bed and hurriedly put his trousers on to answer the door.

'What do you want? If you've come for some money now my lad's dead, you are out of luck,' Robert growled.

'I've not come begging. I came to tell you that he had died and was buried yesterday. However, you seemingly know.' Mary was taken aback.

'Of course, I know – in my position I get to know everything. Did you think I'd be showing my face at his graveside when he'd gone against me all his life and then run away with you, taking half my house contents? The devil may take him and you and all!' He turned to close the door on Mary.

'He did love you, you know – it's just you never showed him love in return,' Mary said quietly.

'Hmm ... If he had loved me, he'd have not run off with you to some shithole of a yard and he'd have tried to work at being the son he should have been. It was Nell and you that made him soft – he could have been something if he'd have listened to me. Now bugger off!' He glared at Mary and then slammed the door in her face.

So, that was how it was; Robert Jones had not even been bothered to show his respects to his only son. Well, she'd no longer have anything more to do with him – that part of her life was now at an end. She would stand on her own two feet and, once more, put the past behind her. Mary walked off up to Saint Mary's in silence; it would not only be a prayer for Toby that she said that morning, there would also be a silent one for herself, for with Toby cold in the ground she no longer had his income to help her and she was going to find it hard in the coming weeks to keep her independence. Perhaps she would have to be like her neighbour, Tess, and hide when George Summerfield came knocking for his rent. But then she would only find herself homeless and on the streets if she didn't pay him. She entered the church with a heavy heart and sat in the back pews as she thought about her life and the life that her mother must have lived without any support other than that of Nell. She would have to be strong and hold her head up high.

Once back home, Mary sat at the kitchen table looking at what money there was left. If she was careful she could, along with her wage, make it spin out another month; after that she would just have to see if she could find extra work to make ends meet. Her one hope was that John Whitelock would think her good enough to step into Lizzie's shoes when she left to go with her beau. However, she had not been there long enough to really believe that he would consider her, despite Lizzie's belief that he would. With Lizzie expecting and about to leave earlier than planned, she knew she had not yet gained all the knowledge she needed to run the bar.

She put her head in her hands and looked around her; the small cottage that had looked so unloved when she and

Toby had first moved in now had curtains up at the windows and a rug on the floor. If she had known Toby was so ill she would not have spent any spare money on making the cottage homely, would even have stayed with Robert Jones. However, that was easy to say with hindsight. She'd have to pay her way somehow, because she had nowhere else to go and she valued her independence. 'Please Lord, let me be all right,' she whispered to herself as she looked into the dying embers of the fire, hoping things would take a turn for the better and she could put her days of heartbreak behind her.

Mary walked into Whitelock's restaurant and knew instantly that something was wrong. She'd not been at work for two days because of Toby's funeral and the need to put her own house in order and the atmosphere could be cut through with a knife when she put her head around the kitchen doorway to say that she was back at her post. Frank's gossip about her had been long forgotten and now there was obviously a new topic of gossip. Nancy came up to her and grinned, a look of 'I know something you don't't' on her face.

'I'm sorry, Mary, you must be feeling low after Toby's funeral but it's a good job you're back! John Whitelock is wanting to see you and he's in a right mood,' Nancy whispered.

Mary felt her stomach churn. Was it her that was in bother? What had she done to upset her boss? She'd told him why she had to have the two days off from work and he'd been more than understanding when she'd told him about Toby's death, just as all the staff had been.

'Mary! Get your arse in my office – I need to speak to you.' John Whitelock charged in, scowling, and stomped through the silent kitchen, nobody daring to say a word as they prepared food for the service at lunchtime. Mary didn't look at anyone as she quickly followed him into his office. 'Sit down.'

Mary felt her stomach churn as he sat back in his chair and stared at her.

'We are in a sorry state this morning and I'm cursing that Lizzie and George. You'll not have heard, as yet, but they've run away together. There was all of us thinking that she was to leave with her unknown beau when it was really George the waiter she was carrying on with. To make matters worse, they've taken three bottles of my best brandy, a canteen of my best silver and left me high and dry without two of my main staff. By God, I'd tan their hides if I could get hold of them!' His cheeks were bright red and purple with the anger that he was feeling.

Shocked, Mary stared at him. 'I'm sorry to hear that, Mr Whitelock. I always believed Lizzie was going to leave with her Harry, I'd no idea that she and George were courting. So it must be George's baby that she is carrying as well,' she said without thought. 'I enjoyed working with her and would hate to think badly of her.' Inside her head, she was questioning where this latest news left her. Would she still be wanted or did this mean that John no longer trusted her, that he thought she must have noticed the love affair that had obviously been blossoming under everyone's noses?

'So, she was with child too? Aye, well, that George was always a bit quiet and shifty, but I thought better of Lizzie. She leaves me in a bad position – and that's where you come into it. The customers have taken a shine to you and you seem good at your job. I know you've only been with us a short time, but could you step into Lizzie's shoes as chief barmaid if I find you a replacement for your own job? I'm asking you because I'm desperate; none of the stock's been checked behind the bar and I've seen to changing the barrels this morning, but all else is as Lizzie left it on Friday night. I knew she was to leave us shortly but not like this,' John groaned and looked at Mary.

'As you say, I've been only here a short time, but I've watched what Lizzie does and I do think I could run the bar. A lot of it is making sure the customers are happy and that the drinks are served quickly and I've got a good memory for who drinks what and I've noted what Lizzie does when she's accounting for what she's taken over the bar of an evening. Yes,' she said firmly, 'I'm sure I could handle it.' Mary looked at him and couldn't believe that her prayers had been answered so quickly, which made her all the more determined to prove her worth and run the bar like a well-oiled machine.

'Aye, well, I'm willing to give you a go. How about we say a trial of a fortnight and I'll put an advertisement out for a barmaid to help you? That and a waiter, the thieving bastards!' John breathed in deeply and shook his head.

'Thank you, sir, I'll not let you down. I'll do my best.' Mary pushed her chair back in readiness to tackle the jobs that she knew would be waiting for her behind the busy bar, but before she went, she hesitated and then said, 'Sir, may I make a suggestion?' Mary felt her legs turn to jelly; it was not for her to say how John Whitelock ran his business but she felt compelled to share her thoughts.

'Well, what is it? I can but listen.' John sat back and looked at the young lass that his customers had taken a shine to and who had been a boon since the day that she had started to work for him. Many of the drinkers had been overheard commenting on the dark-haired lass who always had a smile on her face and could pull a good jar.

'Could I ask that Nancy join me behind the bar? I understand that she wanted my position before but wasn't allowed it.' Mary had felt sorry for Nancy from the first day that she had met her and knew that underneath her dull exterior there was a happier Nancy wanting to break out if given the chance.

'Nancy? Why Nancy? She's got a sharp tongue on her and she comes from the worst part of Leeds that you could think of. She wouldn't be right behind the bar – men want something pretty to look at and that's why I didn't entertain her request last time.'

'Yes, but she's loyal to you and underneath those drab clothes she's quite a bonny lass. Please, let me take her under my wing and I promise that you will have one of the best barmaids in Leeds by the time she's worked with me a week or two. She knows more than me, the truth be told, and she needs a break.' Mary looked pleadingly at him and hoped that he would give the downtrodden Nancy a chance.

'Mmm, I suppose my view of her is coloured because I know her background a little too well. Her father is constantly in and out of Armley Gaol after drinking and brawling when he's had a gill too many. I won't serve him in here and he knows it, so it will be ironic if his daughter is our new barmaid …'

'She'll be fine. I'll look after her – and if she doesn't work out, you'll be the first to know,' Mary said, quietly hoping that she hadn't overstepped the mark.

'Very well, send her in when you go back to the bar – I can get a kitchen maid a lot faster than a bonny face to serve behind my bar. But it's on your head, Mary, both your job and that of Nancy's, so don't let me down. If you prove suitable, it'll mean a rise in your wages, but I'll expect my money's worth from both of you.' John drew a deep breath and calmed himself, knowing that Mary had been heartbroken by the death of her brother. 'And Mary … I hope the funeral went all right, I know it must have been hard for you.'

She nodded her thanks, then turned away to go out and, as she closed the office door behind her, she could not stop the smile that spread all over her face. She'd prove her worth if it was the last thing that she did, she thought, as she caught Nancy by the arm and told her that Mr Whitelock wanted to see her next.

'What's he want to see me for? I know nothing and I've done nothing. Just because there are bottles of brandy and silver missing doesn't mean to say I knew anything about it. Folk always want to blame me, just because my father's a jailbird.' Nancy looked worried.

'It's nothing to do with that, Nancy, he knows that Lizzie and George took it. It's good news for you, I promise.' Mary smiled and looked around at Mrs Trotter, who stood with her hands on her hips, listening in. She watched as Nancy knocked on the office door and walked in.

'Lord help us, what a bunch I work with.' Mrs Trotter shook her head and got back to her cooking.

'There's only me that's squeaky clean,' Frank said and grinned, winking at Mary.

'Well, you can shut your mouth, Frank Gibson. Everybody knows you like looking through bedroom windows before folk pull their bedroom curtains and you've been caught snaffling the odd thing or two from the market. A bloody dirty peeping Tom, you are, so keep your comments about other folk to yourself!' Mrs Trotter glared at Frank, making him blush. 'Nobody's perfect and it's about time you realised it. Still, I'm disappointed with Lizzie, I always thought she was a nice lass.'

'I liked her; she taught me my job and she was all right with me. I only hope she and the baby will do well with

George,' Mary said, forgetting that it was only she who knew about the baby growing in Lizzie's belly.

'She was expecting! Oh my Lord, no wonder they pinched silver and brandy. They'll need every penny because George hasn't any money,' Frank gasped.

'I feel sorry for her,' Mary said and looked at the faces of the kitchen staff.

'She's been leading us all on with her sweetness.' Mrs Trotter shook her head. 'They are the worse sort, the ones that can lie to your face.'

The conversation stopped abruptly as Nancy came out of John Whitelock's office with a look on her face that none in the kitchen had ever seen before.

'Thank you, Mary, thank you! Mr Whitelock says it's you I've to thank for my leg up in the world. I'll not let you down,' she said, grinning with delight.

'What's she wittering on about?' Mrs Trotter asked.

'Nancy is to join me behind the bar. She is to have my job and I Lizzie's, if all goes to plan,' Mary announced, smiling.

'Oh my Lord! As I say, the world's gone mad. And who am I to have to help lay the tables and skivvy in my kitchen?' Mrs Trotter demanded.

'I don't know, but it won't be me, not ever again, because I'm not going to let Mary down. She's shown faith in me, the only person who ever has, so I'm going to be the best barmaid ever,' Nancy said, still grinning

'You have got a lot to answer for, Mary Reynolds. You've only been here five minutes and you've tipped my kitchen upside down with gossip and worry.' Mrs Trotter shook her head.

'Things will be all right, I promise you, Mrs Trotter. It isn't me, it's just life's happenings. After burying my brother I aim to make the most of my life because every day is precious. I think he's still with me and looking after me because, without Lizzie leaving, I would have struggled to feed myself and to pay the rent. Things, I'm sure, happen for a reason.' Mary smiled at Nancy.

'I'll not let you down, I promise,' Nancy said quietly. She had found a friend at Whitelock's and she wasn't going to disappoint her.

That day Mary worked behind the bar by herself. She thought it better that way, just until she could broach the subject of Nancy's appearance with her later that evening. She knew that it wasn't Nancy's fault that her dress and looks were at best a little drab, but she had to help the girl with both if Nancy was to work behind the bar with her so towards the end of the day, before she tackled the act of being accountable for the day's takings, she decided to speak to her. It was a delicate situation and she felt awkward at having to say something that she knew Nancy might be offended by. She chose her moment well when Nancy came through from the kitchen on her own and watched Mary as she washed the last of the day's dirty glasses before tackling the accounts with John Whitelock, who was to be summoned to assist her until she got used to handling that side of her new position.

'Nancy . . .' Mary felt her stomach churning as she plucked up the courage to tackle her poorly dressed friend. 'I'm sorry for what I'm about to say, but it's only because I want you to keep the job that's on offer to you.' She looked at Nancy awkwardly, feeling that she had no right to preach to the lass who had worked at Whitelock's a lot longer than her, but she knew it was in her best interest that she did so. 'Your dress and hair, Nancy, we need to do something about them if you are to serve behind the bar. Folk, especially the men, like to have something bonny to look at.' She saw tears welling up in Nancy's eyes.

'I know I'm a scruff, Mary, but I can't afford fancy clothes or to spend time on myself. There's eleven at our house and any money that my older brother and I earn goes to filling mouths, so we haven't anything left by the time the rent's paid and there's bread on the table. My mother does her best – she takes in ironing and washing – but my father, when he's at home, just spends anything she makes on drink.' Nancy dropped her head in shame.

'Well, at least with your new position you'll be earning a little bit more and that should help.' Mary looked at the lass sadly. Nancy was not on her own – there were plenty of large families in Leeds struggling to make ends meet. 'Look, I've got a dress or two that I've no need of and I can spare an hour or two tonight to help with your hair. Can you wait until I finish behind the bar and then walk down with me to my home? That way, in the morning you can start behind the bar with a new look and surprise all those who have doubted my decision.' Mary smiled, she had nothing but sympathy for the lass who clearly wanted to better herself.

'Me mam would worry where I've got to, Mary, so while you balance the till with Mr Whitelock, may I run home and tell her what I'm up to and tell her my good news? I'll not be long; I'll wait outside until you appear.'

Mary nodded her approval. 'Very well. I'll see you in an hour and we'll walk down to my home. Let's give those who doubted us a shock in the morning and have a new, glamorous Nancy standing in front of us in the morning.' Mary smiled as Nancy turned tail and obviously couldn't get home fast enough with her news. She was glad that she had given hope to her and she would do her best to make sure that her own new position was secure.

Chapter 8

Mary sat at breakfast and thought about the last few days. There was an ache in her heart that she knew would only fade with time. She missed Toby so much; he'd always been there for her since her birth mother had died and she honestly hadn't known if she could face life without him to lean on. She stirred her spoon through her porridge and started to think about the previous day; it was as if somebody had heard her prayers and made everything all right, because she would now have enough money to pay her bills and remain independent – but she'd also have a position of serious responsibility at Whitelock's and would she be up to it, she now wondered. She had come a long way in just a few months and knew she shouldn't be showing doubts about her ability to cope – but she was.

John Whitelock had been amazed by the takings from the bar when they'd tallied the sales up together. So much so that he had realised quickly that it wasn't only the silver and rum that Lizzie had been helping herself to, but a share of each day's takings too. Lizzie's demure attitude and kind ways had fooled even him and now he was left looking the fool.

Mary sided her uneaten porridge; she'd no appetite and her stomach was churning as she thought of the day's work ahead of her. Yesterday she had walked into her work, not knowing what the day was to unfold, but this morning was a different matter; she was now in charge of the bar and she had to show her worth. She reached for her shawl and looked around the basic kitchen, recalling Nancy's surprise that she lived in such a humble place. Obviously, Nancy had thought that she was a little farther up in society and had been taken aback when she entered Riley's Court to find the steam trains rumbling on the tracks nearly overhead and the size of Mary's home. Perhaps it would do the girl good to realise that they weren't that different, that both of them were working to keep a roof over their heads and that both came from humble backgrounds.

Mary smiled as she closed the door behind her and set up out of the court, waving at Tess, who was peering through the window, looking at what the weather was doing. Come Friday, Tess would be playing a game of cat and mouse when the rent collector came knocking, but today she'd be out and about, poking into other people's business and gossiping. Still, as Mary knew now, Tess had a heart of gold and was a good neighbour.

As she hurried through the streets towards her work, Mary couldn't help but wonder what Nancy would look like when she arrived at work. She'd managed to find a dress of hers that had seen its best days but was still much better than anything Nancy had ever worn. It was green with a white lace collar, plainly cut but practical for the work behind the bar, the skirts not too full and the bodice not cut too low. There were many men folk who liked a flash of cleavage but Mary did not want to encourage them, not in Whitelock's, anyway, especially when it was trying to attract the more refined drinker and diner.

Nancy had agreed that Mary could wash her hair, an event that the older girl was astonished to find was only undertaken by Nancy once every few months, making her cautious of head lice when she scrubbed it with carbolic soap and towelled it dry. She then set about wrapping strands of the long, lank hair around strips of rags to give the hair some curl, sending Nancy back out into the night with damp hair and a feeling of shame at admitting that she was not that fond of soap and water or personal hygiene, which she promised Mary to get the better of. This morning she would see the fruits of her labours and so would the rest of the staff at Whitelock's, because under that drab exterior really was quite a bonny lass, Mary had found. There was, however, one thing that she had worried about when seeing to Nancy and that was the bruises that were evident on her body. When asked about them, she'd dismissed them as her being clumsy and the young of the family accidentally punching her, but Mary had her doubts. She knew Nancy's father was a hard drinker, so was she suffering at his hands?

*

'Bloody hell, I never knew you could look like that!' Frank let out a whistle and stared at Nancy as she stood, beaming from ear to ear, in the already busy kitchen.

'Do you like the new me, Frank? My mother says I look a right sight but I like it.' Nancy pulled on her clean strawberry blonde curled hair and grinned.

'Well, let's put it this way, Nancy, happen I've been chasing all the wrong girls, now I know exactly what's under my nose.' Frank winked and then quickly made his way into the bar as John Whitelock checked that all his staff were working and that he was getting his money's worth.

'You look smart this morning, Nancy, I nearly didn't recognise you. Keep it up.' He looked at the lass who had always come over as drab and dark-haired and smiled; somebody had obviously told her to smarten her act up and he'd a good idea who that person was.

'Am I going to get a new maid or does that bar of yours get all the attention?' Mrs Trotter stood and looked at John. She was the only one who dared say what she thought to her employer. She'd known him since he was a small boy and she wasn't going to take any waffle. 'Agnes here is run off her feet; she's doing two jobs this morning while some of us swan about like lady muck.'

'There's a notice outside on the doorway so you'll have a new kitchen maid and a new waiter by the end of the day for there's plenty out there wanting a job. But that doesn't mean I'll not be fussy – I'm not taking on another bloody thief!' John Whitelock respected his cook, but Lord could she moan if she wanted to!

Mary hadn't bothered going into the kitchen on her arrival; instead, she made straight for the restaurant and bar. She aimed to make that her world. It was best to keep out of the kitchen where gossip was rife and she'd learned that it could make or break you. She walked around the already set tables; they weren't quite as expertly laid as Nancy's but whoever had done them had made not a bad attempt. She straightened the cutlery up where needed and ran her hands over the tablecloths, just as she had seen Lizzie do, before settling to her job behind the bar.

Mary looked up as the kitchen doors opened and stared with amazement at the new Nancy. 'Lordy, you look a different lass this morning, Nancy! Even your face shines lovely and clean – and just look at your hair! It's turned out beautifully and you're nearly blonde; I didn't expect that.'

'I know, and I've you to thank for the new look. I've even caught Frank's eye.' Nancy grinned.

'You want nowt with doing that. He's so shallow and, from what I hear, no lass will ever be good enough for his mother. Not that I'm bitter, but you know the rumours he spread about me and my mother; and he got it completely wrong: my mother died of consumption and she was never a prostitute. She did, however, sing in the music hall, so that bit he did get right.' Mary was not about to forgive Frank for telling tales about her and she thought she owed it to Nancy to warn her off him.

'I know, he's a terrible tittle-tattle, but it's nice to see him look at me in a certain way.' Nancy blushed and made her way around the back of the bar.

'Aye, well, I'd keep it at looking and nothing more for he's not to be trusted. Now, let's make a start on the day. You've probably seen what goes on behind this bar more than me, but you can make a start by polishing the glasses because some look a bit grubby and I'll see what we need in drink behind the bar before service begins. When the customers come to be served, try to smile and be pleasant, Nancy. We're here to serve them and we want their money, so none of your scowling black looks, think on now.'

'No, I'll try not to, but you can't change the way you're thinking. Some folk who come into this restaurant deserve scowling at and then there's them that have more money than sense – they're the ones that annoy me,' Nancy said, scowling, and then got on with her job of cleaning the glasses. Mary sighed; she was going to have her work cut out, curbing Nancy's forthright speaking, but she would do the best she could.

The lunchtime service proved to be one of the busiest of the week and Nancy worked well, with Mary only having to give her a warning look once or twice when she was a bit short with the odd customer or two. The trial came when Thomas Winfield entered and, with Frank as the only waiter, he had to wait to be seated properly. Mary knew that he was important so she made her way over to look after the customer such a fuss had been made of the last time he had visited.

'Mr Winfield, sir, would you care to take a seat at the bar until Frank has cleared you a table? I know he'll want you to sit at one of the better dining places near the window and he shouldn't be long clearing and getting it ready for you.' Mary smiled at the dashing businessman and felt herself blushing as he looked her up and down and smiled.

'Thank you, my dear. I've not come for a meal this time. I thought I might indulge myself with a quick tot of whisky before I go and inspect how my latest project is coming along. Have you seen what I'm doing with the building being erected in the shadow of the Town Hall at the end of the Headrow? It's going to be truly magnificent – a new building for a new era, an era to allow a little gaiety and excitement into people's lives. That is, if the builders and architects stop arguing and get on with how I want it to look once finished.'

'I haven't, sir, I've been rather busy of late, but on my next day off, I will walk up that way as I have yet to return my brother's book to the library and I'll make sure I take the time to view it. I'm sure it will be a marvellous contribution to Leeds.' Mary smiled and passed him a glass of the best whisky and a jug of water.

'You're fairly new and I recognise the other girl too – she was tidying the tables the last time I was here, so what's happened to the girl who used to serve here? Is it right what

I hear, that John's been taken in by her and a waiter?' Robert Winfield smiled and waited for Mary to reply as he added a splash of water to his whisky.

'It isn't for me to say, sir. However, I've been fortunate to land on my feet and fall into the position that I am in now. For that, I am grateful to Mr Whitelock.' Mary looked at Thomas Winfield and knew he was looking for gossip on his rival.

'Clever, bonny and faithful – he's a lucky man to have you working for him, the old dog.' Thomas looked around him. 'He's gone very smart with his restaurant but he doesn't have many spirits behind the bar and the décor is very much Victorian. He needn't worry that my new Palace Hotel will be a rival to him – I'm aiming for the middle classes, the ones who would like a good time, to have a drink and enjoy themselves. These are changing times and my hotel will be a place of gaiety and indulgence when it's finished.' Thomas swigged back his whisky quickly. 'I hope to see more of you, Mary Reynolds; you take care of yourself.'

With that, he pushed his glass across to Mary and left her watching him leave the bar, wondering how on earth he had remembered her name when he'd only met her once. So, Thomas Winfield was building a gin palace; gin, she knew, was having a revival, especially in the large towns and cities. It was like any drink: drunk in small quantities there was no harm in it. However, gin had played greatly in the lives of Nell and her mother and she had always been wary of it. It could control your life and ruin it if you let it and she had always vowed she would have no part in drinking alcohol. She was content without a drink in her life and that was the way it would stay; she was happy to sell it, but not partake.

Mary had worked hard and had shown that she could handle her new position at Whitelocks; today was her day off from the toil behind the busy bar and, after cleaning and dusting her humble home, she decided to return the library book that had been on a table next to Toby's bed and had, if she was truthful, been overlooked too long. Books had been Toby's solace and he'd buried his head in one often, losing himself in the world that opened up between its pages. Now she shed a tear as she picked up the copy of Mary Shelley's *Frankenstein* and remembered him looking up from the book and shaking with fear at the thought of the human-made monster coming to life, his imagination was that vivid. She held the book close to her and placed it in the bottom of her basket reluctantly. It was like losing a piece of Toby, she thought later, as she passed it over to the librarian and explained that her brother had passed to a better place and that she was sorry for the late return.

The librarian was very understanding and tactfully closed Toby's account without fuss as Mary stood for a moment, looking around the large hall filled with books and medallion portraits on the pillars of the great and good of the literary world. The library was always busy because the people of Leeds had a real thirst for learning and it was the place to learn at little or no cost, a boon to those who had no money to spend on books or the frivolous things in life. Leeds was expanding and changing and the people who lived within it were seeking change and education, which was evident to Mary as she left the grand library and stood on the steps looking around her. Wool-spinning yards and cramped back-to-backs were still found within the town, but in the centre of Leeds old derelict cottages and yards had been pulled down and more shopping arcades had been built. Hotels were being built, shops being opened on a daily basis and, across from her, she could see Thomas Winfield's grand investment, the Palace Hotel. The name was already prominent on the red brick Burmantofts terracotta walls that were growing higher with each day; it was going to be a truly impressive building. She walked down the library's steps, passing the statues of sleeping lions, and went and looked up at the hotel. Thomas Winfield was right; it was no threat to Whitelock's and it was so much grander; he would need three times more staff than Whitelock's.

'So you have come to admire my handiwork, Miss Reynolds?' Mary turned quickly. Thomas Winfield was standing right behind her and alongside him was a younger version of himself. And whereas Thomas's hair was going grey, that of the young man next to him was thick and jet black and his eyes the brightest blue she had ever seen. She couldn't help but stare at him as she replied.

'Yes, I was just admiring your building, and you are right, it *is* most impressive.' Mary smiled as she stood in front of the men.

'This is my oldest son, William. He's the one who's pushed me into going forward with building this hotel. He keeps me on my toes and keeps me up to date with what is happening in this ever-progressing world.' Thomas smiled and held out his hand to introduce his son to Mary.

'Nice to meet you, Miss Reynolds.' William held his hand out to be shaken, balancing the plans of the new hotel under his arm. 'I don't believe we have ever had the pleasure of meeting before?'

'No, sir, indeed we haven't. It is nice to make your acquaintance.' Mary felt her cheeks flame as William looked at her with intensity. He really was one of the most handsome men she had ever seen and she couldn't quite look in his eyes in case he could read her thoughts.

'Miss Reynolds is now in charge of the bar at Whitelock's and she is making a very good job of it, I must say. She shines with radiance, just like the tiles that John Whitelock has used in his restaurant – he knows a good thing when he sees it,' Thomas said and looked at his son, who had not taken his eyes off Mary since they had been introduced.

'You flatter me too much, sir. I only do my job and hope that I do it well.' Mary hung her head, embarrassed by his comment.

'I'm sure he doesn't flatter you, Miss Reynolds, my father has an instinctive nose when it comes to finding good workers who might benefit him in the long run. Don't be surprised to see him calling on you from time to time to watch your progress and perhaps snaffle you from under your employer's feet.' William laughed and glanced at his father, hoping that he had not revealed too much about his methods.

'Why don't you show Miss Reynolds the plans, William? Just a brief look – unfurl them from under your arm and show her the corner tower that we are planning,' Thomas said, encouraging his son to engage with the barmaid who had caught his attention because he wanted to hear the reaction of an ordinary person to his extraordinary plans, hoping that his ambitions were not too outlandish for the changing Leeds.

'Of course. Here, come and sit with me on the library steps and look at them. I think this is going to be one of the finest hotels in Leeds and also the busiest if we have a bar running the length of it, serving mostly gin. We aim to make it a modern gin palace, a place where you come to enjoy yourself and spend the evening, or just call in for a quick drink. However, this hotel's bar is going to be full of mirrors and glitter, not like the old gin shops, which were seedy and dark.' William spoke with passion as he rolled out the plans and showed Mary complicated drawings of what they were building, sitting close together with her.

'Look, we have a ballroom here, and this is the bar … you can be served whatever drink you want from along it and there's plenty of room for the staff to move around and for the drinkers on the other side of the bar to be comfortable. Now, what do you think of the tower? Right at the top it's going to be encased in a copper dome, which will shine in the sun's light initially and then, with age, a patina will form on it and it will go a beautiful shade of bluish-green.' William was full of excitement as he explained each and every detail of the new hotel and bar and, as she commented on the plans, Mary couldn't help but admire the young man sitting next to her on the library steps. He was so handsome and so full of passion.

'Come, William, we have an appointment with the main engineer and you will bore Miss Reynolds to death with your talk of escarpments and the like.' Thomas smiled down at the young couple, Mary with her skirts gathered around her and William excitedly revealing all their plans while she listened intently. He knew he was right: Miss Mary Reynolds would be ideal to join his team at his new adventure and William seemed taken with her. If she had proved her worth so fast to John Whitelock, then she would be a great asset to the Palace Hotel and he was going to have to persuade her to work for him and him only. She had a bonny face, a good figure and, from what he's heard, obviously a good business head on her – just what he wanted when he opened the glamorous bar at the Palace.

Mary lay in her bed, her mind flitting over her past life and what would perhaps become of her in the future. It was the first time in her life that she had ever been truly alone and the emptiness of her life was starting to press on her. She stared up at the ceiling and listened to the late-running steam trains travelling on the lines into Leeds station. There was always noise but never the company that she craved of an evening when she got home, now that Toby had died. She missed him so much; he might never have had a lot to say for himself but he was steady company and someone she could depend upon. Since her early years, she had always been an independent soul, taking in sewing to earn herself some money as soon as she had left school at the age of twelve and helping Nell with chores around the house. She was a strong woman now, with a mind of her own, and had fallen on her feet with her job at Whitelock's, but something was missing in her life … she found herself yearning to be loved by somebody, somebody who would hold her close and love her for who she was.

Her thoughts wandered to earlier in the day when she had sat next to William Winfield, poring over the hotel plans. He was a handsome young man – she'd thought that about his father as soon as she had seen him – but his son could only be a year or two older than her and she had found him even more darkly attractive. It was, however, no good wasting her time thinking about him, she knew that. He was rich and she was way below him in society so she could but dream. She hugged her pillow and smiled, remembering his blue eyes and his black collar-length hair. 'If only …' she whispered and then closed her eyes to sleep.

Chapter 9

'Nancy, what on earth is wrong with you?' Mary looked at Nancy, who had been quiet in her work all day and now she had found her crying in the yard behind the kitchen, where she had been sent to check how many barrels of bitter were left.

'I'm sorry, please don't say anything to Mr Whitelock! I'll stop my blubbing and come back into work,' Nancy sobbed and wiped her nose on her sleeve.

'Here, use my hanky, else you'll leave snail trails on your sleeves and customers will see it.' Mary pulled her handkerchief from out of her sleeve and passed it to the distraught Nancy. 'Now, what's wrong?'

'I-I can't say because it's family business. It's best you don't know – and anyway, you'll only tell the others.' Nancy breathed in hard and tried to control the sobs.

'I promise I'll not say a word to anyone. Now, come on, Nancy, you know you can trust me. What's to do?' Mary put her arm around the shaking girl and tried to comfort her.

'It's my father. He only just got let out from Armley Gaol yesterday, but already the coppers have come back for him and they'll not let him out now, not after what he's done. What he's done – it's fearful, fearful,' Nancy gasped. 'As soon as he was released he went out on the pop and came home stinking drunk. My ma asked him where he got the money from to go and get drunk and said he should have spent it on his family, not on drink.' Nancy halted for a minute and blew her nose. 'Oh, I hate him, Mary, I hate him! And I hope he hangs this time.'

'Oh, Nancy, don't say that, surely it can't be that bad?' Mary felt so much sympathy for poor Nancy and waited to hear more about what her father had done. She looked at her closely and noticed a fresh bruise on her arm. Nancy's father was a brute, of that there was no doubt.

'It is! It's worse than bad, it's evil, Mary. He got so mad with Ma for lecturing him, he just lashed out and baby Len was howling because he didn't like the noise and that just made my father worse and he picked Len up by one leg and threw him against the wall. He just threw Len like a rag doll through the air and the poor baby came crashing down near the fireplace. I can still hear the screams of my mother and my sister and the tears we all sobbed when we saw his body crumpled and broken on the stone flags. My father killed him, the poor little soul, and he's been taken away to the mortuary and my mother's beside herself with grief. I hope my father rots in hell!' Nancy sobbed. 'I loved baby Len, how could he do that to him?

He was only crying because he was scared. How could he kill his own son?'

'Oh Lord, Nancy, I'm so sorry. The uncaring brute!' Mary felt her heart beating fast, visualising the violence seen in Nancy's home. 'You must have been terrified. But how did the police catch your father and what are you all going to do?' Mary put her arms around the quaking Nancy.

'The neighbours held him down in the street after hearing all the commotion and my brother went and got the peelers. He swore, when they carted him away, that he would kill every one of us if he ever gets out of Armley. My mother's that frightened she's packing up the home and she says we are all to move to Lincolnshire where her family is from once baby Len has been buried. But I don't want to leave Leeds; it's always been my home, and besides, I've just got my job with you and I'm making my way in the world.' Nancy's tears streamed down her cheeks again and her sobs grew louder. Mary, desperately sorry for her, didn't know what to say to the poor young woman whose life was in turmoil.

'Len was the baby of the family; my mother cursed when she found out that she was having him, but when he came we all loved him. I hope my father rots in hell, I really do. He's done nothing for any of us, ever. And now this ...' Nancy sobbed.

'Oh, my Lord, I'm shaking myself,' Mary said quietly. 'Aye, but Nancy, it would be the drink; he'd not know what he was doing. He'll be regretting his actions now that he's rotting in Armley.' Mary put her arm around her and squeezed her tight. 'Now, do you want to go home? I know what it's like when you've lost someone, but never under such bad circumstances. I'll get somebody to stand in for you from the kitchen and everybody will understand and be there for you. Or I can always give the excuse of you not feeling well if you don't want anyone to know the truth. However, I've no doubt that your father's misdemeanours will be made public once the newspapers get hold of the story.'

Nancy shook her head.

'No, I'm not going home, he's ruined the rest of my family's life, but he's not going to ruin mine. I'm not going to let John Whitelock or you down, so just give me a few minutes and I'll pull myself together. Oh, thank you for being so kind to me, you are a true friend.' Nancy breathed in shakily and tried to smile at Mary.

'Are you sure? Because I'll make it right with Mr Whitelock, whatever you want to do. Just tell me when you've composed yourself and made your decision. I'll hold the fort until then. At least we now have a new waiter and service maid; they can help for a while. Take your time; dry your eyes and steady yourself for you can't undo what your father has done but you can make a life for yourself to spite him. I know your heart will be breaking but hold your head up and think positively.'

Mary gently touched Nancy's arm and turned her back to return through the kitchen to her place behind the bar. Terrible pictures of baby Len being thrown against the wall ran through her head as she smiled at the customer entering the restaurant. How could a father do that to his son, no matter how much drink he had supped? Poor Nancy, she would do all that she could do for her. She knew exactly what it was like to come from a poor home, for in her darkest moments she remembered her mother dying in the hovel that they had lived in. It was a memory she tried hard to forget and she knew that the death of baby Len would always be with Nancy, no matter how she tried to escape her past, of that she was certain as she smiled at her first customer of the day and poured a gill while the restaurant filled with customers; she could never show her true feelings to the world, she had learned that a long time ago.

The news of the terrible crime that Nancy's father had committed was soon public knowledge. The *Leeds Intelligencer* reported the infant's murder on the front page with a graphic ink-drawn illustration of what they believed Nancy's father to look like as he committed the dreadful act. The staff at Whitelock's read about it and whispered and looked at Nancy with an air of disbelief or pity. Some of them gave her sympathy and others just ignored her and didn't broach the subject. Baby Len's funeral was highlighted in the newspaper and the streets where Nancy and her family lived were lined with mourners respecting the poor child who had committed no crime other than crying when frightened.

Mary decided that the funeral was more important than serving her customers and made arrangements with John

Whitelock for him to serve behind his own bar while she paid her respects as Nancy's closest friend. She walked behind the small coffin, her arms linked with Nancy's, as his brothers carried the baby from out of the dilapidated terrace house to his resting place in the churchyard. The tears and sobs from the crowd and family filled the air as the small body passed through the onlookers. A photographer stood at the entrance to the church and the flash of smoke from his picture-taking made Mary feel angry at the ghoulish pleasure that some people took in other people's grief. No doubt the photograph would be appearing in tomorrow's newspapers for all to read, with no thought of the family's grief. The family stood heartbroken at the front of the church as the vicar said what words of comfort he could before offering up the young soul for deliverance before they all walked out into the graveyard for the burial under the sweeping branches of an ancient yew tree that would stand guardian to the small body.

Mary stood with her head down after throwing some soil onto the small coffin and stepped to one side as the family wept. Even though she knew them to have little or no money, they were all dressed immaculately in respect to their lost brother and son, all in black, with Nancy's mother's face covered in a veil. She felt her stomach churn, not knowing what to say to her as Nancy bade her mother say hello to her closest friend.

'I thank you for attending with us today, Miss Reynolds, it has meant a lot to Nancy to have a friend to talk to these last few days.' Alice Hudson looked at Mary, her eyes swollen from crying and she looking old for her years.

'I'm sorry for your loss, Mrs Hudson. I don't know what I can say to make things any better,' Mary said quietly.

'Nay, there's nowt you can say. My man's a bad 'en. He liked to have his way but never faced up to the consequences. Well, he'll have a lot to answer for when he faces his maker and he'll be stalking the fires of hell when that rope around his neck finally takes his life.' Nancy's oldest brother put his arm around his mother and whispered comfort to her. 'We'll be long gone on that day, though. Has Nancy told you that we are to move to Lincolnshire this coming weekend? I can no longer live in this town, it holds too much heartache.'

'I knew you were thinking of leaving, but not that soon.' Mary looked across at Nancy, who bowed her head and couldn't look at her.

'Aye, well, we are, but I thank you once again for what you have done for my lass. She owes you a lot and I'm sorry she's going to leave you needing a new bar lass, for you've become friends, I can see that.' Alice Hudson took her son's arm and stopped for a second by the grave's edge to say her final farewell to her baby son and then walked out of the churchyard with all her family bar Nancy.

'I'm sorry, Mary, I was going to tell you, but I was hoping that she would change her mind once we'd buried Len. But my uncle's sending a horse and cart for our stuff and we're to join him in a tied farmhouse in Lincolnshire. He's got us all jobs potato and turnip planting and picking. My mother thinks it will be better for all of us – but I don't want to go.' Nancy was nearly in tears as she looked into Mary's eyes.

'I know that you said you were probably going to go but you hadn't said anything more about it. I'll miss you working with me – and I'll miss you as a friend. But Nancy, potato picking isn't for you! You'll be out in all weathers, in the mud and cold; all of you would be much better staying in Leeds because things will get better and folk will soon forget about your father's mistakes.' Mary took Nancy's hands. 'These hands are not for potato picking. Now, I've been toying with the idea for a while but I will understand if you feel obliged to your family ...' Mary hesitated and then asked the question that she had been thinking about for some days. 'Why don't you come and live with me? I'd expect you to pay your way, but I could do with the company and it would help me with the rent; besides, we get on well together.' Mary smiled and looked at the frowning Nancy, noticing the frown turn into a beaming smile as she listened to her proposal.

'Do you mean it? You're not just asking out of pity, are you?' Nancy looked at Mary with tears in her eyes.

'I wouldn't ask if I didn't mean it. Since my brother died I've been on my own and money has been tight. I've managed to pay my way but I have little left for any enjoyment in life so you would be a welcome lodger – and besides, you can cook, which is more than my brother could, and clean. It would be lovely to have someone share the chores of running the house with.' Mary linked her arm through Nancy's as they looked at the tiny grave that was about to be filled in.

'Then you have yourself a lodger! I'll tell my mother when I get home. She'll not be suited, but our Meg is getting up and Tommy and Adam will be making money down in Lincolnshire, so they'll all manage without me. It looks like I've got you to thank again, Mary. Oh, I'll always be beholden to you and I can't thank you enough.'

'You're welcome; I know what it's like to be the centre of gossip and alone – and you'll be all right with me. We'll look after one another, like sisters. Now, you break the news gently to your mother in the morning – she's had enough heartache for today – and I, in the meantime, will go back and relieve Mr Whitelock from running his own bar. I don't think he was so suited at me for coming today, but I couldn't let you down.' Mary kissed Nancy on her cheek then watched as she ran to catch the rest of her family up as they walked solemnly down the street.

Mary sighed and turned away; she would go back into work, just to show willing, and then she would go home and start to get Toby's old room ready for her paying guest. It would help her financially, that was a fact, but despite what she'd said to the girl, whether she and Nancy could live comfortably together was another matter. They were like chalk and cheese, and even though both had been born into poverty, from an early age Mary's needs and wants had been seen to by Nell and Robert Jones, in a comfortable home where she was fed and clothed, while poor Nancy had been dragged up by her bootstraps. Only time would tell if they were compatible or not, but perhaps she should not have been as hasty as to offer her board and lodgings – after all, her father was an accused murderer and Nancy was known for her moods. Doubts crossed Mary's mind as she made her way back to Whitelock's through the busy streets and she only hoped that she had done right.

'Are those all the possessions that you have?' Mary looked at the few small boxes that had been hastily unloaded from the back of the cart that had all the Hudson family's possessions on it, as well as the family itself.

'Aye, I don't need much in my life and besides, I never have the money to buy anything; my money, up to now, has gone into looking after my lot.' Nancy smiled at her family as she stood in the doorway of her new home in Riley's Court. 'They're wanting to be off for they've got a long haul before they get to my uncle's and he wants to make good speed while the day is young.'

Mary looked at the cart, which was loaded with household belongings and children and adults, and noticed that the bodies outnumbered the furniture and belongings that were going to make their way down into Lincolnshire.

'You'll take care of my lass, she's depending on you!' Nancy's mother shouted down from the front seat of the wagon, where she sat next to her brother, whose face was weather-beaten from the days spent out in his fields.

'I'll take care of her, Mrs Hudson, she'll come to no harm while she is under my roof. We'll look after one another.' Mary stood with Nancy and looked up at the heartbroken woman as Nancy kissed her on the cheek and then did the same to the rest of the family.

'Take care, Mam!' Nancy yelled as her uncle slapped the reins over the two horses' withers and the cart joggled out of the yard. The girls stood and watched and each had a feeling of loss: Nancy of her family and Mary of her privacy as Nancy turned to her and said, 'Right, a pot of tea and then I'll sort my room out. Am I at the front or the back of the house? I hope it's not the back – I'll not sleep for the rumbling of the trains going past and besides, it's not long since your brother died in that room. I don't fancy lying in the same bed as he's been in. Imagine if I caught something from him!'

Like it or not, Nancy *had* been given the bedroom at the back of the house and Mary knew that if she was to keep her own privacy and a full say in how her own home ran, she had to stand her ground. 'It's at the back, Nancy, take it or leave it. And no, you won't catch anything – all's clean and waiting for you.'

'Right you are then, you're the boss – in more ways than one. I'm just the lodger and I should know my place,' Nancy said sarcastically as she gathered her few possessions in her arm before climbing the stairs to her room, leaving Mary to make the brew that she had offered.

Mary shook her head; they might be friends, but perhaps living together would be a step too far for both of them. Time, no doubt, would tell, but just for now they could share a cup of tea together and discuss a few house rules if Mary was to have her way, else chaos would prove the master.

Weeks went by and living with Nancy proved to be difficult sometimes because she was set in her ways and, although the girl was very helpful around the house, Mary sometimes wished that she had never invited her to stay. But what was making a positive difference to Mary's life was the amount of money Nancy contributed to running the home and if it hadn't been for that, she might have been tempted to tell her to look for different accommodation. What made things truly difficult was the fact that they worked together and lived under the same roof, so they were never free of the sight of one another, unless one made an attempt to go out and get away from under the other. This Saturday morning, three months after Nancy had come to stay at Riley's Court, it was different; Mary knew she had to be there for Nancy. Yesterday, they had executed her father and there was a vivid description of his hanging in the *Leeds Mercury* for everyone to read. There was no escaping it – her father was back in the limelight, with people actually watching the hanging and taking great delight in doing so. Nobody had the time of day for a child murderer, whether he had been drunk or sober.

Nancy came and sat down at the breakfast table across from Mary and looked sharply at her. 'You needn't try and hide the newspaper from my eyes before we go to work – I know a report on my father's hanging will be in it.'

'I didn't think that you would want to see it, let alone read it.' Mary picked up the newspaper and stared across at Nancy, concerned.

'If I don't hear it from you now, I'll only hear it being whispered about at work. It's best I get it over and done with before I walk out of these doors. Please, Mary, read it to me; reassure me that I am now free of the man whose name I carry, even though he was no father to me or my brothers and sisters.'

Mary looked at Nancy assessingly and then nodded before her eyes travelled to the report that she knew Nancy would be upset over, no matter that she claimed otherwise. The man, after all, had been her father and he couldn't have been evil all the time. Her voice wavered as she read the extract.

The Hanging of a Child Murderer

Yesterday, at five to nine precisely, the chapel bell at Armley Gaol was rung to prepare the crowds that had gathered outside the walls there to hear of the execution of Harry Hudson. Hudson, who had earlier in the year killed without mercy his six-month-old son while under the influence of drink, had a much-stained record of various assaults, theft, and wife-beating, but the vicious attack on an innocent child was deemed

> unforgivable. The bell could be heard above the noise of the crowd as Hudson was escorted to the gallows by his executioner, William Billington. In his footsteps walked the prison chaplain and the governor of the prison. A white hood was placed over his head and Hudson could be heard to curse his executioner as he placed the rope around his neck before pulling the lever for him to drop to his death. The body took at least ten minutes to be still and was left hanging for over an hour before being committed for burial in the prison graveyard. Cheers rang out from the crowd as his death was pronounced.

Mary placed the newspaper on the table and looked across at Nancy: there was not one sign of regret on Nancy's face, no tears or sobs, only a sigh, and then she sipped her tea.

'The bastard's gone, then; let's hope that he rots in hell,' Nancy said quietly and then smiled at Mary. 'We're free at last from the man who made all our lives hell!'

Chapter 10

Mary stood behind the bar at Whitelock's and tapped her feet as she hummed a tune that she could not get out of her head, waiting for the restaurant doors to be opened for yet another day's service. She knew exactly what the day was going to bring: another day of moaning from the kitchen staff, thinking that they were the only ones who really worked in the place. Another day of the waiters being snide and treating customers who gave them a good tip well, while others were made to wait; and another day for her and Nancy to serve the same customers with the same drinks and for them to smile and listen to the same stories that they had been told a thousand times or more.

Mary had been working at Whitelock's for nearly a year now and for a good amount of that time she had enjoyed it, and John Whitelock certainly treated her well, but now she was bored. In fact, she was bored with everything. She'd no hope of improving her lot in life, no beau and no hope of ever earning more money to make her way upwards. To make matters worse, it was Christmas, and while everyone else was making plans to be with family and the ones that they loved, she had opted to work behind the bar, seeing as she had no one to share her Christmas with and had no other plans. Even Nancy, who she was beginning to find more and more annoying by the day, had found herself a male friend and was about to pack her bags and join her family in Lincolnshire for two days to celebrate Christmas. She watched Nancy, busy flirting and giggling with her beau, Jake, the new waiter, as they waited for the lunchtime rush to begin, when both would touch hands lovingly as he took the drinks from her to be served to his waiting customers. It seemed that everyone was happy with their lot other than her. She stopped tapping her feet and felt angry with herself for feeling pangs of jealousy over Nancy's happiness and told herself she shouldn't be so mean. She, too, could have a man on her arm if she wasn't so picky. She looked up at the clock as it struck eleven thirty. Time to make everyone jump to attention – and for the two lovers to stop lovingly dreaming into one another's eyes.

'Jake, come on and leave Nancy be and open the doors; and Nancy, get yourself behind this bar – and for heaven's sake, straighten your apron!' Mary snapped at the courting couple.

'Sorry, Mary, I was only making the most of a minute or two with Jake, I'm here now.' Nancy blushed and glanced at the lad who had stolen her heart as he unbolted the doors and opened them up for the world to enter in.

'It's all right. I'm happy for you both. It's just folk shouldn't have to wait outside in this cold for too long. Let's hope that they're not too full of alcoholic cheer before they reach us and that we can get this meal on the run-up to Christmas over and then you can be on your way and I can go home for the night.' Mary looked up at the customers entering the restaurant. All were jovial, wishing each and every one a Happy Christmas before sitting down at their tables to talk and exchange good wishes of the season as they ate and drank from the fine menu, which Mrs Trotter, with the aid of her kitchen staff, had prepared. Mary smiled and laughed with her regular customers and, on their leaving, shouted after them to have a good and hearty holiday and then turned to serve her next customer, who she knew would have no concerns about how she would be spending her Christmas. This was the first that she would be spending on her own and her heart felt heavy at the thought of previous Christmases shared with Toby and Nell at what was once a happy home down at the quayside.

After working all day, Mary walked with Nancy and Jake to the railway station to see them board the last train down the east coast to Skegness, where Nancy's family were waiting to greet her and her new beau. The station was busy, with people going and coming home to visit relations, and the steam from the huge trains filled the air as she hugged Nancy and urged her to take care and to enjoy her time with her family. She too had a year of events to look back on, Mary thought, as she waved her off, watching as the lovers disappeared down the track to a poor but festive welcome in the bosom of Nancy's family. She sniffed in hard and tried to stop a tear running down her cheek. She pulled herself together and took a grip of her emotions as she looked at two young children who were begging from the passengers that were alighting from the trains. She might be on her own, but she had a roof over her head, a full belly, and a good job. She shouldn't feel so sorry for herself, she decided, as she reached into her purse and found a halfpenny for the boy and girl dressed in rags with dirty faces and shoes that had been mended more times than she cared to think about. She put the halfpenny into the little girl's hand.

'God bless,' she said quietly as the little girl smiled up at her.

'Thank you, ma'am,' both children said and then moved on to see if they could find more charity that night.

She breathed in hard and watched as the children tried their luck with the well-to-do and poor alike before she walked out of the thronging station and back down the cobbled streets to her home. At least she was with company tomorrow, working until the middle of the afternoon, and John Whitelock had made it easy for the staff who would have to work that day. There was to be a carvery buffet in the restaurant at lunchtime, not the usual three- or four-course menus, and then it was to close early in preparation for the coming Christmas Day. Preparation for Christmas Day! There was no preparation in her case, although she had bought herself a chicken to help celebrate the good Lord's birthday. But there would be no presents, no parlour games like in the past, the small cottage would be filled with just her presence and no one else to wish her Christmas greetings. She sighed and slumped in her chair on arriving home, looking up at the sprigs of holly that Nancy had insisted they put in the windows and on the kitchen cupboard. She could do better than this with her life; now, with no ties to family or loved ones, it was time to make her way in the world. This would be her last Christmas spent on her own, she vowed to herself and it would be the last Christmas spent in this poor excuse of a home though she had made it as warm and homely as she could. No, next year would be different; she didn't know how but she was determined to change her lot in life.

It was the third week in January and Mary lay in her bed and listened to the front door being closed behind Nancy as she went out to her work. She had lain in bed on purpose but although she had no real problem with Nancy, she just needed to have time separate from her. She worked with Nancy, lived with Nancy, ate with Nancy – and unless the girl walked out with Jake, she sat and *talked* to Nancy seven days a week. It was better than being alone, but Nancy and she had little in common and now all she spoke about was her love of Jake Ingram, the waiter. Of course she paid her way and the money she gave her helped Mary pay the rent and bills and she had saved a little to spend on herself.

Christmas had come and gone and Mary had not been bothered by her lack of family and celebrations but now she had decided, after working long hours at Whitelock's, to spend some money on herself with a visit to Leeds market and the shopping arcades and to finish her day off with an evening at the music hall. She yawned and stretched; it was a luxury to still be in bed after seven o'clock in the morning and she decided to snuggle down under the covers for a few minutes more before rising and getting dressed. She closed her eyes and tried to sleep but her head was full of the day that she was to have and the things that she would buy. It was no good: once awake, she had to get up, get dressed and go about her day, no matter how comfortable her bed was.

Dressed and sitting enjoying her breakfast in peace for once, she raised her head when there was a knock at the door and Tess, in her usual informal manner, walked into her kitchen.

'I saw you were still at home so I thought I'd pop my head around and see if there was a brew in the offing. It's nowt being on your own all day and I know you took to spending Christmas Day on your own badly. That was your fault, though – I'd have come to join you, especially if I'd have known that you'd cooked yourself a chicken.' Tess eyed her neighbour up and down. 'You're not ill, are you? I'll not catch anything from you?' Tess said quickly, looking at the scowl on Mary's face and wondering why she was at home.

'No, I've just begged a day off from John Whitelock. I worked long hours over Christmas, seeing I've no family, but I thought that I'd have a day to myself and do things to cheer myself because these long January days are dull and miserable.' Mary reached for a cup and saucer and poured Tess a drink of tea from her teapot.

'Aye, I know all about miserable days, especially at this time of the year. January and February are always the worst months. That's why I was glad to see you at home and I thought to myself that I'd call in and have a cuppa.' Tess smiled and looked at Mary closely. 'You'd have thought that your stepfather would have invited you back to his, this last Christmas, although I know you've told me in the past he'd washed his hands of both you and Toby.' Tess was testing the ground to see if Mary had heard the latest news about Robert Jones that was making Leeds alive with gossip.

'He'll never have anything to do with me ever again, Tess. I'm not his blood – and judging by the way he treated Toby at the end of his life, it wouldn't matter if I was. It seems all he's interested in now is his work, his racing, and his women. Poor Nell would be beside herself – she loved him so much.' Mary sighed and sat back in her chair; she really didn't have time for this conversation this morning – she wanted to be off up the market and in the shopping arcades.

'I hear he's to be posted down south, that he's really dirtied his copybook here in Leeds. You've not heard owt, have you?' Tess leaned over the table eagerly.

'No, and I'm not likely to either. I've washed my hands of him.' Mary looked at the old woman, who was obviously visiting her for a purpose.

Tess sat back with her arms crossed and grinned across at Mary. 'He's been helping himself to the force's funds and running an illegal betting syndicate over at York! They've thrown the book at him and he's lucky he's not in the gaol.' Tess laughed at the shock on Mary's face.

'That wouldn't surprise me; he did like to bet on the horses. Yet he had no time for Toby's love of them.' Mary shook her head. 'Why he's changed into the man he is now, I haven't a clue. He was always so kind to Nell in their early days together and she thought he was a good man – his true colours only started to show over the years.' Mary sipped her tea.

'Aye, well that's what power does to some folk, it must have gone to his head. To make things worse, the baggage that he'd been living with has run off with some of his money. So he's back to what he used to be, a bobby on the beat and on his own. He should have been kinder to his own instead of being so proud and arrogant.' Tess nodded her head.

'That'll mean his house will be empty. I always liked living down there, near the canal. It was on its own and out of the way. I was happy for a time there.' Mary sat back and thought about the years when life had been good, when Nell had looked after her as her own daughter, along with Toby.

'Aye well, it's no good looking back, you've got to look forward. Now, this will tickle your fancy! Guess who's coming for supper at mine tonight?' Tess grinned across at Mary, showing her rotting teeth.

'Go on, tell me!' Mary smiled, seeing the excitement on Tess's face.

'George Summerfield! I've got George the landlord coming to supper. We've played cat and mouse with one another for years but I've finally caught him. He doesn't know it yet, of course, and now I've caught him I'm not about to let him go, not with all his money. I can't stop much longer because I've got a pot boiling on the stove with some brisket in it and I want to have a good clean up. I need company in my old age and there's many a good tune played on an old fiddle – and besides, it'll be easier living with me than chasing me every week for my rent.' She winked as she rose from her chair. 'Now, you have a good day to yourself. And find yourself a fella before your looks begin to fade because you want nowt with being an old maid. Be like the lass that lives with you and walk out with a man.'

Mary watched as the old woman left her and crossed the yard back to her own home. It seemed that everybody had somebody in their life, bar her. She hadn't really worried about being on her own, but now, with everyone else busy courting, she felt quite the outsider. Still, better to be independent than tied down to a man who would probably change as soon as she married him, she thought as she cleared the breakfast table, then put on her new red mantle and matching hat before checking how much of her hard-earned money she had in her purse. She was going to enjoy her day and that was going to be in no way thanks to a man – she was her own woman and that was how she liked it.

Even though the day was dull and overcast, Leeds was busy. It was always busy, being the centre of commerce for Yorkshire and the wool trade. Mary passed the round, highly decorated building of the Corn Exchange, where negotiations for buying and selling corn and grain were being made by farmers and dealers. The noise from the deals being done could be heard loud and clear as she walked up Vicar Lane towards the bustling market, which was now the favourite place for the working folk of Leeds. It was a market in the making, with the guilds building a glass roof over part of the market for the protection of the fishmongers and butchers that traded around the edges. However, some of the markets were still uncovered, and because of Leeds' growth, there were rumours of the stallholders being moved on until a more suitable market was built. Mary, for once, did not visit the fishmongers and butchers, but the smell from them assaulted her nostrils as she entered the large gates into the market. She made straight for the stall that everyone visited for frivolities and everyday useful items.

'Ah, Mary my dear, my favourite customer. How are you this fine cold and frosty morning? Warmer than I am, I hope?' Michael Marks asked in his Polish accent and smiled at this customer who had supported him from his very first appearance on the market. 'I was just saying to my partner here that we should really be thinking of expanding and perhaps look at renting a shop instead of freezing out on this stall.'

'Next year, perhaps, Michael; this year we employ some staff, some young ladies, to help on our stall so that we don't have to stand here.' Thomas Spencer smiled at Mary. 'Michael wants to walk before he can run, but I must admit on a parky day like today a nice warm shop in one of the arcades would be most appealing.'

Mary smiled at the two men who supplied her with all the bits and bobs that made life more bearable, everything from lace to ribbons, hatpins and brooches, down to mundane household goods, and all at the same price. The slogan above the stall boasted: 'Don't ask the price, it's a penny' and was also brandished on banners on each side of the stall, leaving the customer in no doubt at all at how much the goods on the stall would cost them. It attracted many a customer, and people gazed for a good length of time at the rows of haberdashery and household items that the pair of men could supply.

'I'd like two feet of that beautiful blue ribbon, the one with the satin sheen, and a dozen of those small blue buttons and a reel of this blue cotton, please.' Mary picked up her reel of cotton from the display and handed it to Michael Marks as he finished counting her buttons into a small paper bag, along with the ribbon that he measured and cut into the length required.

'You are going to be busy! Are you sewing yourself a new dress, perhaps, to catch the eye of a young man?' Michael smiled and passed her the bag, then took her money.

'I'm going to make myself a new dress, but I doubt if I'll attract a man. I don't seem to have much luck in that department,' Mary sighed.

'You will one day; you are too good-looking for someone not to sweep you off your feet. If I weren't spoken for myself, I'd be asking you to walk out with me.' Michael winked and watched as Mary made her way through the market in search of the material to go with the cotton and ribbon that she had just purchased. He admired the young woman who was independent, but he thought it would have to be a strong man who would win her love.

Mary looked at the lovely blue material that she'd bought, then picked it up and smelled it. There was something about a new piece of material that just made you do that, then smooth your fingers along the length of cotton before planning on what design and cut the garment you were to create was going to take. She stepped back and sighed; was it to be a full skirt or a straight skirt? She'd noticed that straighter skirts were coming into fashion but from what she had seen, they hadn't a lot of freedom of movement. She picked up the two patterns that she had bought, along with the fabric, and looked at the models posing on the front, who looked perfect. She liked both patterns and the white pintuck blouses that she wore on most days would complete the look; however, the sewing would have to wait for another day if she was to catch the show at the music hall, she decided, as she glanced at the clock on the mantelpiece. Quickly, she folded the material away and put the ribbon and buttons together with it. Sewing could wait until Nancy was back sitting with her of an evening – it would give her something to do instead of listening to the endless tales of Nancy's day.

Grabbing the full coal scuttle, Mary banked up the fire; at least she would be warm on her return and Nancy couldn't complain that she had come back to an empty, cold house and she'd been thoughtful enough to buy her a mutton pie for her supper – which was more than Nancy would have done for her, she thought, as she tied her best hat on and pulled the house door to, not bothering to lock it because nobody ever got past guard dog Tess, so all would be safe until Mary or Nancy's return. As she set out on the walk up to the music hall, she couldn't help but notice that the people she passed were looking down at their feet and seemed to be quieter than usual. The mood had certainly changed since the afternoon, but as she quickened her pace she thought nothing more of it than that people were tired and ready for their homes. And she was in no mood to worry about other folk; she was going to wallow in the smell and excitement of the busy hall, laugh and smile at the performances and forget her worries for an hour or two. She had saved the money especially for this evening, and now the time had come to reap the benefit of the long hours of work and having Nancy as a paying lodger. She didn't notice the paperboy on the corner of Briggate had a longer than usual queue, nor the faces of the people as they read the breaking news, her head set on the night's entertainment as she made her way down the old woollen yard to the music hall doors and pushed her way through the crowd of people standing and talking in the lamplight. Then she paused. Was that woman crying? Why was nobody going into the hall and why was it so quiet? Mary looked around her and saw the doorman talking to a couple who, just like her, were obviously wanting to attend the performance. She made herself known and pushed past the doorman, only for him to grab her arm.

'I'm sorry, miss, there's no performance tonight, and it's been cancelled on account of Miss Rosie Bell, who was the supporting act, being found dead in her room. The rest of the cast are beside themselves and there's no way they will perform this evening – it would be encouraging bad luck on their part. Though the boss is saying that the show must go on.'

'Oh, the poor woman! Had she been ill?' Mary gasped.

'No, they don't think so. The peelers think that she took her own life. The boss had just told her he didn't want her back and she must have taken it hard.' The doorman looked at her and whispered, 'She'd taken poison, they found her with a bottle in her hand!'

'Oh, I see … The poor woman!' Shocked, Mary walked away, the news making her think of how her mother must have felt when she had been cast aside for someone fitter and healthier than her. Life, or even death, could be so cruel.

The mood was sombre in Whitelock's; January was always a poor month because the weather was depressing and times were bad – ordinary people were finding making a living hard while some of the great industrialists had more money than they knew what to do with at the expense of their lowly employees. However, Nancy was without a care, too much in love, lost in the arms of her Jake, to care about anything else but them.

'Just look at the Prince of Wales; he's nothing but a playboy from what I'm reading in this newspaper. Lord knows if he will be able to put the country first if anything ever happens to his mother – he's too fond of his women and drink.' Nancy giggled and quickly folded her newspaper, putting it to one side as a string of customers entered, most of them looking sombre and deep in conversation. Whitelock's, as usual, was filling with dreary businessmen and snooty women who talked about one another over lunch. Not the sort of place for a love-struck Nancy to be working at all as she waited for Mary's response.

'He'll be all right, when the day comes, although he has been waiting for his time to come for a while now. I hope that it's not for a good while yet because although the Queen has never got over the death of her Albert, she's not doing a bad job of guiding the country,' Mary said quickly as the first customer of the day came to the bar and ordered a drink and Nancy took the first list of drinks from Jake, who winked at her as he passed it to her. Mary thought she had a rough idea how the Prince felt; he must be bored like her because she had outgrown Whitelock's and she knew it. It really was time to look for a different position, but there wasn't much to be offered to a humble barmaid, because although she was in a position of some authority, that was all she was. A barmaid with another barmaid doing as she told her to do. She had a meagre wage and not much respect from the people she served; she was just there to look pretty and do as John Whitelock instructed her to do. And she knew she could do so much more if given the chance.

Mary smiled and passed the two gentlemen at the bar their drinks. They didn't even acknowledge her – she was a woman who was there to serve them and that was all. She stood back and thought about her lot; no, sooner or later, she would look for another place to work. Whitelock's was not enough to keep her happy; she needed to stretch her mind and have more responsibility if she was to be happy.

Chapter 11

January 1894

'Another year, another day and no change,' Mary whispered and looked out at the wet, dreary streets of Leeds and wished, not for the first time that morning, for more in her life. She should have left this job that was too easy a long time ago, that or find a man to look after her. But the thought of being married and children around the bottom of her skirts did not appeal to her. Christmas had come and gone yet again and, like the previous year, she had worked all hours that God had sent just to give herself something to do. Nancy was now wittering on about marrying Jake but letting it be known that neither of them could afford anything more than where they were already living, making Mary feel unwanted because Nancy hinted constantly that she wished Jake could move in with them.

She was almost crying with boredom as she looked around her at the affluent diners and Nancy flirting with Jake as he waited for the drinks to be poured, when a young lad ran into the bar and looked up at her. His face was filthy but in his hand he held a pristine white envelope.

'Here, missus, are you Mary Reynolds? I've been told to deliver this note to you by that man standing over the other side of the street and wait for an answer.'

Mary looked down at the street urchin and took the note from his hand, glancing out of the window at the man who stood on the street corner, watching her and the boy. She realised at once that it was the young and handsome William Winfield who was the sender of the note and quickly opened the envelope to read what was inside.

'The fella says just to give me an answer of yes or no – he doesn't want to cause bother for you.' The young lad wiped his snotty nose and grinned, assuming that it was a love letter that he had been instructed to carry.

Mary looked down at the note.

Dear Miss Reynolds,

Forgive the hastily written note. My father and I wondered if you would be interested in gaining employment with us at the Palace Hotel? We would like to talk to you at ten thirty this evening on the premises. We think it would be in all our interests for you to attend.

Yours sincerely,

William Winfield

*

'Tell him yes.' Mary said as she quickly put the note in her pocket before anyone else saw it and looked out across the street to where William stood. She felt her cheeks flush as she watched him smiling as the young lad ran to tell him her reply.

How could she say anything other than yes to the offer that had been sent to her? It was perhaps the answer to her prayers, a new place of work – and for one of the wealthiest property developers in Leeds. Besides, it would get her away from the small group of lovely but nosy workers that she was with now. Giving the glasses an extra clean with her glass cloth, she started to hum a tune.

'Mary, stop that humming!' John Whitelock exclaimed as he came in and informed her of a change in the menu.

Mary stopped instantly. 'Sorry, I just felt a need to cheer myself up.'

'You can cheer yourself up by doing some work! Now shut up and get on with your job.' John scowled as he spoke but Mary grinned as soon as he turned his back on her and pulled faces at him behind his back. Ten thirty could not come soon enough.

'Are you not walking home with me? It's not like you to go somewhere at this time of the night.' Nancy unlinked her arms from Mary's and looked at her when she said she would leave her at the entrance to Whitelock's.

'There's something on at the library that I wouldn't mind seeing. I won't be long, it closes at eleven, so I've got to hurry if I want to catch them,' Mary said quickly, not wanting Nancy to know the truth.

'I would have thought that you've enough on, what with working, dressmaking, reading and the like, and now you are trailing off to the library. No wonder you can't get a man: you are too well-educated and men don't like clever women.' Nancy looked Mary up and down. She was grateful for her help in getting her a leg up in the world, but now she believed that Mary thought herself better than anyone else, even though she'd come from nothing.

'It's something and nothing, a new exhibition that they are thinking of putting on. I'll not be long,' Mary lied yet again, hoping that Nancy hadn't noticed that the supposed new exhibition had been worthy of her hair being tidied, her skirts smoothed and her cheeks plumped.

'You wouldn't get me going there – it's full of snobs. You want nothing to do with learning!' Nancy yelled after her as Mary set off with urgency down the gaslit streets to the Palace Hotel to meet the Winfields.

Catching her breath, Mary stood outside the now fully-built Palace Hotel. Even in the gaslight, it looked grand and the copper dome on the top of the buttress shone as the light of the moon glinted down upon it. However, it was the light from inside that caught her eye. The sight was magnificent: sparkling crystal chandeliers hung from the ceiling, lit not by candles or gas but by electricity, a luxury only the wealthiest could dream of. The Palace Hotel outshone any other building on the row and Mary felt her stomach churn as she climbed the steps to the entrance and put her hand on the rotating brass door that led into the lobby of the grand hotel. She felt herself underdressed and insignificant as she stood and gazed at the opulence that surrounded her. Never had she been in such a building.

'Ah, Mary, we were expecting you.' Thomas Winfield smiled and greeted her as she stood in front of him, William, and the most elegantly dressed woman that she had ever seen. 'I was so glad that you accepted our invitation to join us this evening. I'm sorry it was given in such an undercover way, but I did not want to risk your position with John Whitelock and I have no idea where you live.' Thomas smiled, watching Mary tremble in front of him with nerves and with anticipation of what was to be asked of her. 'Don't worry, my dear, we are not about to eat you. As William hinted in the note, we are looking to employ you, if you are willing to join us.'

Mary looked at Thomas and then at William, noting that the woman next to him was gazing at her up and down and trying to show an interest in the person standing in front of her but obviously noting that she was of much lower status than herself. 'Thank you, sir, I feel privileged that you have taken me into consideration for whichever position you think me fit for. I, of course, am loyal to my employer, Mr Whitelock, at present and would not, as you say, like to jeopardise my position with him.'

'Then it will remain our secret until you have made your decision on what William and I have to offer you. However,

I am being rude; William, you already know, but let me introduce you to his fiancée, Miss Faith Robinson, soon to become Mrs William Winfield.' Thomas turned and looked at Faith as Mary made a slight curtsy to her. He urged Faith to say something but she just smiled coldly, making Mary feel embarrassed that she had thought so little of herself in front of the elegant woman that she had felt the urge to curtsy. 'No, no need to stand on ceremony, Mary; you will, hopefully, soon be one of our members of staff and therefore part of the Winfield family. That is how we hope to run this glorious Palace Hotel, making it full of laughter and enjoyment – and if the staff aren't happy, the customers aren't happy, and that would never do.'

Thomas stretched out his arms. 'What do you think of it so far? We've got marble floors, the finest crystal and the largest mirrors in Leeds – we've not skimped on anything. Come, follow me out of this lobby into the main bar because that's what I really want you to see – hopefully to tempt you away from John Whitelock. Although he will give me a run for my money when it comes to delivering good meals, *this* is what we are about.' Thomas opened the huge wide doors at the side of the lobby and showed Mary the crown jewel in his Palace Hotel.

'Lord, I've never seen anything like this!' Mary gasped. 'Everything glitters! Just look at the chandeliers and the grand piano. The bar itself must be nearly twenty yards long and the bottles of drinks behind it – I could never remember them all. Just look at how many different bottles of gin alone you have on the shelves, there must be at least twenty.' Mary stood enraptured and looked around her; never had she seen such luxury. There were tables and chairs covered in the richest velvet for customers to sit in and relax, while on the walls were pictures depicting exotic, scantily clad ladies with flowers around their bodies and in their hair. Tall palms grew in large brass planters but the pièce de résistance was the bar, long and slim with bottles and glasses stacked up behind it ready for the many customers who would soon be flocking through the doors. 'It's wonderful!' she exclaimed.

'I'm glad that you like it. It's cost me a pretty penny. There are thirty bedrooms, as well as the staff bedrooms for those who want one, a laundry room and a kitchen that wants for nothing. All I ask is that it becomes a success because this is to be my gift to my son and Faith on their wedding day.'

'For which we are truly thankful, Father. Not only have you provided us with the business but a home as well. Our rooms are just below the copper dome – they're beautiful, aren't they, Faith?' William turned and smiled at his bride-to-be and waited for her answer.

'Yes, a little small and I would have preferred to be away from your work, but they will suffice for now, until we have a family …' Faith looked at William with a straight face and then glared at Mary. 'You seem to have taken my fiancé and his father's eye, for them to have given you this sneak preview of our world. Can I ask why?'

Mary sensed the hostility in Faith's question and blushed.

'I don't know why; I've only spoken briefly to both of them and served Mr Winfield on his visits to Whitelock's,' Mary answered truthfully.

'I'll tell you why she's here, Faith. It's because she owned the position that John Whitelock gave her from the moment she was behind his bar and she's loyal, as she's proved once again this evening. That is why I want to offer Mary the position of overseeing the three girls and the waiters who are to run this bar for me. She's ideal for the job, as well as being pleasing to the eye,' Thomas said sharply to his future daughter-in-law, then looked at Mary.

'What do you say to that, Mary? We will pay you better than John Whitelock and there is accommodation if you want it. I don't know your personal situation, but I do know that you've no wedding ring on your finger, so you are not beholden to anyone at home, I hope,' he said and looked sombre. 'It'll be different from Whitelock's here and I'd expect you to dress accordingly and to act the part, but I have faith in your ability and so has William. He was the one who convinced me that you were right, the day you looked at the plans together.' Thomas looked at the surprise on Mary's face.

'Me in charge of three girls and some waiters! Well, I must confess I was beginning to find it a bit monotonous at Whitelock's and could do with a challenge.' Mary looked across at William, who smiled and winked at her in encouragement.

'We'd see to your dress; we have employed Sharp and Wright, the best outfitters in town, to see to our needs. Your rent in the room that we would give you would be taken out of your wages and, of course, any meals that you need would come from the kitchen. However, we would expect you to take a firm hand with the girls I employ. Oh, perhaps you would like to take part in the interviews? You seem to have a good sense of people's character,' Thomas said and couldn't help but see the look of disdain on Faith's face.

'Oh, no, if I take the position, I would leave that to you. I'd be lost with what to ask them.' Mary looked at both men. She had instantly liked them – and her new surroundings, which were so much grander than Whitelock's. As a bonus, she would have a new home, away from Nancy and the filth of the railway line. However, she couldn't help but feel that Faith had no time for her and that there had been an instant hostility as soon as they met. She paused and thought about her life and how much better it could be if she took the chance that was being offered her. 'What time would I be given away from work? It's just that I enjoy going to the music hall and I'd appreciate a little time to myself to do as I please.'

'We'd work around that, I can assure you.' William was quick to intervene with an answer.

'Then yes, I would love to join you here at the Palace. I can't believe that you have chosen me to be part of your scheme, although I really don't deserve the position! And yes, I *will* take the opportunity of a room here. I rent a small cottage with Nancy, who works with me at Whitelock's and, to be honest, it hasn't been working well of late. We're not really compatible, it would seem.'

'Then welcome on board, Mary Reynolds. We will expect you to work hard but in return we will treat you fairly. We have decided that our grand opening will be in the first week of March, so you have plenty of time to make things right with your lodger and John Whitelock – I'm sure both will miss you.' William and Thomas shook Mary's hand but Faith turned and went to sit down in one of the chairs and sat watching the three of them as they laughed and congratulated themselves.

'Let me walk you to the door – or perhaps you'd like a wee drink to celebrate?' William made to walk around to the back of the bar to lift down a bottle of gin.

'No, no, please, I don't drink myself. And I aim never to do so!' Mary said quickly.

Faith laughed out loud and exclaimed, 'A woman in charge of the bar who doesn't drink? Now that is laughable!'

'It's the best way to be, I think – at least we know who's not drinking the profits,' Thomas said and glared at Faith.

William quickly stepped alongside Mary. 'Let me show you to the door and thank you for your time. We'll be in touch regarding a starting date and to show you your room and the rest of the hotel. You'll fit in like a glove, Mary, of that I'm sure.' He placed his hand in the small of her back, urging her to join him on the walk to the doorway.

'Thank you once again! I can't believe that I've been so lucky as to be given the chance to work in such a place. It truly is beautiful.'

Mary took a final look around the bar and the lobby as she followed William to the revolving doors out onto the street.

It was beautiful! Her world had changed once again for the better, and what made it more beautiful was the look that she saw in William Winfield's eyes as he wished her goodnight. What a pity he was engaged to be married! He was the first man she actually thought that she could feel something for. It wasn't about the money, the way she thought about him, she just felt as if he genuinely liked her and that she could connect with him, even though he was way above her society. But now, she thought, she was daydreaming. Was it not enough that she had landed on her feet with the best job she could possibly have, let alone wish for the perfect man to go with it? She was lucky enough for now and should be thankful for what she had got, she thought, as she walked back to the reality of her present life at Riley's Court and the interrogation that she knew would be waiting for her from Nancy about her so-called visit to the library.

A good six weeks had passed when Nancy thought fit to tackle Mary over her frequent absences from home of an evening. 'I think that you've got a fella and that you're not letting on,' Nancy accused over the breakfast table.

'What are you on about?' Mary said sharply in reply and watched as Nancy spooned the last mouthful of her porridge into her mouth.

'Well, nearly every night last week you went to the library, or so you said, and now you're telling me that you're going again tonight. Well, I know for a fact that it's closed on a Monday evening – and that it doesn't stay open after eight, so you couldn't have gone there that first night. I know because the old grey-haired fella that looks like he's got no home and who works there always comes in for a drink of a Monday evening because he's not at work. You've got a man in your life, and you don't want me to know!' Nancy sat back in her chair and stared at Mary, saw the colour come to her cheeks. 'I knew it! You needn't deny it, your face tells me everything.' She tipped her chair back, gloating at her knowledge.

'Well, you're wrong, but seeing you've brought the subject up, I'll tell you what I've been up to – and I suppose it is time that I told you because it's going to affect you when I leave here.' Mary looked across at Nancy and noticed her announcement of leaving had taken the wind out of her sails, good and proper.

'Leave, what do you mean, leave? Where are you going? You can't leave me here on my own!' Nancy exclaimed.

'Right, but you can't say anything to anybody at work. Not, at least, before I get to speak to John Whitelock. You'll promise?' Mary gave Nancy a hard stare and watched as she nodded her head in agreement but at the same time gave her one of her well-known scowls.

'I've been going to the Palace Hotel, Nancy, because the Winfields have given me a job there when it officially opens in another two weeks. I've been learning the ropes and making sure I know how everything works before the rest of the staff are taken on, as I am to be in charge of the bar.' Mary stopped talking for a moment and looked at Nancy.

'You bloody dark horse! I thought it was a fella, for sure. Instead it's employment in the swankiest hotel in Leeds. Is it true that they have electricity and a bath in nearly every bedroom? All of Leeds is on about it. How did you wheedle yourself in there?' Nancy looked excited and gasped, hearing Mary's description of her new place of work and how Thomas Winfield had chased her for the job.

Mary sighed and left the worst news for Nancy last; she had been dreading telling her but she had to, to be right with her. 'Trouble is, Nancy, I'm going to be living there, so that leaves you living on your own here. Now, I'll tell Mr Whitelock that you are up to taking over my job behind the bar because that will help you financially. However, at the end of the day, it will be his decision and I feel bad that I might be leaving you unable to pay the rent.' No matter how tired of Nancy's relentless chatter she was, she still felt beholden to the lass that she had taken under her wing.

'What are you worrying about that for? Don't be daft! You go and better yourself, Mary Reynolds – you deserve it; you're always thinking of others and you run that bar like clockwork. Besides, I know you've been bored of late – and it'll be an excuse for Jake to move in with me. I'm not afraid of living over the brush, because there's no way I'm going to be married; I've seen what it does to a woman after watching how my father was with my mam. Though at the same time we're only human – we have our needs.' Nancy winked and grinned.

'Nancy Hudson! Have you no shame, What will Tess think of you? She'll tear you apart with her gossip,' Mary said and grinned, delighted that Nancy had taken her news so well.

'She can say all she wants, but she's no better herself. I've seen old George Summerfield coming away from her house in the early hours, his breeches just about round his ankles, so I know what they get up to.' Nancy grinned. 'You wish me luck and I'll do you the same. We've both got what we want, then, and well-deserved of it we are.' Nancy, for once in her life, smiled broadly and started thinking about life with her lover Jake under the same roof.

'That's put my mind at rest, then. Things are working out well – new job, new home, a new beginning for us both,' Mary said as she cleared the table and reached for her shawl. 'Still, I'm not looking forward to telling John Whitelock that I'm leaving his employment. He's been good to me.'

'He's been good to you because you've been good for him. The place has never been so busy, thanks to you, and I only hope that I can follow in your footsteps if I'm allowed, but I don't attract the men like you do, although you seem oblivious to your charms.'

'Don't be silly, Nancy. I don't attract the men and, if I do, I'm not aware of it. I've too much to do with my life before I get weighed down with a man to look after and a home and family to care for. I learned my lesson from Nell; she gave up her independence for Robert Jones only to be used and replaced as soon as she died. I aim to make my own way in society and that's just the chance my new position will give me. Now, come on and move yourself else we'll be late for work.'

'There, you see? That's the difference between you and me. You're determined and not swayed by anything, whereas I just live for the day, especially since all the trouble with my father. You'll go far in life, Mary, but you just don't realise the gifts that you have yet.' Nancy followed her friend out of the house, knowing that she was going to miss her, but also knowing her leaving would hopefully lead to a better life for her.

'Well, I thought you'd be here until a fella came along and swept you off your feet. And for you to go and work for Thomas Winfield! I'm disappointed in you, Mary. I thought at least you'd be loyal to me – after all, I did give you a leg up in the world when you needed it.' John Whitelock sat back in his chair and looked at Mary, who sat with her head bowed in front of him. 'Still, I can't hold you and I suppose you'll do what your heart tells you. We're obviously not enough for you.'

'It's not that at all, sir,' Mary protested. 'I've enjoyed my time working here and I truly appreciate all that you've taught me while I've worked behind the bar here. You and the staff will always be remembered fondly by me, but I feel it is time to move on and the Palace gives me that opportunity.' She looked at John Whitelock with gratitude, knowing that if she had not been spotted behind his bar, she would never have been considered by the Winfields.

'Aye, well, I can't say I blame you. I hear that he's got a right fancy place there and that he's given Leeds Corporation a few headaches with putting electricity into his hotel. It'll happen make them realise that not only the posh folk need it, but that it would benefit the whole of Leeds.' He looked at her. 'I'll wish you well, Mary Reynolds. I don't blame you for leaving us and I will put Nancy in your place as you suggest – she's a different lass since you took her under your wing.'

'Thank you, Mr Whitelock, I truly appreciate all that you've done for me and I hope that Whitelock's goes from strength to strength. The Palace will not touch your clientele – they really are more of a hotel and bar and they haven't got the skills of Mrs Trotter to hand!' Mary smiled.

'Aye, an old-fashioned gin palace, who would have thought it?' He shook his head. 'Stuff always comes back around and always will. Good luck, lass, I appreciate you giving me some time to organise myself here before you go, I just wish you were staying.'

Mary hugged Nancy close to her and wished her the best. It was moving-out day and she couldn't help but feel a little sad about it; after all, she had been independent in Riley's Court and now she was putting all her eggs into one basket with tied living accommodation going with her job. 'You'll keep in touch, won't you? And don't be too hard on Tess, she'll need you as a friend, never mind her gossip.' Mary held Nancy at arm's length.

'I will, don't worry about me, Mary. Jake and I will be fine, he'll be coming along with his stuff shortly. I just can't believe that you are taking so little of your own.' Nancy wiped away a tear and tried to smile.

'I don't need it, but if you ever decide to leave, let me know and I'll collect the one or two bits that happen do mean a little more to me. I've taken my personal belongings – pictures, letters and the odd ornament or two – but my new room is already furnished and I want for nothing. I'm leaving you that material – I haven't time to make myself a dress now and besides, the colour will suit you. There's everything you need and there's a choice of pattern. It can be my leaving present to you.' Mary picked up her large carpetbag and looked around the small cottage. 'Toby never did like this place, he said we would not be here long and he's been proven right.' She smiled and walked out into the yard, leaving Nancy watching her as she left for her new way in life.

Chapter 12

Mary looked around what was now her new home. She was three storeys up in the Palace Hotel, on the same landing as most of the resident staff, but she had one of the larger bedrooms and the luxury of a double bed, which she had found to be comfortable after her first night in the hotel. The whole room was luxurious compared to Riley's Court; she had a dressing table, a wardrobe and a washstand, and a shared bathroom at the end of the hallway with hot and cold water, something she had only ever dreamed of.

She was blessed, she thought, as she looked around and then went to the window to pull back the curtains and look down onto the busy Headrow that ran through the centre of Leeds. There, she could see horses and carts and cabs making their way back and forward while people hurried about their business and stopped and talked to one another. She'd never be short of something to watch, she thought, as she went over to the wardrobe and opened the doors. Within it was the one thing that Mary was not happy about as she stood in her vest and bloomers …

Along with her new position and room had come the responsibility of dressing the part and she had been sent to see Madame Boulevard at Sharp and Wright's, the dress-makers with whom the Winfields had an account and who had measured her up for four delightful new dresses to wear while working. The dresses were beautiful; all four were delicate and ornately decorated with lace, sequin and fake pearls that caught the light and shimmered as she walked. It was what she had to wear under the dress that she hated – a corset that pulled her waist in and made it very hard to breathe. She hated it, but all the ladies of fashion were wear-ing it, seemingly, so she must do the same. She'd been able to stand her ground a little and insist that she would have a front-laced corset, rather than have to ask the assistance of a maid every morning to pull her laces tight up her back, but now, as she fit the corset around her body and started to lace herself up tightly, binding the tops of her hips and squeezing her waist into the smallest shape yet, she was near to the point of swearing. There was something to be said for being an ordinary working-class lass who didn't need such finery. How was she to go about her work, trussed up like a goose at Christmas, she wondered when she finally secured the ribbons tight and looked at herself in the mirror. If God had meant to make women that shape he would have done so in the first place, she thought, as she slipped the dress of her choice over her shoulders and struggled to button it up without the aid of a maid.

It had taken her half an hour longer than usual just to get dressed and now she would have to see to her hair before going downstairs and eating breakfast in the kitchen, along with the other staff who lived in and whom she had yet to meet. Then she was to be introduced to the waiters and three girls she was in charge of, who were to serve behind the bar before the grand opening at noon. It was to be a big day at the Palace Hotel, one that a lot of people had been waiting for, not least Thomas and William Winfield, who had sunk a lot of money into their new venture and now it was time to see some reward.

She parted her long dark hair in the middle and braided each of the hanks before plaiting it, then coiling it around her head and fixing it in place on each side of her face; she then placed a pair of jet earrings that had been Nell's in her ears. She smiled at her reflection and wondered what Nell would have thought about her looking and living like this. Not to mention her dear mother, who had, so briefly, tasted a fleeting glimpse of the good life, only to have it taken away from her ... She was not going to let that happen to her, not if she had her way.

Mary stood up, quelled the butterflies in her stomach, and tried to forget the restrictions of her corset as she made her way along the corridor and down three flights of stairs to the kitchen, where she knew the staff, who were valued and were key to the running of the new hotel, were to sit and dine together of a morning. She breathed in and composed herself, telling herself that everybody was in the same boat this morning, all new, all wondering who else they were working with and if they would all gel together. It had been obvious from an earlier meeting with all the staff there were going to be teething problems but nothing that couldn't be sorted. She should have nothing to worry about, she convinced herself as she opened the staff's kitchen door and walked into the room.

'Good morning,' she said and smiled at the faces around the table, watching as a young maid bobbed and waited for her to be seated before filling her teacup with tea and placing the toast in front of her.

'Good morning. So, you are employed here with the rest of us? May I ask your name?' A stern-looking gentleman of middle age, sitting at the end of the table, enquired and looked at the rest of the faces as they all gazed at Mary.

'I'm Mary Reynolds. I'm here to manage the bar, especially the girls behind it and the waiters. I feel exceptionally privileged to be joining you all this morning.' Mary smiled and unfolded her napkin on her knee and reached for some toast.

'I'm Mr Roger Birbeck and I'm the general manager. I think you will find that you are answerable to me, as is everyone at this table.' He gestured arrogantly and puffed his chest out with pride as he looked around at what he thought was his domain.

'I don't mean to be disrespectful, Mr Birbeck, but I think if you ask Mr Thomas or Mr William Winfield, they will tell you that the bar area is my domain and mine only. However, I am sure that you will have complete management of the rest of the hotel's staff.' Mary was going to stand her ground; she knew that she was answerable to no one but the Winfields for the running of the bar and she wasn't going to let this pompous man think otherwise.

The rest of the staff looked down at their plates and tried to ignore the conversation unfolding in front of them.

'I think that you are incorrect there, Miss Reynolds. I presume it is *Miss*,' he said caustically. 'I will go this minute and get clarification from Thomas Winfield. This needs to be sorted straight away.' Roger Birbeck rose from his chair, throwing his napkin down on his plate. The rest of the staff were quiet until he disappeared out of the room.

'I'm Raymond,' a thin, tired-looking man smiled at Mary as he spoke. 'I look after the wine cellar, so we'll be seeing a lot of one another. This is Madge who's in charge of the housemaids and Geoff over there is in charge of the stables. Mr Braithwaite is the main cook – or I should say, chef, if grumpy Birbeck was here. We've all been talked to as though we had dirt on our shoes by him, so don't take it to heart.'

'It's nice to meet you all. It looks like I've got off to a bad start with Roger Birbeck, but I know that he has nothing to do with my part of the hotel, no matter what he thinks. He can do what he wants with the rest, but I'm guessing by his attitude he'll run roughshod over the lot of us if he's given half a chance.' Mary smiled and looked at all the faces that were gazing at her.

'He's there for problems and problems only. I'm not having him dallying in *my* kitchen,' Mr Braithwaite announced. 'He'll have to find his position here like all of us and learn to work together with us. None of us are any better than the rest, else we wouldn't need to work.'

'Quite true, Mr Braithwaite,' Raymond said with gusto. 'The Winfields will tell him *exactly* what his duties are. I think he'd like to take command because he's ex-army. Did you not hear him say that he'd seen service in China?'

'Well, he can bugger off back – and he'd better not come near me and my stables. I know what needs doing and with my two stable lads, I'll do it and it'll be without his help.' Geoff grinned and looked around the table.

Mary smiled and got on with her breakfast. With the exception of Roger Birbeck, the rest of the staff sitting around the table were just like her and she was sure Roger would eventually fit in once he got used to his new role in life.

Mary walked up the stairs after eating a very meagre breakfast – if that was how corsets made you feel, she thought, no wonder everyone fainted while wearing them. She'd been served one of the best breakfasts ever seen but had not been able to indulge due to the corset's restrictions. On her days off, she vowed, she would not wear it and just enjoy her food. She was thinking of that when she reached the large hallway and saw Roger Birbeck talking to Thomas Winfield as they stood next to the reception desk. She hurried past them, not wanting to become part of the debate, but couldn't help but notice the redness in Roger's cheeks and the anger on Thomas Winfield's face; she hoped that it was not all of her making as she quickly made her way into her domain and stood and looked around her. In another two hours, the place would be full to the rafters with drinkers, guests and the curious of Leeds. She, along with her girls, would have to put on a show, smile and serve drinks – and they would have to do that every day, come rain or shine. She ran her hand along the highly polished bar and looked at the row upon row of bottles, at the glasses all waiting to be filled and drunk from. This bar was like no other in Leeds and it was bound to be a success – she'd make it a success, she and her girls, who she would encourage to smile and chat with each and every customer and listen to their woes. She leaned against the bar and closed her eyes for a moment of dreaming but was suddenly awakened by the voice of William Winfield.

'Lord, look at you. You look absolutely beautiful, if I may say so!' William smiled. 'Definitely the right person for the right job; my father and I were right.'

Mary blushed as William's glance swept her up and down.

'I hear that you've had a run-in with Roger Birbeck; he's just been complaining to my father but he got short shrift. I think it was a case of him not understanding his initial duties, so we all know where we stand now. He thought he was in charge of the entire hotel, but we have told him he's there in case of any problems and that our staff should find him approachable, not an ogre. To manage with a delicate but firm hand, not to go in ham-fisted.' William looked around him. 'Are you ready to meet your girls? I think that you'll find that we've chosen wisely. There's a brunette, a blonde and a redhead and they are all genuinely lovely, all from different backgrounds but all with lovely manners, which is what counts, and they will all do their jobs well, especially with the help of the waiters, most of whom have come from our other hotel in Leeds, so they are all experienced.' William looked around him. 'My father is proud of this place and I'm so grateful for his gift to Faith and me.'

'You must both be proud and grateful; I think the Palace is the most glorious place that I have ever stepped foot in. I know I'm going to enjoy my time here and I'm grateful to be working here. I'm sorry I've got off to a bad start with Roger Birbeck, and of course I will seek his help if I do have any problems, but I'm rather hoping that will never be the case,' Mary said, looking at William. He was handsome and well-dressed, a true city gent, and she felt her heart flutter as she caught his eye.

'I'm sure you won't. Now, here comes Mr Birbeck and I do believe he is bringing your staff with him, so perhaps now is the time to bury the hatchet.' William winked and then smiled at the three young women and Roger Birbeck as he made his way out of the bar.

Mary waited until Roger and the girls reached her. 'Thank you for showing these young ladies to me, Mr Birbeck. Ladies, would you mind sitting in the seats over there, until I have had a word in private with Mr Birbeck?' Mary looked at the three young women who were all dressed in different colours of the same dress, which had been especially designed and made for the Palace Hotel; they all looked absolutely stunning and did as she had asked.

Roger Birbeck stood in front of Mary and dropped his head. 'I'm glad that you are still speaking to me, Miss Reynolds. I feel I perhaps owe you an apology, now that I have been put in the picture of how the bar is to run. I'm used to everybody jumping to my tune, having been a sergeant major in Her Majesty's army. I feel perhaps that I have overstretched my rank with most of the staff here already.'

'And perhaps I was quick to judge. Now, how about we start over again? We can't afford ill-feeling between any of us if we are to work well together. I will, of course, ask for your advice if I need it and report to you if anything untoward happens. But at present, thank you for showing my girls to me.' Mary smiled and held out her hand. 'Please, call me Mary, and yes, you are right – I am single, else I would not be working here, doing this job. However, now I need to get to know my staff before the doors are open to the world and I'm sure you have many things to do.'

'Apologies it is, then. I look forward to working with you, Mary, and I'll try not to be so brusque in the future. The waiters will be yours, as and when you need them, I'll see to that.' Roger stood and then quickly turned away with his usual military swagger. He'd been put firmly in his place when it came to Mary Reynolds, who seemed to have special favour with the Winfields, so he would pay heed to that in the future.

'Now, ladies, I'm sorry that you have to wait for my attention.' Mary walked over to the three girls who were sitting quietly together, looking around at the bar and room which was going to be their home eight hours or more every day. 'I'm Miss Reynolds, but please call me Mary unless we are speaking in front of Mr Winfield Senior – he would prefer you to show me respect. However, I'm not that worried – as long as you work hard and do as I say, you can call me whatever name you like. Now, each of you tell me your name and a little about yourself. We have time to get acquainted, although before the doors are opened and customers made welcome, there is to be an interview and photography event on the main steps and the Winfields would like all their staff to take part.' Mary smiled and watched the excitement on each girl's face. 'Now you, dear: what's your name and where do you come from and what family do you have?' Mary looked at the girl with the stunning red hair and waited.

'I'm Molly Askew, Miss Reynolds, but my friends just call me Moll for short. I live over at Kirkstall with my mother and father; he works at the iron forge and my mother keeps house. I've been working for Thwaites Brewery, so I know my beer, but I also know how to look after folk and make sure they have what they need.' The other two girls sniggered at her last few words.

'I tell you what,' Mary said sharply, 'there will be none of that, you two. We will run a respectable bar and I expect you to keep yourselves to yourselves while you're at work. What you do after hours is your own business. Thank you, Molly, and now how about you? Let's hear a bit about you.' Mary looked at the dark-haired girl, who was the bonniest of the three, with the bluest of eyes that twinkled when she laughed.

'My name is Shona Brown and, as you can probably tell by my accent, I'm not from around these parts. I came down from Glasgow looking for work in the woollen mills when my ma died, but I hated the grease and the heat and the smell of the wool and I wasn't about to lose an arm or a leg to the spinning machines that move so quickly. I live in a rented room just off Inkerman Street and I was working at the Wheatsheaf until Mr Winfield offered me work here. I can't thank him enough! I never thought that I'd be sitting here, in this posh place, in clothes as fine as these, waiting for my photograph to be taken.' Shona hardly stopped for breath as she grinned and looked around her and then folded her hands, noticing that Mary was smiling at her with amusement.

'And that leaves just you, my dear?' Mary nodded at the blonde girl, who seemed to be the quietest of them all.

'I'm Beth Harper; I live with my mother and my baby in the terraced houses just off Park Lane. My husband died in a pit disaster and I've been making a living as best I can since his death. My baby is only nine months old, but he'll not cause any bother, Miss Reynolds; my mother will look after him when I'm at work. Like Shona, I am ever so grateful for my employment and won't let you down behind the bar. I know how to pull a pint and I know my drinks – and my manners, come to that.' Beth looked at Mary worriedly; she knew that she would be thinking that with a baby came responsibility but she only hoped that Mary would have some sympathy for her plight.

'Don't worry, Beth, I'll not hold having a child to raise against you. You must miss your husband and you must have been very young when you got married – and to be left so soon?' Mary looked at her with sympathy and compassion; she was the one who needed the job the most and the one she would have to protect.

'I was eighteen when we got married and nineteen when I became a widow and a mother. If it hadn't had been for my mother's support I'd have been on the streets trying to make a living – either that or the poor house,' Beth said softly as Shona put her arm around her and gently hugged her.

'Well, you are part of the Palace staff now, my Gin Girls, as I'm going to call you, as I well know what drink the customers will want the most. As long as you smile, serve the customers and make them welcome – but not *too* welcome, Molly,' Mary said, grinning, 'we will work well together. Mr Birbeck is to see that we have waiters when we come back from having our photographs taken and they will serve the people sitting in chairs. Leave them to it unless you can see that there's a table that needs clearing or somebody is asking for your attention. I want you girls behind the bar, encouraging everyone to drink and spend money. The more money they spend, the more secure our jobs – and I include mine in that. I've been low in life too, so I know all about making ends meet. Now, all of you stand up and let me get a good look at all of you. Do you like your outfits? At least they look more comfortable than mine!' Mary looked at her girls as they stood and tried to look as comfortable as she expected them to. 'Very smart and practical! I love the way that they have given you glittering black ties at the necks of your blouses and the same on the ends of your sleeves and your skirts are not too tight but at the same not too flared. You all look really smart.' Mary smiled and stood back.

'I should say, woo-hoo, they all look like the cat's whiskers!' A man carrying a suitcase with a hat perched jauntily on his head stopped and grinned at the group as he walked past them. 'You don't look too bad yourself, if you don't mind me saying,' he added, flashing the whitest set of teeth Mary had ever seen and making the girls giggle.

'I'm sorry, but who are you?' Mary asked sharply, feeling rather embarrassed by the man's comments.

'I'm Leonard T. Barns and I'm here to play that little baby over there. To tinkle on the ivories while you girls get my listeners more drunk by the minute.' He motioned to the large grand piano that was at the end of the bar. 'I'm sure going to have something nice to watch while I play away.' Leonard said with an American brawl.

'I'm sure we all find your comments flattering, but perhaps you should keep them to yourself.' Mary looked at the man who, to her mind, was cheekily outspoken.

'I say as I see and you all look fine, just right for this swanky place. Now, if you'll excuse me, I'll go and admire from afar and set myself up for the crowd that's gathering outside. There are reporters and a photographer – it's a big day for sure.' Leonard grinned and looked back at the girls as he walked over to the piano and placed his case, out of which which he produced a trumpet, on the top.

'Right, a quick look behind the bar, girls, although Mr Winfield has already told me that you've been shown the ropes and where everything is at, and then we'll go and join the rest of them on the steps for the all-important photograph.' Mary ushered her girls like a mother hen to the back of the bar and answered all the questions the girls came up with as they looked at the different drinks and shapes of glasses and managed the three ornate brass cash machines that stood proudly on the shelf behind the bar. She soon realised that any drink request could be dealt with because all three girls had been taught well. The Winfields had made excellent choices, she thought as she walked with them through the lobby to the grand entrance and the steps where it would seem that the whole of Leeds had gathered for the grand opening of the Palace Hotel.

Chapter 13

The streets outside were thronged with people who wanted to say that they were one of the first to have crossed the threshold of the extravagant new hotel, fitted with luxuries that had never been seen before. The photographers and news reporters hovered and asked questions, eager for news for their papers.

'I believe the Palace is a wedding present to yourself and Miss Robinson,' a reporter from the *Leeds Mercury* shouted at William Winfield and his fiancée as they stood in the middle of the group of the most important staff at the Palace. 'How do you feel about that, Miss Robinson?'

'I'm most grateful to my future father-in-law,' she curtly replied. 'I'm such a lucky woman, living so close to my husband's work, albeit in such a grand setting.' She tried to smile. When she had first courted William Winfield, she had in mind grander living accommodation than a two-bedroom apartment in a hotel. She had hoped for a large house set in its own grounds; instead, she had been given work on her own doorstep and a place to live surrounded by other people with no privacy. And she stood high in Leeds society – it was right for her to expect more.

'Is the wedding still set for June the twenty-third? Will the reception be held here? Can we expect any famous names to attend, Mr Winfield?' the reporter shouted at William.

'I'm sorry,' he responded with a friendly smile, 'today is about the opening of the Palace. However, yes, the wedding *is* still scheduled for June the twenty-third and the reception will be here, but it will only be family and very close friends who are invited.' William glanced at Faith; he hadn't discussed the wedding plans with her of late – the hotel had taken up too much of his time and too much of his and his father's money, if truth be told, and this would come as news to her. 'Now, if you'll excuse me, we have, as I'm sure you know, work to do. Father, over to you.'

Thomas Winfield looked down at the crowds and smiled as he waved for the staff gathered around him to go and attend their positions in readiness for the baying crowds. 'It's my pleasure to announce that the Palace is now open! Please join us in our celebrations.'

He cut the ribbon that had been placed across one of the revolving doors and watched as the people swarmed in like bees into a hive as he, William and Faith stood to one side. This was the day he had waited for and it was his proudest moment; he'd battled Leeds Corporation for planning consents, argued with the banks, but today was the day when he would start to see some return for all his hard work and settle his son in a home for life, regardless of how ungrateful his future daughter-in-law had sounded.

William patted his father on the back as they walked into the lobby. 'Thank you, Father, this means everything to me. It is the best present anyone could possibly receive and I will run it with love and care. Just look at the astonishment everyone is showing as they look around – there isn't another place like this in the whole of Yorkshire.' William smiled happily as he looked around, and then he noticed Faith disappearing up the stairs, away from the eyes of the fascinated crowd.

Thomas saw the disappointment on his son's face. 'I don't think Faith shares the same dream as us, William. I heard the note of sarcasm in her reply to the reporters. I only hope that she changes her mind and sees that she will want for nothing when this place becomes the success we both know it will be.' Thomas sighed. He'd not said anything to his only son, but he had, from the outset of William's courtship, wondered if Faith was more interested in William's money than the man himself.

'Oh, she'll return shortly, Father. She'll be savouring our new rooms and thinking of personal touches that she can add once she has moved into the apartment.' William tried to hide the doubt in his eyes; of late, he and Faith had not seen eye to eye over many things, the biggest being that they must live in a busy hotel with William on call twenty-four hours a day.

'Well, I hope she will – she'll be the face of the Palace and I expect that of her at least.' Thomas looked at his son and gauged his mood. 'You know it's not too late to change your mind? You don't have to go ahead with the wedding, William, the hotel will still be yours and it's not as if she is in the family way.'

'Father, please! Don't say another word. I love Faith and the wedding stands. Now, don't let any doubts spoil this day. I'll speak to Faith later before she returns home. As I say, she will have gone to our rooms to rearrange what we have placed in them so far, that is all.' William smiled wanly; he'd say anything not to spoil his father's big day, but he knew by the looks on Faith's face that he would, yet again, be arguing with her over something he hadn't realised that he'd done which had upset her.

Mary and her girls had never seen so many people in one space before and they couldn't serve them fast enough, even with Mary giving the girls a hand behind the bar.

'I hope that it's not this busy every day,' Beth said quietly to Mary. 'We'll be run off our feet.'

'It's curiosity today; half of them have come to have a good nosy. Some of them are just standing and looking at the chandeliers and wondering how the incandescent bulbs will be changed. I hope they don't ask me, because I haven't got a clue. I'm still in awe of them myself!' Mary laughed.

'Here, lass, can I have a gin when you've done talking?' An elderly man leaned over the bar and looked at Mary.

'Certainly, sir, which one would you like? Old Tom, Plymouth Dry, Hendrick's, Sapphire? And would that be with tonic or just neat?' Mary enquired.

'Bloody hell, I just want a gin, not an encyclopaedia! And you can hold the bloody fizzy water,' he replied and stuck his finger out at the Old Tom bottle. Mary served him quickly and watched him battle his way through the crowds as the next customer made their way to her.

'He's one from the old school; I've been mostly serving gin with tonic and a slice of lemon this morning – the way they drink it in India is more popular now and it's not as savage to drink. It's quite refreshing – even I like a tipple,' Shona shouted down the bar as she smiled at her next customer.

'Lordy, we're busy!' Molly laughed as she passed her customer two pints of dark stout and waited until he counted the change out of his pocket. 'I can hardly hear the piano playing. I think he's playing *Daisy Bell*. Oh, I love that song, especially the bicycle made for two chorus. My mam sings it all the time and drives my father crazy because she's always out of tune.'

'Oh, thank goodness for that!' Mary exclaimed. 'Mr Birbeck has sent some waiters to help us out. They can collect the dirty glasses and see to anyone who wants a repeat drink. I thought that he'd gone back on his word.' She sighed with relief as three waiters dressed in dapper eveningwear came in with pristine white napkins over their arms and quickly started to clear any empty glasses which had been left on the tables and enquire of the people sitting if they wanted a drink. 'Beth, you see to the waiters' orders and us three will serve everybody else – I think it will quieten down after the first hour or so,' Mary said, hoping that what she said would come true as she watched customers shove for a position at the bar and try and grab her attention by waving their money.

'Mr Birbeck sends his apologies, Miss Reynolds. He's so busy he doesn't know which way to turn, else we would have been here earlier. Every room downstairs is busy and poor Mr Braithwaite is nearly exploding, he has that many orders of luncheon to see to. Mr Winfield himself is behind the check-in desk, helping out because there are that many people wanting to stay here,' the more senior of the waiters said to Mary as he waited for his tray of drinks from Beth.

'I'm just thankful you're here now. So, Mr Birbeck is doing a good job in his role as manager and I'll tell him so next time that I talk to him.'

'Thank you, miss, I'm sure he'll appreciate that. We've all decided his bark is worse than his bite because he's been pretty fair with us this morning when one or two of us made mistakes,' the waiter said as he looked around the room. 'It's a posh place, this, and I see you have a door that leads out directly onto the street without going through the lobby. That's a stroke of genius, because ordinary folk can come in, nearly unnoticed, grab a drink and then leave. You're always going to be busy in this part of the world.'

'Yes, we're getting a mixture of all sorts of customers this morning and I expect it will continue like that all day. I think the Winfields can be proud of themselves – I certainly would be – and Miss Robinson should be thankful for such a generous gift to get them started in life. Not that we should comment about our employer's lives.'

'From the gossip that I've been hearing, I don't think that she is. Did you not see her face as she walked away after the photographs and reporters? She's not taken part in anything this morning, except the glamorous bit,' the waiter said and shook his head as he balanced the tray, laden with different drinks given to him by Beth, in his hands and then weaved his way through the crowd.

'Trouble at the mill already?' Beth smiled at Mary. 'Sorry, I couldn't help but overhear, but as you say it is none of our business,' she added and then went on to put the next tray of drinks together.

Mary looked around her; how could anyone not appreciate all the work and the craftsmanship that had been put into the building of the Palace? She had taken an instant dislike to Faith Robinson, who was clearly the sort of person who liked to keep other people in their place. The few times that she had spoken to her, Faith had had a sneering look of contempt on her face and she never seemed to agree with her fiancé, William. However, it was nothing to do with her, she thought, as she smiled at her next customer, while still watching that her three girls were doing their duties. She just hoped that there was enough drink in the cellars below to keep the bar topped up for what was going to be a long day …

*

'I don't know about you, Miss Reynolds, but I'm just a little on the tired side.' Roger Birbeck leaned on the bar, which was being closed and cleaned by all Mary's three tired girls before they went home.

'Yes, it's been a long but profitable day. My feet ache and my head is throbbing,' Mary said as she watched her girls finish their work for the day. 'Be careful walking back home, you three, and thank you for your work today – we couldn't have survived without you all.'

'Thank you, Mary,' all three chimed together as they pulled on their coats and secured their hats and walked slowly out of the bar by the side door.

'Mary, is it? Do you not think they should call you Miss Reynolds? Shouldn't you distinguish yourself from them, else they will think that you are no better than them?' Roger looked at Mary, frowning.

'I'm happy with being called Mary, because I *am* no better than them; I'm just a bar girl who is good at her job and I'm not one for airs and graces. Besides, when you all work in such a small space you have to get on with one another, else it doesn't work.'

'As long as you can keep them in line. I'm afraid *I* will be demanding the staff call me Mr Birbeck – it's only good manners,' Roger huffed and looked at the drinks behind him. 'There's plenty to go there. I see that you have my favourite whisky – I'm partial to a drop of James Eadie's Trade Mark X,' he said with a glint in his eye.

'Would you like a tot now? Mr Winfield said I could have a drink on the house at the end of the day and, as I don't drink, there's no fear of me ever doing that.' Mary knew full well, by the look on his face, what his answer would be.

'No, I couldn't ask you to go behind the bar again, it's closed for the night. But I must admit it would be a grand nightcap, something to help me sleep after such a hard day. I have no doubt it will be just the same in the morning, for nearly every room has guests booked in them.' Roger looked over at the bottle that had caught his attention.

'Then let me get you one – and you are welcome to have a free one on the house every night. Just the one, mind, because it's me who will have to account for it if any more is drunk,' Mary said as she quickly went behind the long bar, opened the bottle and poured a dram into a tumbler for the eager-eyed Roger. 'I've no ice, but you can add a splash of water to it.' Mary pushed the water jug, which had the advertisement for James Eadie's whisky blazoned on it, towards Roger.

'Nay, you don't spoil a good thing by watering it down,' he said as he took the tumbler from Mary and quickly swigged it back. 'You are a good woman and I'll take you up on your offer of a wee dram together of an evening. Not every night, but it will be welcome sup with the good company of an evening when I'm feeling low.'

'Are you not married, Mr Birbeck?' Mary asked and looked at him as he placed his tumbler down on the bar. 'Is there no Mrs Birbeck?'

'No, my life in the army never let me settle long enough and nobody would want me now. I'm too set in my ways, and too long in the tooth now that I'm in my mid-forties. Once the army had done with me I thought this job working here was ideal for me, seeing that it came with living accommodation and meals, and I felt it would be time to have an easier life. But after today I don't know if easy is the right word!' Roger put his empty tumbler down on the bar and looked at Mary. 'And yourself, what brings an attractive young single woman to be working here?'

'I like to be independent, Mr Birbeck. I've no family and, like yourself, I have no commitments nor any intention of settling down as of yet. My work here will be my world for now.' Mary stifled a yawn and wished that she could go to bed but didn't want to be rude.

'Please, it's Roger, when we're alone. Now, we are both tired and I suggest we call it a day. Which floor are you on? They've seen fit, in their wisdom, to have put me up in the heavens in a rather large attic bedroom – I think, perhaps, to keep me away from the rest of the staff.' He grinned.

'I'm on the third floor, just above the turret, where I have a good view of the Headrow.' Mary looked at the empty glass on the bar; it could wait to be washed in the morning. The rest of the room would be cleaned and freshened by the maids and another day would soon be upon them all, she thought, as she and Roger made their way up the sweeping stairs to their rooms.

'Good night, Mary,' Roger said as he left her on the third floor. He watched as she walked to her room and then made his way to his. Mary Reynolds was an extremely good-looking woman and he knew she had spirit after the way she'd put him in his place that morning. Perhaps she was the woman he had been waiting for all his life, he thought, as he stripped down to his vest and laid his suit out for the following day before climbing into his bed, plus she came with the benefit of a whisky each night. Perhaps life was going his way after all . . .

Downstairs, Mary lay in her bed; she was exhausted but she couldn't sleep for the noise that was coming from the flat below her. It was after midnight but she could hear William Winfield and his fiancée shouting and rowing over something or other. Everyone, it seemed, had seen the displeasure on Faith's face, although she herself had been oblivious to it as she had been too concerned about the running of her bar. She pulled the pillow over her head as she heard doors bang and plates crash. This in no way sounding like a happy arrangement, she thought, and even with the pillow she could still hear William shouting, 'Please come back, Faith! Let's talk.'

Mary breathed in deeply and closed her eyes. It was probably just a lover's tiff, but everyone above and below must have heard it. William deserved so much better than Faith, she thought, as she at last settled down to sleep. But as long as the hotel and bar were all right, that was all she was concerned about. The Palace might not be owned by her, but she had found happiness in her new surroundings and no way did she want it to change. As she slowly closed her eyes on the day, she hoped that the argument below her was just a momentary thing, that tensions had been running high with the opening day and that it would not affect her or the running of the hotel …

Chapter 14

The hotel was already busy with people coming and going even though it was only early in the morning as Mary made her way from the staff dining room. There hadn't been as many staff around the table this morning, most of them already being hard at their duties. Mary's day was the opposite to most, starting mid-morning and finishing late in the evening, so she realised that having a leisurely breakfast by herself was going to be the one luxury of the working day, the time where she could gather her thoughts and think about what was to come. She was still concerned about the arguing that she had heard coming from William's rooms below hers as she happened to glance him as he was just about to disappear into his office which was adjacent to the lobby. William noticed her and stopped in his tracks.

'Miss Reynolds, do you think I could have a word with you in my office, please?' He looked weary; there were bags under his eyes and he barely smiled as he kept the door open with his hand for her to enter his domain.

The office walls were lined with dark oak and the furniture was dark leather, all of it had been salvaged from the original hotel that had stood there. Mary felt nervous; had she done something wrong? Was she going to be chastised for giving Roger Birbeck a drink of an expensive whisky before they retired?

'Is everything all right, Mr Winfield? Did you want to speak to me about something specific? I did tally the tills up and give your father our takings last night and the girls worked exceptionally well – they make a good team.' Mary wanted to tell him quickly that her part of the world had been very successful the previous day and that he need have no concerns with any of the bar staff. However, she soon realised that it was not business that he wanted to speak to her about.

'Yes, yes, you all did exceptionally well yesterday. The takings on the bar were more than we ever dreamed of and everyone is putting their heart and soul into the running of the hotel – apart from one or two who perhaps could have been more helpful.' William ran his fingers through his slicked-back dark hair and looked at Mary. 'I've asked you into the office to offer you my apologies, because you must have borne the brunt of Faith's and my disagreement last night. I apologise if we kept you awake.' He looked sheepishly at Mary, noticing her blushes.

'It's none of my business, sir. I heard very little and you need say nothing more,' Mary said quietly to the worried man.

'Thank you, Mary, I appreciate that.' William sank into his chair and held his head in his hands.

'Are you all right, sir?' Mary went and stood closer to the desk, looking with pity at the man she respected and admired. He and his father had been nothing but good to her and now perhaps he needed her support.

William sighed. 'She's left me, Mary! Faith threw her engagement ring at me and told me that our wedding was off, that she didn't love me and that she had higher expectations than living in a hotel and waiting for me to return to her at all hours of the day and night!' He looked at her with tears in his eyes. 'My father was right; she didn't love me, she was just after my money. How can I face him and tell him that I've made a terrible mistake?'

Mary looked at the distraught William; he shouldn't be telling her all this but he'd been brooding over it all night and she it seemed was the one who had caught him at his most vulnerable moment.

'I'm sorry to hear that, sir. Perhaps this morning, after she has cooled down and realised that yesterday was a big day and that the hours that you worked were exceptional, she'll come back and apologise. I'm sure she didn't mean half the words that were said.' Mary stood awkwardly and looked at her boss. She wanted to put her arms around him and give him comfort. 'Perhaps she felt neglected,' she added and hoped she was saying the right words.

'Neglected? She had everything that she could wish for at her feet. She could have swanned around this hotel and been treated like a queen. There is nothing that she would have wanted for, nothing that I would not have done for her. The truth is, Mary, she really didn't love me; she expected more than I could give her and she will not be back.' William rose from his chair and turned his back on her, looking out onto the busy street outside his window. 'I'm sorry, I shouldn't be telling you all this, you should get back to your work.' He turned and blew his nose hard. 'Forgive me, yesterday took its toll on me. It might be as you say that Faith regrets her words and returns later in the day. If not, then I should think myself lucky because I have escaped from a loveless marriage.'

'I'll get back to my work then. And sir, don't worry; I'll not say a word of this to anyone and if you need someone to talk to then please just find me. I might not be able to help but I'm a good listener and I'll be a true confidante.' Mary walked to the office door and quietly opened it, then closed William in behind her. Outside in the lobby, people were going about their business, checking in at the desk and being shown to their rooms by the bellboys. Roger Birbeck was busy seeing to a woman's enquiries as she passed him so was too busy to talk to her. The world was getting on with the business of living while William Winfield's heart was breaking, and Mary knew Faith Robinson would not be returning; she'd seen her sort before. Once she had realised that all William's money was tied up in the Palace and that she might one day have to work for her money, she had thought better of marrying him.

Mary had seen what sort of woman she was the first night that they had met. She had, however, put her dislike of Faith down to pangs of jealousy for she had been attracted to William Winfield from the very first day she had set eyes on him, knowing he was way out of her league. She could love him, penniless or wealthy, if he would only let her, but that would never be possible and she knew it as she walked into the filling barroom and smiled at her girls, who were already chattering to one another behind the bar.

'Sorry, girls, I'm late – you're putting me to shame.' Mary smiled and looked at the three. 'Are you ready for another day? I think this one will be quieter hopefully, unless Leonard gets carried away at the piano, seeing that he is grinning so much at you all.' Mary gave Len a warning look. 'It was an opening day bonanza yesterday and while I hope that we will be somewhere near as busy, not with such a crush today.'

'Sorry, we've been talking to Len.' Shona turned and waved and grinned at the flirtatious piano player. 'We've come to an arrangement with him because Moll had a bit of a fright last night.'

'Yes, I was scared stiff, I was. Thought someone was following me all the way home to Kirkstall. It was right creepy and I thought twice about coming back again today. A self-respecting girl shouldn't be out at that hour for I saw all sorts on my way home,' Moll said and sighed.

'Well, we've sorted it now, Moll. What's going to happen, Mary, is that Len's going to walk all three of us home. It's not too far out of his way – he only lives down the road from Moll and the rest of us are en route.' Shona looked at Mary. 'He was only too willing when we told him what happened.'

'I bet he was; do you think you can trust him?' Mary looked across at Len, who had started playing quietly at the piano.

'Oh, yes, he says he's a father of four and wants nothing to do romantically with young, innocent girls. Although some of us are not that innocent and we can hold our own when we are together.' Shona giggled and looked at Beth.

'I'll have a word with him, just to make sure that he knows exactly where he stands. I agree that it is very kind of him to walk you all home, but I need to know that he doesn't expect payment in kind. After all, I need to keep my girls safe,' Mary said and frowned at Len.

Len looked across at the girls and Mary talking about him and knew instantly that if he didn't do what was expected of him, and if he did anything other than be honourable to the three girls who had taken his fancy, it would be the worse for him. Mary would be serving his balls, pickled in one of her gin and tonics, and not think twice about it.

'Well, to be honest, William, I think that you're better off without her. You know what I thought of her and it's best she left you now before you had to go through a messy divorce and put this place at risk.' Thomas Winfield looked at his distraught son. 'Your mother from the very start didn't like her, she said she was just a money grabber, it is why she didn't attend the hotel's opening, she couldn't stand there and play second fiddle to a woman who she knew was going to break your heart.'

I'm too soft. I found myself breaking down in front of Mary Reynolds this morning, to my shame. I started out apologising for the noise that must have kept her awake while Faith and I rowed and, before I knew it, I was telling her my inner secrets.' William sat down and looked up at his father, sighing.

'Well, you could have done worse. Mary will keep your heartbreak to herself – she's discreet. In fact, Faith would have done well to have taken a leaf from her book; from the amount of money that they took over the bar she and her girls must have worked exceptionally hard yesterday. Instead, your wife-to-be hid away and did nothing. Believe me, she's a weight off my mind – she was never right for you. Move on, look at what you've got, find someone else to replace her and put all this behind you. She isn't worth the worry, lad, believe me.' Thomas sighed with relief; he never had liked Faith Robinson and now she was gone after showing her true colours.

'Aye, she's a good lass, is Mary; she was very understanding, I'll have to thank her later. Perhaps you're right, Father, I'm better off without Faith – it's just that folk will gossip and she blatantly stood at the opening yesterday, although she must have known that she was thinking of leaving me then. The papers will make the most of it once they hear of my predicament.' William scowled.

'The papers will write what they want, so take no notice of them. We know why she left. Now, stop moping and get out there and run this hotel. I'll sort the office today while you show your face to everyone and act as if nothing's happened – don't let the ungrateful bitch spoil your life. Someone else will be out there for you and she might be nearer than you think.' Thomas watched his son leave the office with a heavy heart. He was thankful that Faith had left their lives because she hadn't been right since day one. Now, someone like Mary Reynolds was more to his liking, but unfortunately, she was a long way below William's station in life, so she would never do, never mind how bonny and hardworking she was.

'Miss Reynolds, have you read today's paper? I can't believe the slander that Faith Robinson is saying about young Mr Winfield. The whole staff is reading about it because the *Leeds Mercury* is delivered daily for the guests. No wonder William's been keeping out of everyone's way.' Beth passed Mary the local paper folded on the startling headline: **KING OF THE PALACE LOSES QUEEN!**

Mary looked at the report and shook her head as she read the interview given by Faith Robinson, which made William Winfield sound as if he hadn't got a penny to his name and made him out to be a manipulating ogre. She said that she realised that she was being used just in time before the wedding, set for June the twenty-third, that William loved only himself and never took account of her feelings.

'This is rubbish, poor William,' Mary said quietly. 'She really knows how to put the boot in and destroy a man's reputation. Don't you girls believe a word of this; we all know William Winfield is a good, kind person, that he is not the man she is writing about. I think that she wanted an excuse to get out of the marriage without any blame.'

'No, none of us believe it, Mary, we all know Mr Winfield too well. She looked down her nose at everyone and didn't talk to any of us, not once. I don't think she wanted to marry to work, the snotty cow,' Molly said. 'Well, we'll show her! Between us all this will become a right royal palace if that's the way she wants to play it.'

'I'll go and have a word with him, girls, tell him that he has got our support regardless of the lies written in this paper. Keep serving the customers with a smile and, if they ask anything about the gossip in the newspaper, feel free to tell them that it's a pack of lies. ' Mary felt nothing but sympathy for William and, at the same time, she was furious with Faith as she stood outside his office and waited for him to answer the door. How could she drag his name and that of the newly opened Palace through the mud, when she knew how much it meant to not just him but all that worked there? She was the lowest of the low.

William opened his office door and felt the colour rushing to his cheeks as he remembered venting his feelings in front of his bar manager. 'Mary, what can I do for you? Is everything all right at the bar? Do come in and discuss what is on your mind.'

Mary stepped into the office and felt awkward; perhaps she should not say anything, after all, it was not her place. 'Everything is fine, sir. I'm just here to say that the girls and I don't believe a word written in the paper today. We know that Miss Robinson is just being bitter and if anybody says anything we will stand by you.' She glanced at the *Leeds Mercury* on William's desk, folded on the page that the whole hotel had been reading.

'She really knows how to destroy a man, Mary. It's not enough that she's broken my heart, she's also trying to break my business. But she'll not do that, I won't let her, so don't you worry. But I really appreciate your support.' William stepped forward and put his hand on Mary's shoulder and looked into her eyes. 'Thank you, I'm glad my father and I found you.'

Mary looked at William, her heart beating fast, then she mentally shook her head. She'd felt attracted to William from the very first but she had to keep her feelings to herself; he was too far above her for her to even have such thoughts. She blushed and replied, 'I just want you to know that I'll be here for you if you need someone to talk to and you need to know the whole of the hotel's staff are behind you and, as I say, will pay no heed to what they hear or read,' she said quietly.

'If only she had been as loyal as you, Mary, I wouldn't be hurting so much.' William sighed. 'Now, the business must go on and by this time next week, I suspect, her words will be forgotten. It doesn't seem to have done much damage today anyway – we are still busy, I'm glad to say. If anything, she might have given us some free advertising – "Come and stay at the Palace with the ogre"!' William tried to smile as he opened the door for Mary to leave.

'You are no ogre, sir, you are a true gentleman and we all know the truth,' Mary whispered as she left the office and felt something in her heart that she had never felt before, in the way she felt about William Winfield.

Chapter 15

'It's not done us any harm, that load of lies told in the paper.' Roger Birbeck stood at the bar talking to Mary after all the tables had been cleared and the hotel had slowed down for the nightshift to take over.

'She could have done, she could have brought it to its knees if people hadn't realised it was just the rants of someone who hadn't got her way.' Mary leaned on the bar and looked at Roger, who had made her and the bar his regular stopping place before retiring for the night.

'Beware the wrath of a thwarted woman.' Roger sipped at his usual tot of whisky and grinned.

'She wasn't thwarted, though; she just didn't realise what was expected of her if she was to be part of the Palace. I never liked her anyway – she thought she was better than any of us,' Mary added curtly.

'Oh, you women! Once the claws are out, they are out. I'm sometimes glad that I'm a single man,' Roger said and then smiled at Mary, the woman who had taken his fancy for the first time in many a year.

'Only sometimes, Roger? You surprise me,' Mary laughed and joked with her companion.

'Aye, well sometimes you think you could do with someone to share your time with. Just someone to natter to and share your problems, a bit like we're doing now,' Roger said and then thought for a minute. 'I notice on our staff rota that you and I have the same day off, tomorrow. How about I take you out for lunch, to thank you for the kindness you show me, giving me your time and these?' Roger waggled his glass in front of her. 'Because you needn't give me either.'

'Oh, no, really, there's no need. I only treat you as I do everyone else, there's no need to thank me.' Mary was taken aback; she had never thought of Roger inviting her out for a meal.

'I insist. You were the one who pulled me up when I first came and made me realise that it wasn't about giving orders like in the army, but compromising with my fellow workmates. Now, I will not take no for an answer! You know Leeds better than me, so where is the best place to eat?' Roger looked at the doubt on Mary's face. 'It's just lunch, nothing more, I assure you.'

'Well, I was planning to see my friends at Whitelock's tomorrow. Days off are so few and far between and I plan to make the most of my time.' She hesitated and then smiled. 'However, why don't we have lunch there and then you can leave me there to catch up with Nancy and my other friends? I'm sure your spare time is precious too.'

'Whitelock's? Isn't that where you used to work and I've heard you mention how good the food is?' Roger watched as Mary nodded her head. 'Then that is indeed where we will go; and it will be my privilege to pay, so don't concern yourself with that – and no strings attached.' Roger bent over and patted Mary's hand gently. He hoped that this would be not the only lunch he would share with her; more and more he'd thought of late that it was time that he settled down and found a wife, someone to look after him to share his life.

'If you are sure, that would be wonderful. It would be such a nice surprise for Nancy to see me and for me to have a meal there; I could only dream about it while I worked there. It will raise an eyebrow or two, me and you dining there, and it will give them plenty to talk about,' Mary said and smiled.

'Then we'll do it. Meet me at twelve prompt in the lobby and we'll walk out together and then enjoy lunch and let them talk!' Roger swigged the rest of his whisky back and smiled. 'Right, I'm off to my bed, it's been a long day.'

'Goodnight, Roger, I just want to have a final look behind the bar, there are one or two jobs that I have yet to do.' Mary made the excuse because lately she had found it a little embarrassing always walking up to her room with Roger. She had noticed the sniggers of the younger night staff, who seemed to be putting two and two together and getting six as they watched them climbing the stairs together. Mary watched as Roger made his way to his bed; perhaps she should not have accepted his offer of lunch because she really didn't want to encourage him. Although she now realised he was a kind man, he was not attractive to her in any way. Well, she would go and have lunch with him but make it plain that was all it was.

'You're working late, Mary, is everything all right?' William Winfield wandered into the empty, dimly lit bar and noticed Mary placing an empty glass on the shelf beneath the bar and then leant on the bar and looked around her, deep in thought.

'Yes, Mr Winfield, I'm perfectly fine. I'm just clearing the last glass away.' Mary looked at her employer; she always found herself feeling flustered when he caught her by surprise on his walks around the hotel. 'May I ask how you are? Are you recovering from your upset? If I'm not being too presumptuous.'

'Oh, Mary …' William pulled one of the high-backed stools up to the bar and sat down on it. 'I'm surviving, but I don't think I will ever be the same man.' William looked bashfully at Mary; he felt he should not find talking to one of his staff so easy, but she was so good at listening – and she was also very attractive, he suddenly thought as he looked at her in the dim light. 'I can't thank you enough for being there for me after Faith left; I'm afraid I was in a bit of a mess.' He smiled now and looked at Mary. 'Can you pour me a gin with a splash of tonic, please? I just feel I could drink one before I retire. I would also appreciate your company, if you would care to join me? And I promise not to moan and complain about my lot. After all, how can I complain? I have more than some men will ever have in their lifetime – it's just that, at this moment, I have no one to share it with me. Someone, I'm sure, will see me as a good bet – but at least she's put any gold-diggers off my scent with her slander, so I should thank her for that.' He laughed and took his glass of gin and tonic from Mary.

'I'm sure you'll have no problem finding someone who is perfect for you.' Mary's heart fluttered as William's hand touched hers as she passed him his drink. She longed to say, 'I'm here, I'll share your life with you, please look at me and sweep me off my feet.' She had kept her thoughts to herself for so long, since the day she had looked at the plans for the Palace outside the library. Now William was with her and they were alone and he was talking to her as a friend – Roger Birbeck could never make her feel like she did, talking to William.

'Are you not having a drink yourself, Mary? It's on the house.' William took a sip of his long cool drink and looked at her.

'I don't drink, sir. I'm afraid drink played a large part in my early childhood and I saw and heard what it does to families, so I've never touched the stuff.'

'Now that's a novelty – the best bar manageress in Leeds and she really doesn't drink! How ironic is that? I thought you were just saying that in your original interview so as to secure the job.' William shook his head. 'Was it your father who drank? How somebody could drink before putting food on the table I can't understand.'

'No, sir. I never knew my father; it was my mother who had a love of gin towards the end of her life. I believe she drank it only to shut the real world out because her life was falling apart.' Mary dropped her head, feeling ashamed of her upbringing.

'The poor woman! It must have been hard, bringing a child up on her own. Society is all too fast to judge.' William looked at the glass of gin he was drinking. 'And it would be all too easy to lose yourself in drink, although, unfortunately, the worries of the world do not disappear that easily, I know that – so don't worry, this is just the one for tonight.'

'I'll serve you for long as you want, sir, everyone needs a release sometimes and I'm not here to judge,' Mary said and smiled sympathetically.

'How do you always know what to say until it comes to my name? Please, Mary, will you drop the sir? I'm William when we are by ourselves. You have seen me at my worst and at my best and you have not said a word to anyone about my struggles. Now that is the sign of a friend, not an employee, and I'd like you to think of me as such.' He swigged the last bit of his drink and stood up. 'Remember, from now on it's William! Right, I'll leave you in peace. Goodnight, Mary.' He waved his hand and walked out of the bar, leaving Mary wondering if it had been the drink talking or if William Winfield really did regard her as a friend. How much she hoped that it was the latter!

*

'Miss Reynolds.' Roger Birbeck held his arm out for Mary to link into as she smiled and walked towards him in the busy lobby of the Palace.

'Good morning, Mr Birbeck, it's a lovely day for luncheon together.' Mary returned the smile and put her arm in his. Walking through the lobby and into the bar she noticed the girls looking at them as they made for the street entrance onto the Headrow. Holding her head up high, she smiled again and turned to wink at them all and then watched their faces as Roger pulled the door open for her as she held onto her newly bought hat, decorated with feathers, that had caught her eye in the hatters across the street from the hotel. The three girls behind the bar, giggled and nudged one another; Mary, their boss, was walking out with the hotel manager – now *that* was a tasty bit of gossip. She must see something in Roger Birbeck that no one else saw, because he wasn't that blessed with looks or an affable manner, but perhaps their work had brought them together. The girls went quiet and got on with the jobs as William Winfield entered the bar.

'Did I just see Miss Reynolds arm in arm with Mr Birbeck?' William asked with some concern in his voice.

'Yes, sir, they looked as if they were walking out together. Didn't Miss Reynolds look beautiful? I'd say that was a new hat that she was wearing especially for the occasion,' Molly replied, wondering why William was so put out by the sight.

'Well, I don't like my staff to fraternise with one another so publicly; I'll have to speak to them once they return,'

William said sternly, frowning, while in the Headrow, Mary kept her arm linked in Roger's.

'Well, this is most pleasant,' she said as they walked down down the street to where Whitelock's sat in the corner of a yard thronged with customers waiting to be seated for lunch. Mary and Roger joined the queue.

'It is indeed pleasant, Mary, I'm so glad that you accepted my invitation to lunch, it makes this old man very happy,' Roger said. He was very blessed to have such a beauty on his arm, he thought, looking at Mary in all her finery, but he sighed at the length of the queue for lunch. 'Do they always make people wait to be seated? Do you not think that it's bad management?'

'Now, Roger, you are not at work now! Plus, it isn't bad management: people like the personal touch and it makes folk think, when they see people queuing outside, that the food and drink must be good. Which it is, as you will soon find out.'

Mary and Roger stepped a few places nearer the doorway.

'I think I'd do it differently, but if it works, it works,' Roger said and watched as the next four people in front of them were taken in and the waiter came out and looked at them.

'Bloody hell, Mary, I didn't recognise you with that posh hat on your head! And look at your dress, you look a right toff!' Jake grinned as he looked at the woman who had helped both him and Nancy in life. 'And who is this fine gentleman on your arm? Have you got yourself a suitor?'

Jake opened the door and ushered Mary and Roger to a table as she replied.

'You mind your language, Jake Ingram, and no, Mr Birbeck is *not* my suitor, we are just good friends.' Mary looked around her and noticed the table next to the bar and placed back in a quiet corner was available. 'Can we have the table over in the corner, Jake? Then we are seated out of the way of everyone's gaze. I recognise half the people who are dining here and I used to serve most of them and I don't want to have to talk to them when I'm having lunch myself.'

'You tell me that you two are not courting yet you need the most discreet table in the restaurant? I've heard that one before!' Jake showed them to the table and Roger looked at him in disbelief at the familiarity between a lowly waiter and the woman who had charge of the Palace bar. 'Hey, Nancy, look who I'm serving here!' Jake yelled the full length of the bar to gain Nancy's attention. 'It's Mary and she's with a fella!'

The whole room turned and looked at the couple.

Nancy scowled and walked up to the end of the bar where Mary and Roger sat. 'Well, I think the whole world knows that you're here now, lass, thanks to big gob! It's good to see you. How are you keeping? Very well, it looks, by the way you are dressed. Now, who's this, then, and is it serious?' Nancy looked Roger up and down as he sat at the table next to Mary. She didn't think much of what she saw – he looked stuffy, full of self-importance and older than Mary.

'I am Roger Birbeck; Miss Reynolds and I work together at the Palace and we are friends only,' Roger replied before Mary had the chance to say anything, and then he hid behind the menu that Jake had given him.

'Yes, Roger and I work together, Nancy, we've just come for lunch as a treat and then Roger is going to leave me so that we can talk while you work if you have the time, although you look as busy as ever.' Mary looked at the people and waiters lined up at the bar, waiting to be served.

'Yes, I'll try and make the time, but I can't promise. Now, Jake looks as if he wants to take your order if you're ready.' Nancy looked down the busy bar; she'd no time now to talk to her old friend – besides, she looked that much grander in her swanky outfit and she had not shown her face to any of them since she'd left. But she did miss her friendship, especially now that her home life was once more in turmoil.

'I'll have the braised beef, Mary, what are you having?' Roger looked across at the woman he was so proud to be with and waited for her reply.

'I don't know, I think I'll have the plaice, it always looked so nice and fresh when it was being prepared in the kitchen.' Mary had no idea how Roger Birbeck was affording this meal but she was going to enjoy every mouthful. She looked up at Jake. 'Say hello from me to Mrs Trotter and the rest of the kitchen staff.'

'I will, and I'm sure they will be glad to hear that you are dining with us.' Jake smiled and took the order into the kitchen with Mary watching him and hoping that someone would come out of the kitchen and say hello to her; after all, she had worked as a team with them.

'Are you all right?' Roger looked at Mary as she forked her food around her plate, looking a bit down in the mouth as she gazed around her.

'Yes, I just thought that I'd be made more welcome by my friends here, especially Nancy,' Mary said quietly and she ate another mouthful of her lunch.

'She's busy – and perhaps they think you have moved on, which you have. Just think of your position now compared to working here. Your very dress speaks of your rising in the world and they are probably jealous,' Roger said and then sat back as he cleared his plate clean. 'The food was excellent, so enjoy your meal and then join me on a walk around the arcades. Forget them, you have new friends at the Palace and I'm sure Nancy doesn't mean to appear rude, she's just doing her job.' Roger reached for Mary's hand but she ignored it and carried on with her meal.

'I think I'll go back to my room after I've finished my lunch. I could do with a little time to myself and it will be nice just to sit and perhaps read a book, which in itself is a luxury these days.' Mary continued eating until she had cleared her plate and then she sat back and looked around her at the busy Whitelock's. 'I learned a lot when I worked here; I enjoyed it and thought it was the centre of my world. However, you're right, I've moved on, but I'm no snob: fine clothes do not change you and I'm still me. If folk see me in a different light it's because they don't know or care about anybody else's life other than their own and see only what they want to see. Sometimes in life you have to move on and perhaps be a little selfish, grab that something that you wish for more than anything in life. My mother discovered what she wanted in life just as she found out she was dying and I'm not going to do the same as her, which is why I wasn't going to waste my time serving behind a bar with no further prospects.'

'I know, Mary, and I admire you for your determination. Now, don't you get upset. Are we having dessert or a tea or do you want to leave?' Roger asked quietly.

'I think I'd prefer to leave and return to my room. Thank you for the lunch, it was delicious; however, next time we will eat somewhere else. I think perhaps Nancy and the staff thought I was rubbing their noses in it, dressed like I am and with you on my arm.' Mary looked across at Roger.

'So there may be a next time?' Roger smiled as he stood up, ready to pay his bill.

'Yes, if you are willing to ask me?' Mary smiled.

'That goes without saying, my dear,' Roger said as he paid Jake and left a handsome tip. 'Birds of a feather flock together and we will make our own little flock.'

Mary sat down in her chair looking out of her bedroom window down onto the busy street of the Headrow. It was thronged with traders and shoppers going about their business, involved in their own lives and making the best of their lot. She'd been in no mood to walk among them on the arm of Roger. He was a gentleman and he would make a good secure partner for life, but she had no feelings for him. He was, as Nancy has quickly pointed out, too old and, being a bachelor and having been in the army for so long, too set in his ways. She would keep him as a friend but not give him too much encouragement. She didn't need a man in her life anyway – she was independent. Besides, the only man she could have any feelings for was way above her station in life and would never have feelings for her, no matter how kind his words had been of late. William Winfield was the man of her dreams and that was where he would always stay, no matter what she did or said.

Chapter 16

Mary and Roger stood in front of William Winfield in his office. Both were bemused as to why they had been summoned to appear in front of him.

William looked at his members of staff and knew that neither of them had a clue why they were there.

'I've asked you to come and see me as I noticed that you have become friendly of late and I noticed you parading your friendship as you walked the length of the hotel, arm in arm. I'm afraid I find this unacceptable; it doesn't set a good example to the rest of the staff. I will not have you fraternising with one another under this roof, although what you do in your own time, out of sight of me and the staff, is your own business.' He glared at the pair of them, hoping that they would accept his decree without any argument.

'I'm sorry, sir, it won't happen again,' Roger, used to taking orders from the hierarchy and knowing that he had to obey William, said quickly. 'We just had lunch together, that's all, sir, nothing more.'

'But we weren't working for you on that day – it was our day off,' Mary said. 'And all we did was link arms and, as Roger said, have lunch together. There's nothing wrong in that, surely?'

'That I find it unacceptable is what you should worry about, Miss Reynolds. Never mind if it was on your day off or when it was, I don't want to see it happening again, else I will have to review either your or Mr Birbeck's position at the Palace.' William looked sternly at Mary, hoping that she would not push him further.

'Very well, if that's what you wish. However, I can't see any harm in it. We are just friends and you should be glad that we work well together.' Mary looked at Roger for his support but found none. Well, Roger needed to keep his position for a man of his age would struggle to find work.

'It is right, Mary … Miss Reynolds; leave it be. Mr Winfield is correct, we should not have acted so free with our friendship; it does not set a good example to the others. I apologise, Mr Winfield, it will not happen again.'

'Then we will leave it at that and I will accept your apologies, Mr Birbeck. Now, if you'll forgive me, I've work to turn my hand to, as I'm sure you both have.' William sat back in his chair and picked up some correspondence from his desk as Roger and Mary left, only to have Mary change her mind as Roger left her and re-enter his office and stand in front of him.

'I think you are completely out of order, Mr Winfield. My private life is nothing to do with you,' Mary found herself saying sharply. It wasn't that she was fond of Roger but she would not be told what to do in her own time. The Palace nearly owned her, body and soul, as it was and on her one day off she would do as she wished. The feelings that she had experienced for the dashing William had suddenly vanished. Perhaps Faith Robinson had been right: that his love of his gin palace was his one and only love and came before anything else. She stood and looked at him with fire in her eyes and watched as he raised his head and looked at her.

'I'm sorry you find my wishes are not to your liking but I'm saying them for a good reason, believe me.' William looked with sympathy at her; not only did he find her attractive and had felt a pang of jealousy after seeing her walking out on Roger Birbeck's arm, but he also found himself wanting to protect her – and Roger was someone he thought she could do with keeping clear of. 'Please, Mary, it's William and don't think badly of me, it's for your own good.'

'Perhaps for the good of the Palace, like everything seems to be in your life!' Mary said and instantly regretted her words as William's eyes gave his sadness away. She didn't want to fall out with this man she really did like and respect, but at the same time, she had to stand her ground.

'Mary, you've got me wrong. I think there is something you need to know about Roger Birbeck, then you might realise why I am against you walking out together.' William looked at Mary; she looked even bonnier when she had a fight coursing through her veins. 'He came to us through a family friend, someone that we owed a favour to. He couldn't get work after leaving the army and the reason for that was his army record. When he was serving there was, without going into details, a lot of misdemeanours against native women. He is not a good man, Mary. Yes, he's good at his job, but I would not trust him with any of my female staff.' William looked at her face. 'Especially with you ... I would not want his hands anywhere near you.'

Mary blushed and realised that she should have known there was a reason for William to take such a stance on her relationship with Roger.

'I see. I didn't realise and I apologise for my harsh words. I know that he's quite direct in his attitude, but I never thought of him like that. Perhaps it was fighting with the army that made him do the things he did. It affects people, doesn't it?' Mary didn't want to think badly of Roger, but she remembered the first day when he had sat at the kitchen table and nearly demanded his own way and got quite irate about it. Perhaps now he was just keeping her happy for a purpose. 'I'll keep him at arm's length from now on, although I'll be civilised so that he doesn't know that we have had this conversation.'

'Thank you. You take care, Mary. I'll be coming down to the bar shortly because I have two new drinks that I was introduced to by my father's American friends and they should work well at the Palace.' He shook his head. 'I'm also feeling somewhat lost, personally ...' William sighed.

'I should rise above it. Looking back, I don't think I did love Faith and our marriage would only have led to unhappiness for both of us.'

'I'm sorry, William, but I'm sure true love will show her face to you. There will be someone who will love you for who you are – a good man.' Mary looked at William, her heart wanting to tell him how she felt, but she knew she must keep her thoughts to herself. 'I'll get back to my work now and I'll be on my guard against Roger – I will also keep a discreet eye on my girls, just in case he tries to attach himself to one of them.'

'I'd be grateful if you don't mention what we've discussed, but yes, just watch them, for they are all good girls. As you are, Mary, and I am grateful for your support.'

William watched as she left his office; he found her so attractive and had felt so much jealousy as she had smiled and joked with Roger Birbeck. Perhaps he should do something about his feelings and to hell with what folk thought . . .

A few weeks later, Mary and the girls stood back and admired the bar. They had climbed ladders in their long skirts, laughing and giggling as they draped Union Jacks and banners all along the bar and had flags hanging over each wall lamp in celebration of the birth of the Prince of Wales's grandson earlier in the day.

'Everyone's looking forward to the celebrations tomorrow. My mam is going to take baby Archie to watch the soldiers who are to march through the city. He's got a set of toy soldiers for when he gets older that I bought on the market,' Beth said as she stood with her hands on her hips. 'I'd have liked to have taken him myself but work comes first.'

'Think of the money, Beth. Besides, the streets will be crowded. Everyone and his uncle will be out there waving their flags to show their support for the Queen's soldiers – who will one day be this new baby's. Nearly every street in Leeds is going to be out. It doesn't take much for folk to have an excuse for a drink and have a knees-up,' Molly said as she rolled up the last piece of bunting and passed it to Mary.

'Well, we're ready for it. We've got a singer coming in to sing along with Leonard to boost the atmosphere and the kitchen is supplying us here in the bar with various delicacies for our drinkers to enjoy at no cost. And Mr Winfield says we can all wave and cheer out at the door when the battalions go past – that is, if you can get through the door for other folk.' Mary glanced back at the bar. 'Can you remember what I showed you on how to mix those new American cocktails, the Pisco Punch and the Ramos Gin Fizz that Mr Winfield's so keen on? I can't see them catching on in Leeds, but we are ready if anybody asks for them.'

'He kept looking at you, Mary, did you not notice? I think he's sweet on you.' Shona grinned and looked at the other girls, who were smirking at her words.

'That's enough of that. Mr Winfield is in no way sweet on me. I am his manager and that's all.' Mary could feel herself blush. She only hoped that her enjoyment at being close to William had not shown as he mixed the drink and poured it out with a gleam in his eye. He'd then insisted that she try a small sip of the Ramos Gin Fizz and watched her close her eyes and take a sip, smiled at her when she'd opened them again and wrinkled up her nose at the taste. 'The drink, I suppose, was all right, and it made me realise that I might have an occasional one because just one drink doesn't mean I'll drink the bottle dry and I'm beginning to realise that I can't run a bar without knowing what I'm selling behind it.'

'We need ice, don't forget the ice, it makes all the cocktails a little special,' Molly reminded Mary.

'I'll catch the ice seller and his cart early tomorrow morning and will take it down to the cellar to keep it as cool as we can. That'll be just another thing we'll have to think about with these fancy drinks.' Mary sighed, she couldn't see any sense in wasting good money on a piece of ice in a drink. Because ice was a real luxury, shipped in from Norway across the North Sea in huge blocks to stop it from melting and then stored in deep ice cellars until it was distributed by the ice sellers that came around early each morning before the sun rose and started to melt it. 'I know cocktails are popular in London, but I doubt they'll catch on here in Leeds; I wish William would change his mind,' Mary said without thinking.

'Ooohh! William, is it?' Shona teased.

'You just mind your own business and concentrate on your job,' Mary said as she found her cheeks colour, especially seeing William Winfield walking into the bar.

In William's hand was the latest edition of the *Leeds Intelligencer*, which he put down on the bar top in front of the three girls and Mary and looked at their faces as they wondered if he had come to show them more slander told by Faith Robinson.

'Look, all the details of what is to happen tomorrow.' William looked around him at the flags and bunting to celebrate the birth of a future king.

Mary picked up the paper and read where and when the soldiers would be parading. She knew her father had been a soldier, a sergeant in the regular army and well respected within his garrison. However, he might have been respected by his fellow soldiers, but he'd been no gentleman according to what Nell had told her, giving Mary a dislike of anything to do with the military – and if they all acted like her father, she could see no reason to stand on the streets and wave flags at them. She sighed.

William frowned. 'Today should have been my wedding day, you know …'

Mary looked at him with sympathy. 'Never mind, it was perhaps for the best. Try and forget what could have been and look to the future, Mr Winfield.'

'Yes, you're right, we would never have been happy together so I'll do my best to celebrate – and tomorrow will give everyone a boost.' He looked at Mary and urged her to walk with him back out of the bar. 'Are you and the girls all right? Have you sorted out what you are to do tomorrow?'

'Yes, we have all in hand, thank you,' Mary said and stopped just short of the lobby as she saw Roger Birbeck looking at them before going about his business.

'He's not giving you any problems?' William asked quietly.

'No, but I've not given him as much of my time and he's given over visiting me for a late drink of an evening as I close up the bar. I think he must be going somewhere in Leeds after he has finished his shift,' Mary said and felt slightly guilty for giving Roger the cold shoulder.

'That might account for his slack attitude to his work this last week or two. I've caught him cutting corners and the housemaids and waiters have complained about him of late. Not to my face, but I've heard them talking; they may not know it, but my ears are always open to my staff's worries,' William said and smiled.

'Are you all right? I do understand that it must be a hard day for you, thinking of what might have been.' Mary looked at him with concern.

'Mary, I know I had a narrow escape and I'm sure there is somebody out there for me – or perhaps I already know her. No, I'm sure it was for the best.' William smiled. 'So I'll put my wedding day behind me and we will celebrate tomorrow in style and I'll keep a smile on my face.'

Mary watched as William walked away. Had he already found somebody to replace the disloyal Faith? He'd said 'perhaps I already know her' and she couldn't help but feel a pang of jealousy for the woman who had obviously influenced her handsome employer as she walked back to her work at the bar.

Mary stood outside the Palace's back doors and looked about her. It was going to be a good day for the parade; the sun was starting to break through the dark clouds of the night and the birds could be heard singing above her head, not drowned out by the noise of the streets of Leeds as they would be later in the day. It was just tradesmen with their horse and carts rushing to deliver their goods and flower- and milkmaids heading for the best places to sell their wares on the corner of the market and on the large wide street of Briggate that were astir. The banners and flags fluttered in the slight breeze and rumbling up the street came the cart that she had been waiting for, the ice seller on his way to the hospital and the fishmongers of Leeds.

'Sir, can you stop, please? We are be in need of your services today. We need some ice.' Mary caught the burly man's attention and looked at the already exhausted horse on its uphill journey to the Headrow.

'Ice, here? I've never delivered here before. I hope that you have ready money, else I won't be able to leave you any unless you open an account with us at the cellars,' he said gruffly as he climbed down from his seat and walked around to the back of the cart, uncovering his load of still-frozen blocks of ice that had been unladen from a shipment from the canal and now stood glistening in the morning sunshine.

'Yes, I have indeed got the money. Can you leave me two blocks and take them down to our cellars? I don't think I could carry them myself,' Mary said, looking at the huge blocks.

'Aye, I wouldn't expect you to carry them – you'd take all day and there'd be a puddle of water before you got them out of the heat. Right, I've got these tongs to pick them up with so you show me the way and I'll bring them to you.' The ice delivery man picked up a pair of large, cast-iron tongs with spikes and grasped a huge cube of ice, grunting and groaning with the weight as he pulled it down from the wagon. 'Get a move on, lass, I don't hang about when I'm carrying this weight,' he said sharply as Mary showed him the way through the hotel's labyrinth down to the coldest cellar. Once there, he laid the block of ice on a slate slab in the cold and dampness of the candlelit cellar that had been overlooked when the new lighting had been added in the rest of the hotel.

Mary shivered as she waited in the gloom for the next block to be delivered and for her to pay the man for his trouble. The cellars were centuries old, part of the previous building and were rarely visited except for the wine waiters who supplied the restaurant. She was thankful when the second block of ice was put in place – the cellars were not a place she felt comfortable in so she was glad when she paid the delivery man and looked at the ice as he left her alone in the cellar. It was a new venture for William and she hoped that the cocktails would be a success as she made her way out of the cold and headed for her new vibrant world through the unwelcoming old pathway.

'Not so fast, Mary! I need to talk to you and sort things out.' Standing in front of her, blocking her way in the last part of the underground pathway, was Roger Birbeck.

Mary stopped in her tracks and looked up at the man she had been cold-shouldering of late, feeling a slight sense of panic. She could smell drink on his breath as he grabbed her by the shoulder; he had obviously been out drinking all night and had just returned, the worse for wear.

'I know that bastard's told you all about me. He's told you all the lies that have followed me from the army. Well, you'd better not be spreading those same lies, else it will be the worse for you.' Roger pushed her against the pathways wall, his face inches from hers. 'We were friends, I thought, but now you've turned your back on me, like every woman I've ever known.' He pinned her tightly against the wall with his body and let his hands wander over Mary's breasts. 'If that's what you believe of me, then let me show you what you've been missing, Miss Perfect Miss Reynolds, who thinks herself better than any man, running her bar and making the women under her just as arrogant as her!' Roger bent forward and forced a kiss on Mary while she tried to push him away, pounding her fists on him.

'Get off me, you bastard! I didn't want to believe it, but you are proving it to be true. Leave me alone if you want to keep your job. This is not doing you any good! Touch me any more and I'll make sure that everyone knows *exactly* what you are!' Mary yelled at him and then shouted for help, although no one would be near the cellar's entrance and no one knew she was down there.

Roger's hands ran down her body and he fondled her breasts again as he laughed and tried to lift her skirts in his drunken stupor. He lost his balance for a second and Mary grabbed her chance. She kneed him in his privates, making him catch his breath, giving her the chance to escape his grip and run like the wind along the twisting paths of the cellar then back up the steps into the staff area and headed for their dining room. Everyone stared at Mary, her clothes in disarray and her hair hanging down with tears running down her cheeks, as she burst through the door.

'Help me, please! Roger Birbeck has just assaulted me! He's down the cellar, drunk and not in control of himself,' she cried as everyone looked at her. 'Please, go and get Mr Winfield – and somebody please tackle Birbeck if he shows his face in here.' Mary sat down in one of the chairs at the table and watched as three of the strongest waiters didn't wait for Roger to appear. Instead, they went down into the cellar to find him and the head waiter went to get William Winfield from his apartment.

'Do you know, when that man first came here I knew I didn't like him, the pompous bastard! But then he won us all over for a while, only to start showing his true colours of late. Here, have a sip of brandy, that'll fetch the colour back to your cheeks,' the head chef said as he sat across from her.

Mary shook her head and lowered it, hearing a commotion and kerfuffle as Roger Birbeck was restrained and dragged into the kitchen for all to see.

'Two-faced bitch, I know your sort!' he yelled and struggled for release from his restraints.

'Take him into the office, lads, and make sure he doesn't escape. I'll send Mr Winfield to you once he's here. I don't want the brute in my kitchen and poor Mary is shaken up enough without having to look at his ugly face again.' The chef looked at the protesting manager and shook his head as he bent down on one knee to be on the same level as Mary. 'Now, how are you? I hope that Mr Winfield gets the bobbies and they lock him up.'

'I'm all right.' Mary looked up and wiped away her tears. 'It's just the shock. I don't know why he decided to follow me down and try to do what he did. At least I fought back.'

The chef patted her hand and rose again to his full height and ushered the astonished onlookers to go about their business as William Winfield rushed into the room.

'Mary, are you all right? What has he done? I've just told the desk clerk to go and get an officer to come and arrest the brute! I don't want him on my premises a minute more. I should never have been persuaded to employ him.' William pulled up a chair next to Mary and took her hands in his.

'I'm all right, just a little shaken. He'll be hurting more than me, I've no doubt, for I kicked him rather hard, just where it hurts a man the most,' she said and tried to smile.

'No more than he deserves – he'd get more than that if I had my way.' William looked at the pale-faced girl he thought a great deal of. 'I think this day is cursed. The sooner it's over the better. No wedding and now this. Mary, come with me and sit for a while in my apartment, out of harm's way. Just until Roger Birbeck is off the premises and then you must have the rest of the day off.' William helped Mary to her feet and walked with her across the dining room. 'Chef, could you send some coffee and something sweet to my room? Miss Reynolds, unsurprisingly, seems very shaken by her experience.' William took Mary's arm and walked with her up the stairs through the lobby, where two police officers were just arriving with the desk clerk. 'He's in there, my office. Please take him away and lock him up, Miss Reynolds can be found in my apartment if you need to speak to her,' William said to the officers and then concentrated on helping the shaking Mary climb the stairs.

'I should never have put you at risk of that man.' William opened the door to his apartment and led Mary to a large sofa in the middle of the room and bade her sit down. 'I could never have lived with myself if something had happened to you. I-I'm sorry but this is rather delicate, but he didn't manage to have his way with you, did he?' He looked at her with concern and worry and she shook her head.

'No, his hands just – just wandered over my top half, and when he expected more, that's when I kneed him.' Mary blushed; she felt awkward, talking so openly.

'Thank the Lord for that!' William stood up and looked out of the window and ran his fingers through his hair. 'Mary, I've been meaning to say that—' William went quiet as there was a knock on the door. 'Enter!' he shouted.

'Sir, here's the coffee and biscuits you ordered and there's a police officer here to see Miss Reynolds.' The maid placed the tray in front of Mary on the table and looked quickly at her before curtsying and leaving while the tall, thickset sergeant who had followed her in stood looking around the fanciest apartment in Leeds.

'Morning, sir, I understand you've had a bit of bother with that Mr Birbeck downstairs. Is it right that he's employed by you and it was this young lady here that he attacked?' Sergeant Andrews looked at Mary with a solemn face.

'Yes, you're right on both counts. I hope that you are to take him to the cells – I don't want him on my premises,' William said curtly.

'We will, but if we are to press charges we have to clear up the matter of the accusation that Miss Reynolds was to blame; that she had, on this occasion and on other occasions, led Mr Birbeck on. That is what he's saying, in a very loud voice, I must add.' Sergeant Andrews stood and looked sternly at Mary as she shook her head and her eyes filled with tears.

'I did not, officer! I never encouraged him to do what he did this morning. He came down to the cellar in order to threaten me into keeping my silence. Which he had no reason to do as I had not discussed anything about him since Mr Winfield had warned me about him.'

'Warned about him? What do you mean?' Sergeant Andrews said and looked sternly at Mary and William.

'I told Mary about his service record when he served in the army. I was afraid that something like this would happen when I saw them walking out together. I should have sacked him then or, better still, never have given him employment.' William shook his head. 'His details are downstairs if you wish to look at them. I just wish I had never listened to my father when he urged me to employ him as a favour to a friend.'

'I don't think there's any need to look at his details of employment with you, sir, your word is good enough for me. Now, miss, what exactly did he do to you?' Sergeant Andrews looked at Mary and saw her embarrassment. 'Sorry I have to ask.'

'He threatened me and pinned me against the wall and then his hands touched me,' Mary sobbed. 'He tried to lift my skirts and force himself on me, but I managed to stop him and run for help.'

'Really, officer, surely that's enough? Miss Reynolds should not have to give any more detail. The man is a known scoundrel and I should have known better than to have employed him. As I say, if it hadn't have been for my father's connections with his brother, I would not have looked twice at him. Miss Reynolds, here, is just the opposite: she is trustworthy, loyal – and I have never known her to lie and drink, unlike that scum you now have in your care.'

'Very well, sir. We will hold him in our cells, at least until he's sobered up. I presume that you will want to see him charged, miss?'

'I don't know … He can be such a kind man when he's sober,' Mary said hesitantly. 'However, I saw a different side to him this morning. He can't go around threatening women like that or even worse. Yes, officer, I think I will be bringing charges against him.' She sighed and then looked at William.

'Well done, he needs to be put away or at least given some treatment if it what he experienced while fighting in the army. Personally, I don't believe it for one minute, no matter what his brother told my father – I think that he's just a bad lot.' William patted Mary on her shoulder. 'But I admire your courage.'

'Right, if you'll excuse me, then, I'll see that my men have got him behind bars in the station and I'll be in touch shortly. Enjoy your coffee.' Sergeant Andrews looked at the two cups on the tray and wished that there had been one for him as he walked out of the plush apartment. These posh folk knew how to live; never had he been in such grand rooms, he thought, as he walked down the stairs and was thanked and shown through the revolving door by the doorman.

'Are you all right, Mary?' William sat next to her and watched as she wiped tears away from her eyes. 'Here, have a sip of coffee and a biscuit, something sweet to make you feel better.' He passed Mary her cup of coffee and looked kindly at her.

'Thank you, I'm all right. I just can't believe the difference in Roger Birbeck's behaviour – he was almost a monster.' Mary took a sip from her cup and tried to smile.

'After you've finished your coffee, go and take time to yourself, I don't expect you to work today. You've trained the girls in the bar well and they'll cope, no matter how busy we get today. I'll stand in as manager until I decide who I can put in Birbeck's place. I am definitely not having him back working here, regardless of my father's connections with his brother. He may be Lord Birbeck, but he will hold no sway over who I employ here.' William sighed.

'Lord Birbeck! His brother is a lord? I'd no idea,' Mary gasped.

'Roger is his illegitimate half-brother, No, you couldn't tell, could you? His brother doesn't want it spread about, but at the same time feels a sense of responsibility for him. The man needs help, not just placing somewhere out of sight for him, hopefully, to behave himself.' William looked at Mary. 'I could never have forgiven myself if he'd hurt you. I don't know if you realise it, Mary, but you do mean a great deal to me, not only as an employee but hopefully as a – a friend.' He looked shyly at her.

'Thank you, William. That means a great deal to me. I'd like to think of you as a friend. However, I think your father, and especially the rest of the staff, would not be happy if we were to make our friendship public. The owner of the Palace Hotel and a mere bar girl friends? I really should know my place.' Mary blushed.

'My mother was "a mere bar girl" when my father married her. He worked his way up in the world and never belittles the class that he came from. He will have no problem with our friendship – in fact, he always asks after you and he took a liking to you from the very first time he met you. As for the staff, they should be too busy working or dealing with their own affairs to worry about us, so I'll not be dissuaded by their glances and whispers. I know that this is perhaps not the right time to ask you this, but will you accompany me to dinner at my mother and father's next Saturday? The dinner table conversation can sometimes be very trying! And now I've no Faith on my arm, I've no one to talk to and escape with.'

'Oh, I don't know …' Mary bowed her head; she was still shaken after her earlier ordeal and now William was asking her to dinner at his parents. 'I couldn't possibly be seen with you at your home – what would people think?'

'It doesn't bother me. I'll introduce you as a friend, that's all, and I know my mother would make you welcome. But perhaps I'm pushing you into it … Go and have a rest and let me know. Perhaps I'm asking too much of you under the circumstances – although my advances can be rejected a lot more easily than those of Birbeck's.' William smiled, remembering Mary telling the officer how she had kneed Roger Birbeck to stop his assault.

'Thank you, William – I just need time to think your offer over quietly. I'll go back to my room now and have the morning to myself, but I'll work as usual this afternoon

– there sounds to be a lot of excitement out on the streets already.' Mary looked towards the window where she could hear crowds gathering down the Headrow, in readiness for the procession.

'Yes, it's busy, and the weather is being kind. Come and join me, I've got a good view of the street from this window.' William rose from his seat and waited for Mary to join him looking out. 'Look at all those people and the flags they are waving, happy that the royal succession is secured for a third generation.'

Mary stood next to William and felt her heart beating fast; she had gone from fearing for her life that morning to hoping that the time would stand still forever as she stood in the William Winfield's sumptuous apartment, with him next to her and with the love she felt for him in her heart. However, she knew that at the moment she would have to treat it as friendship only – unless he showed her different.

Chapter 17

'I told one of the waiters who always admired that creep Birbeck to shut his mouth because he just doesn't know what he's on about. I never did like that Roger – I always thought he was slimy. Besides, he only liked him because he thought he could get one over on the other waiters. Anyway, he's just as big a creep.' Shona stood with her back to the bar, spouting her thoughts to the other two bar girls.

'I'm just glad Mary seems to be all right after her ordeal. At least Mr Winfield is standing by her. Sometimes the men can gang up on us women and say that we have been leading them on and that we deserve what we get,' Beth said and shook her head.

'Nah, William Winfield would never do that with Mary – have you not seen the way he looks at her when he thinks we're not noticing? Mark my words, he has desires on her himself, if she did but know it,' Shona said, laughing.

'Now, that would be a scandal, a common bar lass marrying the owner of this place!' Shona grinned.

'Well, my mam says the Winfields came from nothing anyway, that they've worked for every penny they've made, so why shouldn't he look at someone who's just ordinary?' Beth added and then glanced up, noticing Mary talking in the lobby with the visiting crowds before walking towards them. 'Shush, she's here. She must be feeling well enough to join us. I thought that it would be a cold day in hell if she didn't show her face for the celebrations.'

The girls left off their tittle-tattle and made busy serving their stream of never-ending customers.

'We *are* busy, I see. I knew I'd be wanted. I suppose the word and the gossip has got around?' Mary looked at the girls and knew instantly that she had been the centre of their conversation that day.

'Yes, Mary. So, are you all right? Mr Winfield came to tell us and he was so concerned; we didn't expect you back at work today,' Molly said and put her hand tenderly on Mary's shoulder.

'Roger Birbeck's certainly not going to stop me from doing my job! Besides, look, we are full to the rafters with folk. I'm surprised you had time to stop and discuss me and the ogre Roger Birbeck.' Mary smiled dryly, knowing full well the chatter and gossip they would still be indulging in without her presence.

'We have, but we've also been rushed off our feet, so it is really good to have you back – as long as you're feeling up to working. We want you to know that none of us believe that you would have encouraged Roger and that we all disliked him from the moment he came to work here. Mr Winfield was very sympathetic towards you and he didn't hold back on his anger about what happened,' Molly said and looked around at Shona and Beth, who both supported her words with smiles as they served their customers.

'Yes, well, don't let him spoil our day. It's a celebration and he's not going to get the better of me. Now, how are Mr Winfield's fancy new drinks selling? Anyone tried one yet?' Mary looked behind the bar and noticed that the newly purchased ice bucket had no ice in it.

Shona, noticing her gaze, replied quickly, 'I'm sorry, but none of us wanted to go down to the cellar to get the ice. Not after what happened to you. It's dark and it's cold down there and you don't know who's lurking in the shadows.'

'Oh, don't be so silly, nothing's going to happen down there. It was just me he was after. Here, give me the bucket.' Mary took the ice bucket and looked at the girls before marching off through the lobby and the busy dining room and kitchens to the cellar. She caught her breath and halted as she looked down the stairs and remembered her ordeal. No, she had to conquer her fear; Roger Birbeck was safe and sound behind bars and there was nobody lurking down there, just as she'd said to her girls. Quickly, she went down the stairs, past the place where she was attacked, and made for the block of ice, which was just how she had left it that morning. She lifted the ice pick up from where it had been left that morning and came down hard with it, again and again, filling the bucket with shards of ice before hurriedly returning up into the light and bustle of the kitchen.

Mary smiled and nodded to herself. She had overcome her fear – Roger Birbeck would not get the better of her. However, she couldn't help but think that the story might have been different, had he attacked her with the ice pick. She should be thankful she had her life.

The noise in the bar and along the streets was deafening. The dining room of the Palace was heaving – the townsfolk of Leeds didn't need any excuse to enjoy themselves when given the chance. It was mid-afternoon and the streets were crowded with people waving Union Jacks and watching the parades; the dignitaries and the rich and famous rode proudly by in horse-driven carriages.

Mary told the girls to go and watch for a while when the main group started to go past the windows of the Palace. They needed no encouragement to grab their flags and go and wave and cheer, leaving her to hold the fort at the bar. She didn't mind, they would soon return to her, along with the drinkers who had joined them outside cheering the parade on. She herself didn't feel like cheering; the morning's happenings were weighing heavy on her mind. She couldn't help but wonder if she had led Roger Birbeck on when she had only intended friendship. Perhaps she deserved what he had done to her because she had turned her back on him of late … However, what her mind was thinking about most was the invitation from William Winfield to join him at his family home for dinner. She had decided that she couldn't possibly accept; he'd asked her out of pity, surely? What would a gentleman like him want with a girl like her? She'd dreamed about it but had never expected him ever to realise that she existed apart from running the bar.

'How're my new drinks selling?' William, seeing the bar nearly deserted, wandered in, giving a quick glance to Leonard as he played a soft, soothing melody before taking a seat and looking at the woman who had more pluck than any man serving with the Leeds Police Force.

'I'm afraid they aren't. I've tried hard since I came back to get people to try them, but they shake their heads. They do, however, enjoy having a sprinkle of ice in their plain gin and tonics. I've sold more, especially to the ladies, as they think it might have medicinal purposes as well as being an enjoyable drink. So ordering ice will be put onto my list of things to do.'

'Perhaps my ideas are a little too progressive. My American friends always fill my head with ideas but it takes the people of Leeds a little time to catch on to new ways to have their drink. These new cocktails will be popular sometime soon, I'm sure.' William smiled and then looked at Mary with concern. 'Are you feeling all right? You've got over your shock?'

'Yes, I'm feeling fine. I braved the cellar again to get some ice – I'm not going to let him win and make me scared of my own shadow.' Mary leaned on the bar and looked out at the busy street. Leonard was now playing a slow waltz.

William looked at Mary. 'The crowds will be back in shortly and it's a shame to waste an empty room and the slow waltz that Leonard seems to think we need, by the look of mischief on his face. Let's not disappoint him; come out from behind that bar, take my hand and let us have this dance together, our way to celebrate.' William smiled and looked at the surprise on Mary's face.

'Oh, no, I couldn't, everyone would talk!' Mary gasped.

'Everyone? There's nobody here apart from one or two hardened drinkers over in that corner and they're too busy playing cards to notice us. The rest are outside. So, dance with me, Mary, just once …' William held his hand out and waited for her to join him, hoping that she would take up his offer. The music, the joy of the day and just seeing her beautiful face made him feel like taking her in his arms and losing himself in the music.

'I've got two left feet – and what will the girls say if they see us?' Mary looked at the dashing William and knew she couldn't resist his offer. She loved the waltz music that Leonard was playing and he knew it – she suspected that was why he was playing it.

'Come on, take my hand.' William grinned as Mary succumbed and made her way from behind the bar. 'Leonard, play again from the start. Miss Reynolds and I are just going to celebrate my freedom.'

'Right you are, sir. And I'll play until you tell me to stop.' Leonard grinned, watching as Mary took William's hands and looked shyly at her partner. A handsomer couple he had yet to see as they stepped out in front of him, oblivious to the crowds cheering outside and the mutterings of the drinkers in the corner.

'I thought you said you couldn't dance? But here you are, looking like an angel on my arm.' William smiled at Mary and held her waist tight.

'I'm sure I don't, but my foster-mother taught me; she believed in living life to the full and taught me all that she could so that I would be accepted in any society,' Mary said quietly and dared to glance into William's eyes. He gazed at her as if they were reading her very soul.

'She taught you well. Now, have you thought about my offer of dinner at my home? I meant it, you know, and it wasn't out of sympathy ...' He held her tightly as they danced around the outer edges of the room and he waited for her reply.

'I don't know, William. I'd be out of place; your home is no place for me,' Mary whispered and held her breath as he swept her around the floor with grace and ease.

'No, it's just the place you belong. Please, Mary, please join me? My mother, I'm sure, will be as enthralled with you as I am,' William whispered in her ear.

Mary's cheeks flushed as he looked at her and she knew, in that instant, that he had the same feelings for her as she had for him. 'Then yes, I'll come – and I'll try not to let you down.'

'You will never let me down, Mary Reynolds. My father and I knew that the moment we saw you. He may be a stuffy old devil, but he's a good judge of character, most of the time. Now, one more time around the floor and then I suppose we will have to behave before the hoi polloi catch us together. Not that it is any of their concern!' William smiled and swept her round the floor as Leonard played and watched the love affair developing in front of him. Now that was a turn-up for the books – the hotel owner and the bar girl? It was history repeating itself for sure.

'You made a lovely couple. We watched you through the window, you made better watching than the procession. He's a good catch, is Mr Winfield. That Faith Robinson wanted her head seeing to,' Molly said some time later in front of the other two girls and they all smiled as Mary looked uncomfortable, knowing that they had been watched.

'It was only a dance while the bar was quiet. And it was Leonard to blame; he played my favourite waltz and Mr Winfield noticed my love of it.' Mary was quick to blame poor Leonard, who was now playing something more boisterous for the celebrating crowds.

'I think there was more to it than that!' Beth giggled, then decided to spare her boss the agony of any more questions and get the conversation back to the celebrations as she reached to serve a customer with a pint of beer and a glass of whisky and water. 'My, there were some people out there! I hope my little lad and my mother are enjoying themselves.'

'I'm sure they will be; there are street sellers and allsorts going on.' Mary turned and served a customer, thankful that the bar was beginning to get heaving because it would save her from being questioned further about her moment of heaven, waltzing in William's arms. He'd won her heart completely if he had but known it.

It was after midnight before Mary climbed the stairs to her bed. Once in her room she closed the door behind her, quickly pushed her shoes off to relieve her aching feet and undressed. The relief of being out of the restricting corset and formal clothing and into her nightdress was heavenly as, after giving herself a wash, she sat at her dressing table to brush her long dark hair ready for bed.

She unpinned the buns on either side of her head and ran her fingers through her hair before looking at herself as she brushed her hair. It was just an ordinary, plain face that she saw staring back at her, nothing special in her eyes, not special enough to keep and capture the heart of William Winfield, surely? She brushed with vigour. It had been a day and a half; when she had got up that morning, she had not expected to be the one to put Roger Birbeck behind bars and to be asked to the home of William Winfield, let alone dance cheek to cheek with him. The celebrations for the royal baby had taken second place to what had happened to her in the day, a day she would never forget.

She looked long and hard at herself and sighed. What would she wear to visit the Winfields' home? Would she be accepted by them or would eyebrows be raised? After all, she was a nobody, the lass that came from down by the canal, whose mother and foster mother were still probably remembered down there by the exploits that they'd got up to. She'd no right to expect anything of William, she thought, for she was as common as they came, although she had tried over the years to rise above it all. Anyway, time would tell. She would go along to the dinner and, if she was accepted, that would be fine but she was prepared also to accept that William's parents would have something to say about his infatuation with her. After all, if they'd disapproved of Faith Robinson, then why would Mary Reynolds be good enough for them?

Chapter 18

Mary ran down the stairs. She'd been late getting up after tossing and turning, thinking about William and Roger Birbeck. Her thoughts had run away with her as she'd lain in her bed, little things becoming all-consuming, worrying about what dress to wear and what she should say to William's mother, who seemed to still hold a large sway in his life, no matter that he was a grown man. She was half-way down the stairs when she noticed William and a police officer coming up them.

'Good morning, Miss Reynolds.' William kept it formal as he stopped on the stairs. 'I'm just showing this officer up to Roger Birbeck's room – he needs to clear it and take Birbeck his possessions. Could you, before starting work, wait for me in my office, please?' He smiled and then continued on his way, following the police officer up the stairs, leaving Mary wondering what he needed to speak to her about as she walked across the lobby and entered William's office, sitting on one of the green leather seats that matched the green baize that topped the desk that William sat at each day, which was covered with the papers he had to deal with on a daily basis. On his desk, too, was a picture of his mother and father and Mary couldn't resist picking it up and looking at the dapper couple who looked so happy on their wedding day. She looked particularly at his mother, whom she had never met. She knew that Thomas Winfield was a good man, but William's mother was an unknown quantity. She was lovely, Mary thought, petite with blonde hair and a beautiful face – no wonder his father had fallen in love with her, regardless of her position in life. She quickly placed it back down on the desk when she heard William opening the door but he noticed her putting the photograph back in its place.

'They are a handsome couple, aren't they? And they are still as happy as the day they married – you can't say that about a lot of couples. I'm glad that you agreed to meet them. My mother will make a real fuss of you and my Uncle Rob will no doubt chat you up – he's the confirmed bachelor of the family but still has an eye for the ladies even at the age of sixty-five. He's coming to dinner to view my father's latest purchase, an automobile, would you believe? A Benz Motorwagon. I never thought I'd see the day my father would forsake his horses for a piece of machinery. Well, not that it could replace his horses just yet for everyday use, but he does love new things.' William looked at the horror on Mary's face as she thought of being chatted up by Uncle Rob and taking in the news that Thomas had purchased an automobile. 'Don't worry, Rob will just josh you, he's harmless enough.'

'Your father has bought an automobile? Have you ridden in it yet? What's it like?' Mary asked excitedly.

'I've not been near it of yet but I'm sure he will be eager to demonstrate it to us and show off. So, be prepared for a ride in it. Now, my news today is a little disconcerting; as you saw, a police officer has been for Roger Birbeck's belongings and that is because his brother has intervened in the situation. Not for the best, in Roger's case – I think he would have been better standing trial and going to prison rather than what his brother has done to him.' William sat down in his chair behind his desk and looked at Mary.

'What has he done? Where's Roger? He's not been let out, has he? He'll be coming to find me!' Mary exclaimed, panicking. God knows what he'd do if he came near her.

'No, no, no, my dear, I wouldn't let him touch a hair of your head, let alone come anywhere near this place. No, I'm afraid Roger's life of freedom has come to an end; his brother has decided to inter him in the lunatic asylum at Menston. More for his own sake than Roger's. Being Lord Birbeck, he cannot have the scandal of his brother going around attacking women.' William stood up from his chair and came round to Mary.

'No! Not the asylum at Menston! I have heard that it's a terrible place. Oh, Roger doesn't deserve to be put in there. He just needs to stop drinking; I believe it brings out the devil in him when he takes too much.' Mary shook her head and leapt to her feet.

'It's a case of out of sight, out of mind and no lord that sits in Parliament wants any family scandal, so he's hushing the whole affair up. The policeman asked me if you were likely to go to the papers with your ordeal and I gave him the assurance that you would not. What good would it do? Only more heartache for everyone, so it's best forgotten about.' William put his hand on Mary's shoulder and looked into her eyes.

'No, I'd never tell the papers anything – they just make something out of nothing. I saw the damage they did when my friend's father killed the baby of the family and when your fiancée told tales when she had no cause to.' Mary bowed her head. 'Poor, poor Roger – he will never be allowed out once he's in there!'

William put his hand gently under Mary's chin and raised her face to look at his. 'That's why you are so special, Mary Reynolds, you always see the best in people, but at the same time you are nobody's fool. I'm so glad my father found you …' William bowed his head and felt Mary tremble as he gently pulled her near and placed his lips on hers, kissing her tenderly. 'I've been wanting to do that for some time but I thought that you would think I was taking advantage of you …' He put his hand on her cheek and looked at her with passion.

'I'd never think that – and I've been wanting to do that too but fought against it for the opposite reason. I thought you'd think I was a gold-digger and a common tart,' Mary whispered and looked up into William's eyes.

'You are neither, believe me. You are a true lady, my Mary, I knew that from the minute you and I sat down together looking at the plans for the Palace. You showed more interest in me and this place that day than Faith ever did. When I looked at you, I was smitten – but at that time promised to Faith . . .'

Mary slipped from his grip and looked at William. 'I'd better go – my girls will be waiting for me and we still have a little catching up to do after the busy day yesterday. Oh, William! I feel guilty feeling the way I do about you – I've never felt this way about anybody before.'

'Nor I, but Mary, there is no reason to feel guilty for this can't be wrong as it seems to make us feel happy.' William watched as Mary left his office and he smiled; every time he saw her his heart missed a beat and he'd never felt like this when he was courting Faith!

'Oh, have you something to tell us, Mary?' Shona asked cheekily when she saw Mary come into the bar, flushed and smiling, and grinned across at Leonard, who was idly playing the piano, waiting for the drinkers to arrive.

'You know I'm in charge of you lot? And yet you have no respect for me!' Mary looked crossly at her girls and the grinning piano player.

'He's so good-looking, is Mr William Winfield. I wish it had been me that he had swept off my feet – and he looked like a really good dancer last night. Did he whisper sweet nothings in your ear while he was holding you close?' Molly asked cheekily and then, giggling, went back to washing the few glasses that had been left the night before after the long day of celebration.

'He's extremely light on his feet – and, as for the rest, you'll have to be content with your own imaginations because I'm not telling you girls anything!' Mary said and made herself busy.

'Mmm, he's a really good catch, is Mr Winfield, but you also marry the job, you know – that's what Faith Robinson didn't want,' Beth said as she dried the glasses that Molly passed her.

'Well, that's no problem for our Mary – she loves this place anyway,' Molly replied.

'Will you all shut up? I *am* here, you know! We are just friends, nothing more, so now get on with your work,' Mary snapped. She would not have her private life discussed by one and all. It would all end in tears anyway, when she met his family on Saturday, which was approaching too quickly for her liking.

Thank heavens it was the Saturday that she was scheduled not to work, Mary thought as she took her clothes off in the communal bathroom at the end of the staff bedroom corridor. Most of the live-in staff were busy at work, so no one would notice her bathing and pampering herself, ready for the evening in front of her. She'd washed, styled and dried her hair the previous night – and that had caused enough comments at breakfast because she had kept her hair down and the full length of it had been seen by the staff. She sighed. The only problem with living and working in the same place was that everybody knew your business and there was no privacy. She'd seen the staff smirking and heard giggling from some maids when she had been seen discussing business with William, so her three bar girls and Leonard had obviously spread the gossip and now everyone was putting two and two together.

Mary lay full-length in the bath, making sure her hair didn't get wet, and she was frightened the damp would take the curl out of her hair so didn't lie too long after she had washed, stepping out of the bath and drying herself and dressing as quickly as she could. Usually, a bath was something she wallowed in, a real luxury after never being used to having hot water on tap. However, today her stomach was churning with anxiety and her heart pounded as she tightened her corset and pulled on the dress she had chosen to wear to her dinner with William and his family.

She left the bathroom and quickly walked along the passage to her room. There she stood in front of the full-length mirror and looked at herself. She sighed; the dress was the wrong colour – it didn't show her at her best. Nobody in their right minds would want their son to be seen with her, she thought as she sat down at her dressing table and looked at herself yet again. She closed her eyes and breathed in; this was stupid! William saw her every day and his father had seen her when she was at her worst as well as her best and the blue dress, with its high neck, was of good quality. She calmed herself down and attached a silver brooch with a lovebird flying through a horseshoe to the high neck and then added a pair of jet earrings to her ears before adding just a touch of rouge to her cheeks. There! She looked quite presentable, not bad at all for a lass who had come from nothing, she tried to tell herself as she picked up her small beaded blue bag.

And now, tongues would really wag, she thought, when she met William in the lobby as arranged and took his arm and they made their way to his horse and carriage. Their secret would truly be out and there would be even more tittle-tattling behind her back … She shook her head; she didn't care, just as long as William was being true to her and not using her, like so many men in power did with lower-class women. But he couldn't be, not William; he was a gentleman and had always acted as such …

William stood in the lobby and looked up at Mary as she walked down the stairs towards him. She looked stunning, and so beautifully dressed, just right for the first meeting with his mother.

'You look beautiful,' he said as he offered her his arm, making the staff behind the lobby's desk forget what they were doing for a brief second. 'I can't wait for my mother to meet you – and my father already knows that you are joining me. When I told him he just looked at me and gave an annoying, knowing smile,' he said ruefully and grinned.

'If I know your father, at least, accepts me as your guest, it makes me less nervous.' Mary took his arm and glanced around her, seeing that all eyes were upon them as they walked out of the main entrance of the hotel and climbed into William's personal carriage.

'Stop worrying, Mary. My mother and Uncle Rob are harmless and they will make you more than welcome. Just enjoy the evening – I'm certainly going to! I can't wait to see my father's car, I'm surprised he hasn't been to visit us and shown it off outside the hotel as of yet.' William took Mary's hand. 'Now, sit back and enjoy yourself. I'll be there to look after you, no matter what.' William squeezed her hand and leaned over and kissed her cheek.

'I'll try to. Do you not need special clothing to ride in this automobile? It may be dangerous in long skirts and I've heard they can reach up to fifteen miles an hour, that is really too fast.' Mary decided to keep her fears at bay by talking about Thomas Winfield's new purchase but found herself chattering with nerves as the carriage took them to the outskirts of Leeds and to the new upper-class housing of Roundhay, where they pulled into the drive that led up to William's house. It wasn't a stately home by any means, but it was newly built in the latest style, detached, two-storeys high, square-set with double-fronted bay windows and a pillared archway in front of the main door. She knew that it was one of the most desirable houses in the area, with well-tended gardens on either side of a beautiful green lawn – and, standing in pride of place in the drive was the machine that was Thomas's pride of joy, the automobile, shining in the summer evening's sun.

Hearing the sound of the horse's hooves, Thomas and his brother Rob came out and stood on the steps that led up to the door into the house.

'Now, what do you think of that, my lad? Isn't she fine?' Thomas smiled, not bothering to welcome Mary and his son, so besotted was he by his precious automobile.

'Aye, and William's lady friend is a bonny one too,' Rob whispered in Thomas's ear but was ignored as Thomas ran down the steps and slapped his son on the back as the horse and carriage drove away.

'So, the reprobate has brought you along for company, Mary, or could it be to show off this magnificent machine? After all, our automobile will be one of the few in the country. But you mark my words, the streets will be full of them before long, because they are marvellous machines.' Thomas went and stood next to his precious purchase and stroked it with as much care as he would a woman.

'Lord, Thomas, are you not going to introduce me to this divine creature? Or does she have to do it herself – because it seems that she has a rival in that fearful contraption by the way you two are gazing at it with such passion? Never mind, I'll introduce myself.' Rob smiled and held out his hand. 'I'm Thomas's brother, Rob, and, for my sins, uncle to this wastrel.' He turned and grinned at William who, once he had walked around the automobile, joined Mary at the foot of the steps.

'Glad to meet you, sir. I'm Mary, Mary Reynolds.' She glanced up at Rob, aware of him looking her up and down.

'Drop the sir – it's Rob to everyone I know. After all, I'm the black sheep of the family, according to my big brother here. Now, William, you have found yourself a very bonny filly in this one; she looks a lot more appealing than that mealy-mouthed Faith you were smitten with.' Rob grinned and William visibly winced at his outrageous speech.

'Mary and I are just friends – and she is my guest here tonight, so you behave yourself,' William said and grinned as he turned to her. 'You'll have to excuse my Uncle Rob, he says it as he sees it, and hence he has earned his Black Sheep title many a time.'

'Yes, take no notice, Mary,' Thomas said, shaking his head at his brother. 'Let's go and join Jill – she's been dying to meet you since William said you were joining us for dinner. I left her frowning and saying that the dress she had chosen would never do. It looked fine to me, but I know what you women are like and I've learned not to comment, no matter what my thoughts are.' Thomas took her arm and walked up the steps into the hallway, which was filled with the scent of roses from the elaborate display of them on a hall table; they had obviously been freshly cut for the occasion. 'We'll go and sit in the drawing room until Jill joins us. Dinner won't be long – I can smell good aromas coming from the kitchen and the dining room is set and ready for us – and after dinner, would you like a spin in my new baby? I'm sure you are curious about what it feels like.' Thomas smiled as he opened the door into a sumptuously furnished drawing room.

'I'd like that very much, but I must admit to feeling a little nervous about the experience.' Mary looked at Thomas and then William for reassurance.

'You've been on a train before, I take it?' Thomas quizzed.

Mary nodded her head.

'Then it is similar to that, but without the smoke and grime. You will enjoy it, believe me. Now, would you like a drink?' Thomas moved over to a walnut sideboard and lifted a decanter full of whisky and motioned to a bottle of gin.

'No, Mr Winfield, I don't drink – or should I say I prefer not to drink?' Mary turned to look at Rob as he let out a huge, roaring laugh.

'Bloody hell, William! You've got a cracker here: bonny, good figure and she doesn't drink. Get her wed, lad, before somebody else snaps her up.' Rob poured himself a whisky and looked at his brother, who scowled at him. 'Sorry, I'll keep my thoughts to myself.' He swigged a mouthful of his drink back and sat in one of the comfortable chairs positioned around the fireplace.

William raised his eyebrows as he caught Mary's eye and then went to stand next to her in support.

'Ah, there you are. I thought you must have gone into Leeds to purchase a new dress, the length of time that you've kept us waiting,' Thomas joked to his wife as she entered the drawing room.

'Oh, you are always exaggerating, Thomas.' Jill Winfield smiled at her husband and then walked over to William and kissed her son on the cheek before turning and looking at Mary. 'You must be Mary, my dear. I'm sorry that I've kept you waiting, but you know what we are like, we just want to look right when meeting someone special.' She leant forward and gently kissed Mary on her cheek. 'I must say you look absolutely beautiful – you put my efforts to shame.'

'Oh, no, no, Mrs Winfield, you look so glamorous, I-I could never compare to you.' Mary looked at the woman who was dressed in a truly beautiful dress, adorned by a single string of pearls, elegantly cut to show off, even at her age, her small waist. However, her voice told any listener where she originally came from and the strong accent of Leeds came through as she spoke.

'Are you behaving yourself, Rob? And Thomas, have you bored Mary with the talk of that monstrosity that stands out in the drive?' Jill Winfield turned again to Mary. 'Don't listen to a word either of them says – there's only one man with any sense with us tonight and that's my darling William. Today he's excelled himself by bringing you to dinner with him and I look forward to learning about you when the boys go and play with their new toy after dinner. But for now, let's see if Cook and the staff have done us proud. I believe it's guinea fowl for the main course and Cook has promised me one of her delicious strawberry trifles as we have a glut of strawberries out in the kitchen garden.' She linked her arm through her son's, leaving Thomas to take Mary's as they walked through into the dining room, where the table was set out with exquisite cut glass and the finest silver cutlery. As soon as they sat down, two waiters placed napkins on their knees and made sure they were comfortable.

'There now, isn't this lovely?' Jill said as she looked at the bowl of soup placed in front of her and looked up at her son. She knew nothing about the girl he'd brought on his arm, although Thomas had reassured her that she was no gold-digger, that she was from a working-class background and was a hard worker. All she wanted was for William to be happy; it didn't matter if the girl had no money, but if she was going to break his heart and take him for what money she could get out of him then it was her duty to know about it. She was certainly nothing like Faith Robinson, thank the Lord, she thought as she watched her eat her soup. Manners yes, good looks yes – but no money, you could tell that by the way she dressed, although she would give her credit for she had taken care of what she was wearing for their first meeting. By the end of the evening she would have found out all about her and then, if William was serious about the girl, she might just give him her blessing.

Chapter 19

'So, Mary, my son seems to have taken a shine to you.' Jill Winfield sat in a chair next to the window so that she could watch the three men admiring the automobile and taking turns to drive it.

To Mary's amazement, Jill reached forward to an onyx cigarette box and lighter and started to smoke a cigarette without giving it a second thought until she saw the shock on Mary's face.

'Are you against women smoking? I'm afraid that is something you'll have to get used to if we are to be seeing more of you. As far as I'm concerned, what's good for the goose is good for the gander.' Jill looked at Mary and inhaled a puff of smoke as she enjoyed her cigarette.

'No, I'm just not used to it. There just aren't many women I know who smoke.' Mary looked down at her feet.

'Now, if we are to see more of you, let me hear a little about you. Thomas and William say nothing but kind words about you and Rob couldn't keep his mouth closed as he looked at you across the dining table. But he's like that with every woman – he's not our black sheep for nothing.' Jill crossed her legs and sat back with her cigarette in her hand. 'Let's start with who your parents are, as I already know that you are a manager at the Palace.'

'Both my parents are dead, they died when I was very young, and I was brought up by Inspector Robert Jones until I found fit to leave. We used to live in the old weighing house, down by the canal docks.' For the first time in her life she was ashamed to mention Nell, presuming that the family would not appreciate her being brought up by an ex-prostituteNell.

Jill stubbed her cigarette out in an ashtray and looked at Mary hard. 'Didn't he marry Bonfire Nell? I'm sure he did, because he was the talk of Leeds. Everyone made a joke of it, that one day he was arresting them and the next he was bedding them. You aren't her daughter, are you?' She scanned Mary's face for any resemblance to Nell.

'No, I'm not her daughter; and no, he never got around to actually putting a ring on her finger, although he'd promised to do so. Did you know Nell? She was the one who brought me and Robert's son Toby up. She – she was a kind woman.' Mary's voice faltered, both in remembering her past life and the fact that hope of her ever returning to theWinfields' posh home was diminishing as Jill probed into her past life.

'Everybody knew Nell! She was part of Leeds, stood her ground and took no prisoners, did Nell, and nobody got the better of her. The fellas loved her when she was in her prime.

But, if you aren't Nell's and you aren't dirty Bob Jones's, whose daughter are you?' Jill looked long and hard at Mary, whose face reminded her of someone, someone she had long since forgotten about.

'As I say, my mother and father are dead, and I never knew my father. My mother was Eve Reynolds and she died when I was just four years old. She was just getting famous at the music hall and then she found she had consumption. Nell was her friend and she let my mother and I live with her when we had nowhere else to go. She saved my mother from committing suicide, I believe, when she was at her lowest ebb and had nothing and no one.' Mary held her head up high but could feel a tear trickling down her cheek. 'I'm not about to lie about my past, Mrs Winfield, I come from nothing, but I know I was loved by my mother.'

Jill closed her eyes briefly and shook her head. 'It doesn't matter that you've come from nothing, not in this house. Both Thomas and I came from nothing and have made good lives through sheer determination.' She looked at Mary and started to smile. 'Now, I remember! I should have recognised those eyes and that chin – you are the spit of your mother.'

'You knew my mother!' Mary gasped and caught her breath.

'Aye, I knew your mother; she used to live in the Black Swan Yard with Nell and I know she went there because she was carrying you and didn't want to get rid of you. She worked in the Mucky Duck for a while after the Bluebell but she was far too classy for that place. She was a good woman, Mary, too innocent for Leeds; she should have gone back to Woodlesford, stopped in the countryside and have never met your father.' Jill smiled. 'You probably know I was a barmaid – no one ever wants me to forget that, the way they all gossip about it. It was at the Bluebell, one of the roughest public houses in Leeds that we first met, on one of their dogfighting days. She was as green as the fields that she had come from and folk liked her for that, but some also took advantage of it too.'

'I'd no idea! William did say that you were a barmaid some years ago but he never said where. I can't believe you knew my mother! I can only just remember her because I was so young when she died. Nell told me everything about her; she said, as I grew older, that I was a lot like her apart from my dark hair.' Mary went quiet and thought about her past. 'Did you know my father? I've never known him and Nell would never speak of him.'

'I knew him; all the young women of Leeds knew him or of him. He was dashing and good-looking, full of wit and a good dancer. He'd come into the Bluebell, swaggering in his crimson soldier's uniform, and talk to most women, but your mother caught his eye good and proper; he wanted her and she was smitten as soon as she met him. It was a recipe for disaster because he was worldly wise and she was young and innocent, so he took advantage of her and left her carrying you,' Jill said with a hint of sadness in her voice. 'She was a good woman and I liked her – she gave her heart to the wrong man and so fell on hard times. Sergeant John Oates was his name, a right charmer, but also a right bastard. I hope you take after your mother!' She smiled, knowing already that she did, else she would not be on the arm of William.

'Nell used to say I did. Otherwise, I don't know who I take after. I didn't know my father was a soldier; he must not have been very honourable.' Mary looked at Jill and wondered if her knowing all about her would be in her favour or not. 'My mother was never like Nell, she never sold herself because she had too much pride. I think she thought that she was in heaven when she had the good luck to be found and paid for singing at the music hall, but it ended almost as soon as it started, with her having consumption.' Mary sighed.

'I went to see her, with Thomas, and I remember telling him that I once worked with her. He'll not have realised that you are her daughter so he'll be thrilled. Her voice was absolutely beautiful – I never realised that she had that blessing when she worked with me. But you must have had a rum upbringing with Nell and Robert Jones. I never thought Nell would give up the streets to live with him, she was that independent.' Jill looked at Mary and thought of the life that she must have had but still had pride and ambition.

'I think she knew that she had given her best years to the streets and that time was against her, especially when she saw friends dying of syphilis and the likes because of walking the streets. Robert Jones gave her security, as he did me, but gave her little else once she lived with him,' Mary said and looked directly at Jill, who had not taken her eyes off her.

'And was it the same for you? Was he good to you?' Jill asked.

'He was all right; his son Toby made living with him a little easier and we grew up like sister and brother, but once Nell died, I knew it was time to leave, else Robert might expect me to fill her shoes in more ways than one.' Mary blushed.

'He always was a dirty old dog – you knew you could bribe him with temptation if you needed to. I could see him taking advantage of you as soon as Nell was cold in her grave. Anyway, now my William has his eye on you and he must be serious, else he'd not be bringing you home with him. What do you think of him – or should I say his money?' Jill leant over and lit another cigarette and looked at Mary, scrutinising every movement of her face.

'Please … I'm not here because of William's money, I'm here because I'm very fond of him. He's charming and lovely and I'm so grateful for his invitation to bring me here this evening,' Mary said firmly and looked straight at Jill.

'Only fond! I've seen the way you look at one another. I think it's a little more than fond. Let's put it this way, I never saw Faith Robinson look at my lad the way you do. Or he look at her the way he looks at you. She was just after his brass, the little social climber, and I never did like her. She's got engaged again and is to marry someone from York at the end of the year – no doubt he's got money, because that's all she's interested in. So I think love is in the air, not just fondness, and he's brought you here for my approval because he's his mother's lad at the end of the day,' Jill said, smiling, and drew on her cigarette.

Mary looked across at the woman she knew held her future in her hands. 'It's true, I do love him, but I don't think he knows and I'll leave now if you don't think I'm good enough for him because I understand that you would like him to marry well.' She held the tears back. 'Not that it might ever come to that.'

'Mary, my love, William's happiness more precious to us than anything – and at this moment Thomas and I have never seen him as happy. Don't you do yourself down – we don't judge folk from where they come from, because neither of us had a penny as I said, but through love, hard work and pulling together, look what we have built together!' Jill stood up and looked around her. 'Both Thomas and William speak so highly of you and now I've met you and know exactly who you are, I'm not going to stand in the way of your romance. Your mother should have found a man like our William – she deserved so much better in her life. I wish you well, Mary; my lad will look after you, either way, because his heart is true and you can trust him if you give him yours.' She walked over and gave Mary a hug, then wiped the tears that trickled down her cheeks. 'Now, stop your crying and let's go and watch these idiots in this new contraption. Won't we look just fine with our Sunday best on sitting on top of it and driving around the grounds?'

Mary looked at Jill. 'Thank you, I'm so grateful that you are giving me a chance to love your son.'

'Mary, he'd love you no matter what I thought. Lord help you, he's a stubborn devil, you know, and he's got a mind of his own. I look forward to being a grandmother to some very stubborn grandchildren that I can absolutely ruin!' She linked her arm through Mary's and they walked out to the driveway, where the men were talking and laughing in the warm rays of the setting sun.

'Mary, quickly, we've just time to have a ride in her before the sun sets. Climb in and I'll take you for a quick spin.' William pulled on Mary's arm and urged her to climb up into the automobile's cushioned wooden seat.

Mary looked at the contraption and pulled her skirts up to climb up onto the seat next to him. 'Don't go too fast,' she begged.

'I won't, hold on!' William let off the long handbrake and shouted, 'We'll be back before long!'

As the two of them started off down the driveway, Thomas turned and said to Jill, 'Well, what did you think of her, does she make the grade?'

'I'd blinking well say she does!' Rob butted in and got a warning glance from Jill.

'She's a grand lass and it turns out I knew her mother. And you, if you did but know it, Thomas, have heard her mother singing at the music hall. Can you remember the night we went to watch the Yorkshire Linnet and I said I once worked with her? Well, that's her lass and she's a lot like her mother, so William will be happy with her and she'll fit in well, if it's serious.' Jill smiled and took Thomas's arm to walk back into the house.

'Well, I never! And she's a lot like you when I first met you. That's why I took her on at the Palace. I didn't know then that she'd catch our William's eye but I think our lad loves her, if I know the signs. So I suppose we'd better give them our blessing and hope this time it works out for him,' Thomas said as he poured himself and Rob a drink. 'And I do like her, but I worry that she is perhaps not quite good enough for our son.'

'Of course she is, Thomas, she's perfect! So I think I'll go shopping for a new hat and dress tomorrow, because once our William sets his mind on something he does it quickly and I need to be ready for the wedding.' Jill smiled again.

'Not that quickly, I hope, Mother! Let's have a white wedding at least,' Thomas said, shocked.

'That lass is virtuous – she'll have learned that from her mother, of that I'm certain. However, I think a spring wedding will be in the offing because I *know* she is the one for our son. A mother just knows these things.' Jill smiled as she sat down and waited for William and Mary's return; it would be longer than a quick ride around because time together in the shelter of darkness should be taken advantage of by any courting couple in love.

'As long as they're not looking into one another's eyes and not watching where they're going in my automobile. That's more my worry than a blasted wedding!' Thomas said as he gazed out of the window, watching for any signs of their return.

'I know what I'd be getting up to if I were him,' Rob grunted and was completely ignored by Thomas and Jill, but they were both thinking the same …

Chapter 20

The autumn leaves falling went unnoticed by William and Mary as their love grew and though winter was soon upon them, its cold winds only made their love stronger and warmer. The staff at the Palace noticed the couple touching hands when they could and William having more and more pretend staff meetings between Mary and himself. The girls behind the bar giggled and gossiped about the all-too-obvious love affair and the waiters winked at one another as the courting couple walked past them, while the doorman tipped his hat and just smiled as William and Mary stepped out onto the busy streets of Leeds. There was no doubt about it: they were made for one another and both had the look of a couple deeply in love.

'I'm going to close the hotel over Christmas and Boxing Day. I will, of course, pay the staff their wages, but I think it will be for the best. We've no rooms booked because people want to be at home with their loved ones at Christmas, and even if we keep the bar open, it will mean one or other of us will have to be on duty. Besides, we are invited to stay at my home this Christmas.' William looked across at Mary. 'My mother insists!'

'Oh, that's very kind of her. I'll look forward to that – but can you afford to close the hotel? The bar will definitely be busy, even if the rooms aren't let and we are going to be run off our feet most days in the run-up to Christmas.' Mary looked at William, trying to keep the conversation business-like as she sat across from him in the office.

'Well, that's another thing; I'd like you to join me at some events – there's the Leeds Business Ball and the Guild Ball just to mention two – and the girls should be able to manage without you if they have everything in place for them. They all seem very capable of the positions they are in, thanks to you, and it's time I showed you off to everyone.' William got up from his chair and went and stood behind Mary, running his hand along her shoulders and whispering in her ear, 'I want to show everyone what you mean to me.'

'Oh, William, I don't know … folk will talk. Can't we just keep our heads low and stay as we are?' Mary looked up at him.

'What, and let them think that I'm ashamed of our love for one another? No, we will declare ourselves a couple to the great and good. Let them talk – it'll give them something to do and will give some other poor devil a break.' William bent down and kissed her passionately on the lips. 'Besides, there is no better-looking woman in the whole of Leeds, especially after I've treated you to a new dress or two from Madame Boulevard, who will make sure you look the part. You'll be the most glamorous woman in Leeds – not that you aren't already,' he added hastily.

'Really, William, you needn't. I can pay for my own clothes. I'll go shopping on my next day off, but I must admit I've never shopped for such grand events before. I feel quite nervous.' Mary not only felt nervous, she was also worried that she was about to spend all her hard-earned savings on dresses that she might only wear for one season, but she did not want to be reliant on William's kindness.

'You will certainly not pay! Madame Boulevard will see you tomorrow and the dresses that you choose will be with you by the end of the week, ready for the Mayor's little gathering. Please let me buy the dresses for you? It's because of me that you'll be attending the events, so it's the least I can do; besides, if it's up to me, they will become regular events now that we feel the way we do about each other. I would feel lost without you by my side.' William kissed her again.

When their lips parted, Mary said quietly, 'I just can't help but think that they will all look at me with disdain because I'm only a working-class girl, a barmaid.'

'What? Like my mother, you mean? Now listen, you two are just the same, not overpowering but forceful, and you don't let anything or anybody stand in your way. So tomorrow, go and enjoy yourself with Madame Boulevard; the party season is to be enjoyed and enjoy it we will!'

*

'I'm sorry, girls, but this afternoon I'll not be at work; I'm having to go somewhere for Mr Winfield.' Mary looked sheepishly at her three girls as none of them said anything but all of them smiled knowing smiles.

'That's all right, Mary, we understand. Looking at the weather, we won't be that busy anyway – just look at that rain coming down. It's not fit for a dog out. I hope that you're not going far?' Molly quizzed.

'No, not far at all, an umbrella should keep me dry. I'll be back for the evening. By the way, has Mr Winfield told you that we are all to have Christmas Day and Boxing Day off, with pay? He's closing the hotel for two days because we have no bookings and he believes in Christmas being for the family.' Mary smiled as all three faces broke into delighted smiles.

'Oh, that is so good of him! That means I can enjoy time with my mam and my little lad,' Beth said and sighed happily.

'Yes, and I can spend some time with my dad. What are you going to be doing, Shona? Who are you going to spend it with?' Molly asked.

'I don't know, I've no plans so I'll probably be on my own unless my Prince Charming turns up out of the blue ...' Shona sighed.

'Then you come and spend Christmas with us. My dad will like that and my brother might even visit. You'll like him – he's a pain if he's your brother, but he's good-looking and he's got a good job in the wood yard. Not that I'm trying to pair you off with him!' Molly grinned.

*

With the girls happy, Mary braved the weather and walked quickly down the wet, nearly empty, streets of Leeds to where the double-fronted shop of Sharp and Wright's stood. The exterior was immaculate, one window filled with the best tailoring for men shown off in the best light and with the other window full of the latest fashions for women. With it being Christmas, it was filled with highly decorative dresses with long evening gloves and handbags to match and Mary just couldn't help but stare at some of the designs and their price tags. She would have had to work for at least two years to be able to pay for one of the dresses that took her eye and she couldn't help but feel that the divide was too wide between the working classes and the upper echelons. She put the catch down on the brass-plated door and entered the dressmakers, remembering how, the last time she'd been here, she had felt overwhelmed by the straight-talking Madame Boulevard as she closed the door behind her. The highly polished wooden floor creaked as she walked across to the desk where the shop girl stood in front of rows and rows of wooden drawers filled with undergarments, socks, handkerchiefs, and anything else that the discerning dresser required.

'Yes, can I help you?' The young girl looked up from folding a beautiful dress in tissue paper before placing it in a cardboard box to be delivered to the lucky recipient.

'Yes, please,' Mary said quietly, still feeling overwhelmed by the splendour of the clothes around her.

'It's all right, Miss Preston, I'll see to Miss Reynolds – I've been expecting her.' Madame Boulevard dismissed the young girl and turned to smile at Mary. 'Mr Winfield told me that you'd be calling in for a Christmas wardrobe and I've already chosen a collection which I think you would look absolutely beautiful in. Please follow me up to the ladies fitting rooms – I found your measurements from when you first came to us, so providing you have not altered in size, the dresses I have chosen will fit you perfectly.' Madame Boulevard smiled and walked slowly up the stairs to the fitting room that Mary had visited when she had needed her clothes for her place at the Palace.

Mary followed her, partly dreading the experience of having to be looked at and spoken to as if she was just another everyday customer who had to be dressed as cheaply and as smartly as the employer had instructed.

'May I say, Miss Reynolds, it is a pleasure to have you returning to us? Mr Winfield is a wonderful man and he is one of the best supporters of our business. Now, he's told me money is no object, so I have put out six complete outfits for you to try on and see if you feel comfortable in them. It's important for us ladies to look our best at this time of the year, our men expect it of us. Mr Winfield and you will make such a handsome couple when you are seen together at the many social events around Leeds this Christmas.' Madame Boulevard smiled at Mary and sat her in a small, velvet-covered chair while she showed her the collections that she had put together. 'Would you like a coffee or tea? My girls will get you one.'

Mary sat down and looked at Madame Boulevard and couldn't believe the change in the seamstress. It was obvious that she was being treated with more care than on her last visit because she now realised that William and Mary were courting and her confidence grew as she realised that Madame Boulevard would not want to put a foot wrong and that William's money was influencing her manners. 'I don't need a drink of any kind, thank you. I prefer just to look at the gowns you think might be in my style. Also, my size has not altered, so there is no need for you to take new measurements.' Mary looked at the tape measure around Madame Boulevard's neck and was glad that she would not have to undergo the experience of being measured from head to foot and being commented on.

'Of course. Now, Mr Winfield said you had to choose three outfits so I've asked my girl to place six for your perusal to give you a choice.' Madame Boulevard looked at the young woman whose confidence had grown since the last time she had visited and watched as she stood up and looked at the three dresses placed on mannequins in front of her and the three cheaper ones hung up on hangers, waiting for her to try them on.

Mary couldn't help but feel excited as she looked at the exquisite garments in front of her. Never had she thought that she would be choosing such expensive dresses, one of which was a copy of the dress she'd seen in the window. The long satin skirts, falling gracefully onto the dressing-room floor, would show her figure off to its best advantage, and the delicate fake roses around the neckline would show her shoulders and neck off beautifully. She let her hands feel the fineness of the purple satin.

'That one is the top of our line – it would suit you perfectly. A good choice, if I may say so.' Madame Boulevard smiled, thinking of the price.

'It *is* beautiful, but I would never feel comfortable wearing something so expensive when people are begging in the streets. No matter what I choose, I will think of myself as a hypocrite,' Mary said quietly.

'But you are to accompany Mr Winfield to some of the leading events this Christmas,' Madame Boulevard said mildly and held the fine skirts out to show them at their best.

'I know, but this would just be an extravagance and I like the blue taffeta one with the black beading, which is more me. Plus, I see there is a matching clutch bag with black beads and that sprig of fake blue roses would go just perfectly in my hair.' Mary picked up the bag and roses and smiled as she looked at them. 'I'll take this one definitely, but I'll not try it on here – I can always return it to you if I find it doesn't fit. I also like that quite plain red dress; it will go with that red ostrich feather fan and I already have a hair comb that will complete the look.' Mary looked at Madame Boulevard.

'And the third? Also, do you need shoes and gloves to complete your wardrobe?' She looked at the woman who had so far chosen the least expensive of the six.

'I don't need any shoes and as for gloves, I already have a pair, but I will take the other dress that's on the hanger; it's beautifully simple and green is my favourite colour, and I have a handbag and necklace to make it shine. I'd hate to spend William's money for the sake of it. If you could deliver them straight away to me at the Palace that would be perfect?' Mary got up and made for the stairs down to the shop floor.

'We have a perfume and jewellery counter if you care to have a look before you go!' Madame Boulevard raced after her escaping customer.

'I'm fine, thank you, and I think I have spent quite enough of William's money today. Goodbye, Madame Boulevard.' Mary held her hand out to be shaken by the limp-wristed dressmaker and noted the look of disappointment as she shook it and then closed the door behind her.

'Well,' Madame Boulevard complained to the sales lass, 'she's certainly different from Mr William's ex-floozy and I think I preferred Faith Robinson – at least she spent serious money with us. She wouldn't have hesitated to buy the most expensive dress in the shop and anything else that took her eye. This one makes do and mends by the sound of it – cheap and no breeding!'

The girl didn't reply as she started to wrap the precious clothes up, ready for delivery. Mary Reynolds had seemed perfectly well-mannered to her, and beautiful – she didn't need anything to help her shine out in the crowd and her choice of clothes was perfect for her . . .

Mary stood back and looked at the clothes that had just been delivered from Sharp and Wright, her breath catching as she studied them hanging up outside her wardrobe. The red ostrich fan was spread out on her bed end and she picked it up and looked at herself in the wardrobe mirror, flirting over the edge of it in her reflection. These clothes couldn't be hers, surely? She'd never dare wear them – her everyday dress as a manager was more than she had ever dreamed of wearing when she had first come to the Palace. Now, she had to wear them and face the great and good of Leeds. What had she done – and could she carry it off, being the perfect lady on William's arm?

It was the night of the Mayor's Ball and Mary stood outside the door of William's apartment, wearing the blue dress that had taken her eye straight away. She had taken hours combing and pilling her hair high upon her head and placing the blue roses through her dark coils. Around her neck she had placed a Whitby jet necklace that matched her earrings and when she moved, the black beads jangled gently, making everybody look twice at her as she walked past. She knocked on William's door, feeling her stomach churn with apprehension as she waited for his reaction to her.

William came to his door in his immaculate evening suit, with his hair smoothed back and smelling of cologne.

'Lord, Mary, you are beautiful!' he exclaimed as he looked at her in the doorway. 'I don't deserve you on my arm tonight ... In fact, you won't be on my arm for long – every man in the room will want to dance with you looking like that.' He opened the door wide and watched as she passed him and then stood before him. 'Am I a lucky man or what?'

'Don't tease, William, I'm still me underneath all this.' Mary stood back and looked across at the love of her life. 'I'm not overdressed, am I? I don't want to look out of place and let you down.'

'You are absolutely gorgeous! Now, take my arm and let me show you off to the world. There will be open mouths as we walk out to the event – I'm afraid our secret is well and truly out tonight.'

Mary walked down the stairs proudly with William, noticing that everyone in the lobby below them had stopped to glance at the glamorous couple coming down the stairs. She was on the arm of the man she loved and she was about to be made public to some of the wealthiest people in Leeds. How her life had changed since she'd been a scruffy urchin growing up in the yard of the Mucky Duck as the Swan had been nicknamed; her mother would be proud of her, she thought.

The Mayor's Ball was held in the grand town hall just across the road from the Palace Hotel and Mary picked her skirts up as she made her way across the busy street, catching her breath and breathing in heavily as she climbed the Portland stone steps up to the impressive building. She could hear the music playing and the buzz of people talking as William passed his invitation to the doorman.

William patted her hand and smiled reassuringly; the Mayor's Ball was a good opportunity to introduce Mary to society because, while it wasn't that large, anyone who was anyone would be there and, living just across the way as they did, they could leave whenever they felt like it if Mary, who was the most important thing in his life, felt overwhelmed.

'Champagne?' William took two glasses from the silver tray that a waiter greeted them with as soon as they entered into the grand hall.

'I don't know, I've never had it before.' Mary held the glass in her hand and sipped delicately; she had decided to end the ban on drink passing her lips. She'd decided that if she drank with care, she could perhaps submit to its pleasure without fear. 'It's just like fizzy flavoured water. I like it,' she said as she gazed around the room and took note of the men and women looking at them and openly talking about them.

'We'll not stop long; we'll show our faces, have one or two dances, and then I've got a much better idea of how to share this night together. The Mayor and his cronies aren't keen on me and my father – we are too progressive in our thinking and the town council has not forgiven us yet for our push for electricity to be supplied to the centre of Leeds,' William whispered, noticing the look on Mary's face.

'Good, because everyone is looking at us!' she whispered back.

'Come on, take my hand and let's show them how it's done!' And before Mary could protest, she was being waltzed around the dance floor, with most eyes on them as they laughed and danced.

Mary soon forgot her fears, especially after she had drunk another glass of champagne; after all, she was just as hard-working and respectable as any of the pompous people who were judging her and talking about them. All of them had got into the positions they were in by manipulating others or marrying into money: they had no need to judge her. Both she and William danced and talked to the people that they knew until William decided that he had had enough enough and he turned to whisper to Mary after a long and boring conversation with the Mayor's wife, who had kept looking Mary up and down with disdain in her eye.

It was then Mary saw somebody making a beeline towards them, her blonde hair and marvellous figure causing all the men in the room to look at her as she stood in front of the happy couple.

'William, how lovely to see you, I've missed you so much!' Faith said as she ran her finger down William's lapel, completely ignoring Mary.

'Faith, what a surprise seeing you here!' William took hold of her hand and placed it down by her side, looking at her icily.

'Dance with me? You are such a good dancer and I'm bored by my present beau – he's too busy talking about the price of corn, the boring farmer,' Faith whispered loudly to William.

'I don't think so, Faith. In fact, you'd better go back to your "boring" farmer as I'm here with Mary and have no interest in you,' William said, looking at Mary and trying to push the rather worse-for-drink Faith away from him.

'You are with her, your barmaid? Well, you *have* fallen low, William!' Faith stood back and looked at Mary. 'After his money, are you, dear? Well, he's not got that much, not enough to keep *me* happy anyway. You can have him; now I look at him again I realise I did the right thing, he's not the man I want.'

'Well, you'd better leave us then before I say what I truly think, because you are certainly no lady and will never be good enough for William.' Mary's face was calm as Faith stood still, glued to the spot, and then leaned in to whisper in her ear. 'Now clear off and leave us alone, you're not wanted here.'

'Cow! You're with a cow, William, and you'll regret it,' Faith said as she walked unsteadily away with people watching her, shocked and amused.

'I'm sorry, Mary, she's worse for drink,' William said as he held his hand out for hers.

'It's all right – I've always wanted to have a run-in with her and she never was good enough for you,' Mary said quietly, looking at William with love.

'Let's go back to the hotel and share a nightcap together in my quarters,' William said with a twinkle in his eye.

'Do you think we should? Think of the staff!' Mary looked slightly concerned but couldn't help but think that would be the perfect end to the evening. She and William had made a point of not spending time together in his rooms, knowing that it would only cause more gossip.

'Well, everybody has seen you on my arm tonight, so it goes without saying that we are more than friends. Come on, let's go. I'll order a bottle of champagne to be sent to my room if you wish another drink?'

'No, no, I've had enough; in fact, I've probably had too much judging by what I just said to Faith. Yes, let's go – I really would like us to be on our own tonight.' Mary looked up at William with love in her eyes.

Mary sneaked back into her room just as the clock was striking five in the otherwise quiet hotel; her hair hung loose down her back and her dress was crumpled. As she undid her corset and lay back on her bed she thought of the evening just past; she'd drunk champagne, danced until late – and then she and William had lain in his apartment, lost in one another's arms and making plans for the future. More than ever she knew that he loved her just as much as she did him and that the weeks ahead, filled with balls and parties, were to be relished. It didn't matter who she was or what she was, she was in love with the most wonderful man in the world. Mary yawned and stretched; for now, she would have to try and sleep just for an hour or two if her racing mind would let her. She pulled the pillow around her head and closed her eyes, her heart and her head were lost to William and always would be.

Chapter 21

'William has been showing you off to one and all.' Jill Winfield sipped her sherry and looked across at Mary as they sat around a blazing fire in the parlour of the Winfields' home at Roundhay Park. 'He's truly smitten with you, isn't he?' William's mother glanced at the pair of lovebirds sitting together on her sofa and felt the loss that only a mother felt when she knew that she was no longer the keeper of her son's heart.

Mary blushed. 'I don't know, but I certainly am with him.' She reached for William's hand and squeezed it.

'Well, I'm glad that he's happy and glad that you are staying with us this Christmas. I'm also thankful that Rob has found somebody else to annoy this year – we have had him to stay for several Christmases on the trot and it will be nice to get up and not find the whisky decanter dry every morning,' Jill said, laughing.

'Yes, Mary's not the last of the big drinkers, is she? There's us sipping sherry like it's going out of fashion and she's only drunk one glass in two hours. Are you sure you won't have another glass, Mary, before we all retire to our beds?' Thomas smiled at the lass who he knew genuinely loved his son for himself, not for what he was.

'No, thank you, Mr Winfield. William's been leading me astray on champagne at the balls we've been attending so I think tonight, on Christmas Eve, I'll just stick to this one glass. I'm so looking forward to tomorrow – I really can't thank you enough for inviting me into your home.' Mary looked at William and could see him looking at his mother in an odd way.

'Yes, and I think it's time for us to retire to our beds, Thomas. You don't want to have a hangover in the morning. You've got to give the servants their presents and make sure all is in order.' Jill nodded her head towards the hallway and staircase.

'I haven't *that* much to do. I was thinking of having another drink and discussing with William the plans for the new houses I'm going to be building down in Headingly.' Thomas stood up and made for the decanters on the sideboard.

'No, it's time we went to bed, Thomas, and left these two alone. Can't you remember when we were young?' Jill scowled at her thick-skinned husband. 'Now, Nelly showed you where your bedroom is, Mary, and I believe Cook says that we are allowed a late breakfast tomorrow with it being Christmas Day. So, we will see you at nine in the dining room.' Jill put her empty sherry glass down and walked over to take Thomas's arm before going up the stairs to bed.

'Behave yourself, my son – I don't want to hear the mice playing dominoes in the middle of the night,' Thomas said and winked before being made silent by Jill as she pulled on his arm and made him escort her to their bedroom.

William looked at Mary. 'I'm sorry, my father has all the tact of an elephant in a china shop. I dread to think what he was like when he was younger.'

'It's all right – it's better he says what he thinks and I like him for that.' Mary sighed and looked around the well-furnished parlour. 'Your home is beautiful, William; it's so warming and welcoming and the Christmas tree is absolutely lovely. It makes me feel quite heady with the smell of the pine needles and the logs burning on the fire. Never in my wildest dreams did I think that I'd be spending a Christmas like this.' She turned to William, who was looking for something behind one of the large velvet cushions that were plumped up along the back of the sofa.

'Well, I hope this is going to make your Christmas even more special.' William found what he was looking for and slowly dropped to his knees and looked up at her. 'I wanted us to be on our own when I did this, so I have an early Christmas present for you, my love. Mary Reynolds, would you do the honour of marrying me and becoming my wife?' He looked up at Mary's face as she looked down at the green shagreen box which held inside the most beautiful diamond and sapphire engagement ring.

'Oh, I couldn't! I mean, yes! I could, I mean … Oh, William, I would love to become your wife.' Mary watched as William took the ring from the box and placed it on her finger tenderly.

'It fits, so thank heavens for that, and if it is a little loose the jewellers down Victoria Arcade will alter it. I hope that you like it. I chose the stones especially for their meaning, the sapphire in the middle stands for honesty, purity and trust, while the unusual pink stones are morganite and stand for divine love and prosperity.' William leaned forward and kissed Mary and held her tight. 'I will always love you, Mary, and be faithful and be by your side until the earth stops turning.'

'Oh, William, I love you too. I'll always be yours; I'll never need anyone else and I'll try to be the perfect wife. I can't believe I'm sitting next to you, in this perfect home, with the most beautiful engagement ring that I've ever seen on my finger.' Mary looked down at the delicate gold ring with the perfect precious stones mounted on it. She shook her head and brushed a tear away from her cheek. 'I don't deserve this and I definitely don't deserve you,' she said as William kissed her and held her tight.

'Yes, you do, my love, and more besides. We will make the hotel our home for now, but once we have our children, I will find us a home just like this one. A home with a garden and staff and an automobile in the driveway. The Palace is making money now and I can safely promise you all these things and for you to know that I offer you security and a good life together.' William held Mary tight. 'Tomorrow is Christmas Day and we will tell my parents, although I think my mother already has a good idea that I am serious about our relationship.'

'I don't have anyone to tell for I've no family, my family's my girls behind the bar and they are a law unto themselves. I wish my mother and Nell and Toby were still alive, they would be so happy for us,' Mary sighed.

'We will make our own family in time.' William looked at her. 'Stay with me tonight? Ignore my father's comments, we are engaged now so there's no harm in it,' he whispered.

'You know I love you dearly, but no, I'll not stay with you tonight. My mother made a mistake like that and I have always vowed I would not lie with a man until I'm married. I do not want to be left like she was. I know we talked and kissed until the early hours after the Mayor's Ball and on other occasions since, but I will not go to bed with you until we are wed. So forgive me, William, or take back your ring.' Mary felt her heart beating fast as she hoped that her beliefs would not lose her the man she loved.

'Of course, I'll forgive you. Indeed, I respect you more for not making my lot easy. It is only right that I wait – it's just that you arouse me and I want to show you . . .' William kissed her and looked into her eyes.

'There will be time for that. I too have feelings, but I daren't fulfil them. Our time will come, once we are wed. Now, let us sit and set a date to surprise everyone with tomorrow and perhaps have another drink to celebrate – only one, mind, in my case. Else I might default on both my promises to myself! You can wait, can't you, William? You won't look at anyone else just because I will not lie with you?' Mary looked worried and thought perhaps she shouldn't be so stubborn now she had an engagement ring on her finger.

'Stop it, of course I can wait – it has to be right for both of us. Now, how about spring or early summer? The flowers will be out then and St John's is such a pretty little church and just a stone's throw from the Palace. I presume you would be happy marrying there?'

'Yes, that would be perfect and then we can celebrate at the hotel. With not having any family, the smaller the celebration the better.' She kissed William on the cheek. 'I love you, William Winfield.'

It was Christmas morning and, as they sat around the breakfast table, William had broken the news of his and Mary's engagement.

'Now, we can't better that for a present, can we, Mother?' Thomas Winfield looked at the young couple, so happily in love with one another. 'It's like history nearly repeating itself, except you are a bit better off than I was when I met your mother, William. Although I was already making brass and getting a name for myself.'

'Well, I think it's splendid news! However, I must confess, I did have an inkling that it was going to happen. Welcome to our family, Mary – I will cherish you as my daughter-in-law.' Jill walked over and hugged Mary tightly, kissing her on the cheek. 'Now, if we have all finished breakfast, I do believe Father Christmas has been kind enough to visit us last night. Although when he found the time to enter and place the presents under the tree, I don't quite know, because I heard you two talking below us until the early hours of the morning.'

'He's magical, did you not know, my dear?' Thomas said, laughing. 'I hope that he's brought me something that's useful.'

'Just be grateful for whatever he brings, for there are children with empty stockings in the backstreets of Leeds and I will always appreciate what I have. I remember when, like your mother, Mary, all I had were the clothes that I stood up in. But let's put those days behind us now and celebrate this day as it should be celebrated, as a family that will always be there for one another. Now, who's going to open the first parcel?' Jill looked down underneath the sparkling Christmas tree; she knew she would never forget this Christmas Day, the day she had lost her son – hopefully to a woman who would love him just as much as she did.

'Look at that diamond! And the pink stones are absolutely beautiful!' Molly, Shona and Beth gathered around Mary as she held out her hand and paraded her engagement ring for the girls to see.

'It must have cost a small fortune. I wish I could find somebody who loved me that much,' Molly sighed.

'You've got me – I love you. I love all of you girls,' Leonard added quickly and grinned as he joined the adoring group.

'You are a married man and you say it to all of us, so bugger off back to your piano!' Molly said quickly and glanced at Shona and Beth, hoping that nobody had cottoned on that, after an illicit date or two with him, there was perhaps a little bit of truth in Leonard's words.

'William gave it to me on Christmas Eve – I couldn't believe it when he got down on one knee in the Winfields' parlour and proposed to me,' Mary said joyfully. She breathed in and caught her breath. The last few weeks had flown past like a whirlwind and she still couldn't believe that she was to be married to a man she had thought far beyond her reach a few months ago. Visits to William's home, where she had been introduced to all manner of people, some with new money and some with old, had made her realise that she would be happy living the life that William and his family lived. She had fitted in well and, when asked, had not lied about how they had met, nor was she ashamed of herself after talking to William's mother. Jill had made it in society and so would she. So, when the odd person gave her a disdainful look, she ignored them and pitied them for their narrow-mindedness.

'So, when's the wedding set for? Are we invited?' Molly grinned cheekily at her two friends and Leonard, who had let out a long, low whistle at the sight of the ring.

'We're looking at the first Saturday in May; it should be getting warmer by then and spring weddings are always so beautiful. And the blossom will be out on the cherry trees in Saint John's churchyard, so I'll not need confetti if it's windy – and of course you will be invited!' Mary felt warm and loved as she looked at the faces of the three girls.

'We all wish you well, Mary – it couldn't happen to a nicer couple. You have always looked after us and Mr Winfield is the most caring boss I've ever known. He's a true gentleman and we truly do wish for you to both be happy.' Shona spoke on behalf of all of them as they sighed and looked at Mary, so content and full of love.

'You never know, Shona, you might not be far behind Mary. After meeting my brother at Christmas, neither of you has shut up about the other. I hear he's taking you out on Sunday afternoon,' Molly ribbed her friend.

'It's only our first outing and time will tell – but yes, I do find your brother interesting. However, the dark horse among us is Beth.' Shona looked at Beth, who tried to silence her. 'She's gone and got herself a fella, but she's keeping it quiet.'

'How do you know? You know nothing, Shona Brown!' Beth said sharply.

'She's walking out with our coalman and he told me himself when he delivered our coal for Christmas.' Shona looked at Beth. 'He wanted to know all about you because he knew we worked together.'

'Oh, the bloody gob on him! That's his problem, he never shuts up!' Beth glowered. 'But I suppose he's a good man – there's not many men would court a woman with a ready-made family.'

'Well, it seems that Cupid's arrows of love have been busy this Christmas. Your turn will come, Molly, somebody is out there for you,' Mary said quietly and put her hand on her sleeve.

'Oh, I'm not bothered about a man. I'll be an independent woman and stand on my own two feet. Men are only good for one thing – and that's if you're lucky, so my mother used to say,' Molly said, looking directly at Leonard, her cheeks flushing as she spoke.

'Molly Askew, remember that you are a lady and that sort of talk is for a common barroom, not the bar in the Palace,' Mary said curtly and then turned to Leonard. 'Leonard, I'm sure your wife will not talk about you in such a way; I'm sure Molly did not include you in her assumption of all men.'

'She can say what she wants, Miss Reynolds, it's her without a man at the end of the day. It doesn't bother me,' Leonard said and then went back to his piano. Molly's words had hurt him; he knew that she used him as much as he used her, but there was no need for what she had said. Perhaps it was time to be faithful to his wife; he could do without a woman like Molly – she knew her own mind too much.

Chapter 22

Madame Boulevard looked at Mary and tutted and strutted around her. 'How do you feel to me making it high-necked, with a large sash to be tied at the back? And the pin-tucked breast panel is all the fashion, so we must have that.' She stood back and waited for Mary to comment.

'I'd rather have a low neckline,' Mary said and regretted it as she saw the look on the dressmaker's face.

'Oh, no, a high neckline shows your virginity and keeps you looking virtuous. I presume you *are* to be wed in white?' Madame Boulevard looked at her bride-to-be and waited for her reply.

'Yes, I am, there is no doubt of that, Madame Boulevard. However, I would truly favour a lower neckline, if possible, and for the material, I really do like the white satin that you've shown me.' Mary stood her ground.

'I'm not keen on the satin; I always think it looks slightly common with the sheen that it has on it. How about the taffeta instead? And a neckline somewhere in between your wants and mine? Look, something along these lines …' Madame Boulevard quickly drew a sketch of what she thought Mary's wedding dress should be.

'A dress like this and a simple headdress would be ideal. In fact, let me show you what I've just acquired from Paris, new for the wedding season.' Madame Boulevard walked to the back of the shop and came back laden with six cardboard boxes, all of which she opened to show the contents to Mary. 'Aren't they beautiful? You'd think the flowers were real – just look at the roses and the orange blossom on that one especially. They are sculpted in silk and I don't think I've ever seen anything so gorgeous.' She picked one of the small hairpieces attached to a comb and passed it to Mary.

'Oh, they *are* gorgeous! I love the one with orange blossom – you can almost smell them. And it would go, as you say, with white taffeta. I like what you have drawn, but perhaps more shape in the bottom of the sleeves and then I'd be really happy.' Mary stood back and waited for Madame Boulevard to comment.

'We needn't make it fit over a corset, because I know that you hate wearing them. And a more natural shape would perhaps be more becoming on your wedding day, especially as your figure is one to be admired.' Madame Boulevard smiled, she quite liked this lass who knew her mind and obviously had the assets that William Winfield found attractive enough to make her his wife.

'No corset? That would be heaven! I hate being trussed up like a turkey.' Mary smiled happily.

'Right then, leave it to me. I'll make sure you are the most glamorous bride in Leeds and that your husband will not be able to take his eyes off you.' Madame Boulevard reached for her pattern book and placed the box of chosen flowers to one side. She'd make sure that the dress was one to be admired as all eyes would be on the couple as they walked out of the small church of their choice. It might not be a large wedding, but it would be spoken about in the top society news columns. A grand dress would bring more custom her way, so it had to be perfect . . .

Mary left her dressmaker's feeling carefree; she knew she was going to be made to look beautiful by Madame Boulevard – she'd never seen such fine materials and such beautiful flowers – and how lucky she was to be able to be pampered in such a way. She made her way down from the Headrow, back through the busy market streets, stopping just the once to buy three bunches of snowdrops from the flower stall. She had three ports of call before returning back to the Palace and her work. She smelt the small white perfectly formed flower with its green inner markings and held back the tears of joy and sadness as she opened the gates into the churchyard of Saint Mary's. Once inside, she made her way to the three graves that held her most loved ones, all unmarked and unknown except to Mary.

The first bunch of snowdrops she placed on her mother's grave, saying a silent prayer and whispering under her breath that she was to be married to a good man and hoped that her mother was resting in peace. The remaining two she placed on the graves of Toby and Nell, fighting back the tears as she also prayed for them and told them her news. All three should have been there to attend her wedding because they were the people she had once loved most in life, the people who had made her what she was ... Then she walked back through the churchyard and onto the well-trodden route to her old home at Riley's Court.

Riley's Court looked more squalid than ever, she thought as she made her way down under the railway arch to the first home she could call her own. The trains rattled above her head, the steam and soot drifting and settling on her clothes as she knocked on the flaking dry wood of Tess's door. The house looked deserted; indeed, the whole yard looked deserted, and she stood back and yelled Tess's name but got no response. Moving from Tess's house, she walked across to the cottage where she and Toby, and then she and Nancy, had lived. She knew Nancy and Jake would be at work at Whitelock's but she couldn't help having a quick peek at her old home. She cupped her hands around her face and looked in through the grimy windows. She shook her head and thought that Nancy had got lapse with her cleaning when she saw unwashed dinner plates and cups piled up in the earthenware sink below the window and the table cluttered with old papers and rubbish that should have been cleared away; even the fire was unlit. She walked away; what Nancy was doing not keeping all clean she didn't know – it was totally out of character. Whatever the reason, she'd soon find out as Whitelock's was her next call because she wanted to ask Nancy if she would do her the honour of being her bridesmaid.

The staff at Whitelock's had just finished serving luncheon as Mary walked into the restaurant. Nancy was busy wiping and washing glasses behind the bar with a younger girl Mary didn't recognise as she walked up to the bar and smiled at Nancy. She couldn't help but notice that Nancy looked tired and pale and that she had gone back on herself with the care of her hair.

'Afternoon, Nancy! I've waited until after lunch to catch you because I knew you'd be busy.' Mary smiled and looked at her once good friend whose face showed no sign of interest in her visit. 'I'll not keep you long. I wanted to tell you that I'm about to get married, the wedding is arranged for May the seventh.'

Nancy looked across the bar. 'Aye, I've heard that you've turned into a bit of a gold-digger and that you are to marry William Winfield. You'll be having a fancy wedding, no doubt,' she said with a sneer.

'I'm not marrying him for his money,' Mary protested. 'It's for love, Nancy. You should know me better than that.'

'Well, you'll not be wanting me anywhere near. Besides, I'll be gone by then.' Nancy made her way to the end of the bar, showing Mary her predicament. 'The baby's due in another two months and I'm off to live with my mother and family in Lincolnshire.'

Mary looked at the swollen stomach under Nancy's skirts and sighed. 'Where is Jake? Is he not standing by you?'

'That bastard! As soon as I said I was with child, he packed what little he had and left me.' Nancy sniffed. 'I tried to get rid of it, but it seems I failed for it's still growing anyway.'

'Oh, Nancy, how could you!' Mary gasped.

'Because I was desperate! You've soon forgotten what it's like to be poor and without hope,' she spat.

'That I never will – you know where I came from, Nancy. You know that when I lived in Riley's Court I had hardly a penny to my name. I've just been lucky of late – and I've worked hard for what I've got in life,' Mary said and then looked at Nancy with pity. 'Wouldn't old Tess help you look after the baby? Then at least you could keep your job.'

Nancy laughed bitterly. 'She's gone to live with George Summerfield – even she's looked after her own scraggy old neck. He's selling the houses at Riley's Court to Leeds Council and they're to be demolished and new stuff built in their place. Not fit for inhabitancy, they said when they looked around them. That's why I'm going to live with my mother.' Nancy picked up her cloth from the bar and, turning her back on Mary, went back to her work.

Mary looked around her. Whitelock's was still the same but Nancy had lost her way in the world. Perhaps it would have been a kindness not to have given her the hope of a better life for herself, she thought, as she saw the pain on the younger woman's face.

'I hope all goes well for you, Nancy. Write and tell me what your baby is when it is born and that you are both well,' Mary said as she turned to leave her old world behind. There was no reply from Nancy, just silent tears that only she knew she was crying.

'I have not one soul to ask to our wedding other than Tess,' Mary said sadly as she sat next to William on the sofa in his apartment.

'Well, I'm only asking my parents and Uncle Rob and my old friend from school, Jimmy Roberts, to be my best man. That's why I suggested Saint John's, because it is small but nearby and private. I know we have lots of acquaintances and business colleagues but this time I want a quiet personal wedding with no fuss. The last wedding was far too public. It is better for the pair of us.'

'I haven't even got a bridesmaid or someone to give me away!' Mary sighed and, thinking of Nancy, started to cry and tell William about her friend's predicament.

'She'll never pick herself up if she's got low and desperate.' William looked at Mary thoughtfully; he knew that Nancy meant a lot to her even though she felt let down by her and if she had not been with child, she would have asked her to be her bridesmaid. 'Why don't you go back to her and ask her would she like to work here? She could see to the laundry and clean the silver, even after the baby is born; I'm always wanting staff for those two jobs. And she could have accommodation here if the baby is a good one. I'd hate for you to see her slip back on herself.'

'Oh, William, you are so kind! It would put my mind at rest and Nancy will be so grateful – I know that she'll not want to go and live with her mother. I'll tell her tomorrow and I'm sure she'll accept.' Mary hugged William and then sat back down. 'I've still no bridesmaid, though.'

'Bridesmaids are no problem. The girls behind the bar would love to help you out in that department. As for someone to walk you down the aisle, Rob would be beside himself with glee if you asked him. He keeps saying that you should be marrying him, not me.' William smiled. 'The only thing that matters is that *we* are there and that we love one another. What does it matter who else is there?'

'I know … Oh, William, I love you more than I can ever tell you in words. And you're right, I'll ask the girls to be my bridesmaids. Would you mind if you paid for their dresses? I know they won't be able to afford them, especially Beth – she never has any money because of raising her little boy – and Rob would be the ideal person to give me away because I like him so much.' Mary snuggled into William's side and looked around her; soon this would be her home instead of the lonely room that she was in at the moment. Here, she had a bathroom of her own, two bedrooms and a large living area that overlooked the Headrow. It was a perfect place to live, albeit perhaps a little too near for their work, as Faith Robinson had screamed at William. However, that did not bother Mary one bit. It was warm and modern and she'd be with William. She would be content to live there for the rest of her life, didn't even want to think about moving to the new house her father-in-law had promised them once they'd been built.

'What are you thinking about, my darling?' William kissed Mary on her brow.

'Nothing, except how lucky I am. Compared to my mother and Nell, I have had a charmed life, a life I don't really deserve.' She looked up into William's eyes and kissed him.

'You deserve it all – and our wedding day will be the icing on the cake. I know there are only a few of us at the actual wedding but I have instructed the chef to prepare a banquet big enough to feed all our staff and any guests who are staying here that day. The bar and the lobby area are to be opened up for that purpose and I've hired outside waiters so that everyone can enjoy our day, even the cleaners. So, we will be celebrating with those that matter the most to us, my darling.' William smiled at the look on Mary's face.

'William, that will cost you a fortune, you can't do that!' She sat up and looked at him, shocked.

'I can and I have. And yes, tell Madame Boulevard to make your three girls dresses – that is, if they agree to our wishes. The cost of those is not what I'll be worrying about.' William kissed Mary. 'It'll be whether Chef manages his kitchen without losing his temper on our big day. I've told him to prepare as much in advance as he can so that he too can join in our celebrations.' William laughed. 'Now, everything is in hand, so stop worrying.'

It was the day of the wedding and Molly and Shona looked at one another in their finery. 'It's such a pity Beth didn't wish to become a bridesmaid, but I'm so glad that she will be at the church with her little boy, Archie. And she's going to sit on the bride's side of the church so that it doesn't look so empty. She'll be the next to get wed, of that I'm sure.' Molly looked at Shona and herself in the mirror and grinned. They had been allowed to change in one of the main bedrooms before meeting Mary on her wedding day. She had been given the run of William's apartment to prepare with her own maid, while William had stayed with his parents overnight.

'I think she was wrong when she said she was too old to be a bridesmaid – she doesn't look much older than us. And I love these dresses, although Madame Boulevard was such a tyrant when fitting them. We didn't have much say in what we wanted, did we?' Shona admired herself in the plain cotton dress which had been made charmingly special by the addition of lace around the sleeves and neckline and a bow of ribbon around the waist. 'At least it's a style we can wear after the wedding if we take the ribbon away – and this pale blue suits us both.'

'I bet the bride looks fabulous! William Winfield will have made sure of that. I think she's the luckiest woman in the whole of Leeds. She's going to own all of this with

William, and she can have whatever she wants – she's come a long way from the backstreets of Leeds, hasn't she?' Shona sighed.

'Well, I wouldn't mind just one night of passion with William Winfield. The rest you can keep.' Molly nudged Shona and laughed.

'Behave yourself! It's their wedding day. Come on, time to see the bride – I can hear the church bells at Saint John's starting to chime. Let's go and see what Mary looks like.' Shona urged Molly on as they made their way down to the second-floor apartment which all the staff at the Palace admired. 'I bet she's beautiful – Madame Boulevard will have made sure of that,' Shona whispered as they knocked and waited to be let into the bride's sanctum.

Mary's maid opened the door, revealing Mary standing alone in the middle of the room. Both girls caught their breath at the sight of the glamorous vision that stood in front of them.

'Oh, Mary, you're like a fashion model straight from the pages of *Harper's Bazaar*! You are absolutely beautiful!' Molly walked towards Mary and smiled at her manageress, who was more of a friend than her boss. 'You've no corset on, yet you have the perfect figure and the material of your dress shines and catches the light and makes you look magnificent. Madame Boulevard has excelled herself!'

'I love the flowers in your hair and the sash around your tiny, tiny waist. You are the perfect bride,' Shona said, looking in awe at Mary.

'I don't know … do you not think it's a little over the top? I'm not used to all this frivolity. A simpler dress might have been better, do you not think?' Mary turned and looked at herself in the full-length mirror and hardly recognised her reflection. Her hair was immaculate, piled up at the back of her head, the flowered comb resting on it. Her waist was tiny and the full-length skirt flowed to the ground while the pintucked bodice showed off her bust but very discreetly. 'I just hope William likes it.'

'If he doesn't, then there's something wrong with the man,' Molly said as she sneaked a look out of the apartment's window to the streets below. 'Oh, Mary, there are photographers waiting for you and the street is full of well-wishers! Thank heavens the sun is shining else you would have got wet on your walk to Saint John's.'

'I insisted that I should walk to the church. William wanted me to have a carriage but it's only a matter of a few yards and it would have been stupid. Oh, every time the bell tolls my stomach churns! I can't believe it's my wedding day.'

'Well, we'd better get a move on, else you'll be late. I could hear people gathering in the lobby, wanting to wish you well, and Chef has been setting out his wedding banquet since before it was light. *Everyone* is looking forward to your big day!' Shona smiled.

'Oh, I need my flowers! I put them in the bathroom to keep cool. They smell so beautiful – William must have known I love lily of the valley and there's a sprinkling of forget-me-nots running through the bouquet to match your dresses. And you both look beautiful too – I really couldn't have more loyal friends.'

'Here, ma'am, I've got the flowers,' the maid said as she passed them to Mary and watched as the wedding party made their way down the wide, curving stairs into the busy lobby, which was filled with well-wishers and tables of wine glasses and plates, ready for the onset of the wedding banquet.

'Mary, wait just a minute! I wanted to catch you before you went to the church.' Nancy came rushing down the corridor, her three-day-old baby in her arms. 'I want to give you this for good luck. It was my grandma's and you and William have given me and Richard so much. I never imagined living and working here!' She pushed a silver wishbone bracelet into Mary's hand and smiled.

'Nor did I, Nancy. But here I am. Thank you, my dear friend. Now, you go back to your room and rest, because I know you didn't have an easy time with this young man.' Mary smiled at the baby in Nancy's arms and then turned to let Shona fasten the bracelet around her wrist. 'It's beautiful, but I must return it to you after the wedding, Nancy.'

'No, I want you keep it. I have everything I need – you've both seen to that, so God bless and be happy …' Nancy turned and made her way back to the room that she shared with her newborn.

Tears filled Mary's eyes; Nancy was indeed a true friend – she had given her the most valuable thing in her life bar her baby and Mary vowed that she would always be there for her and her son.

Everyone gasped as they watched Mary and her bridesmaids walk down the stairs and pass out onto the street. This was going to be the wedding of the year for Leeds and people wished Mary well while photographers angled their huge cameras for the best view, changing the glass plates quickly in a bid to get the best photograph of the new bride.

Mary's heart pounded as she reached the churchyard and walked through the iron gate to make her way along the paved path to the church's porch. The vicar who had taken them through their vows and had read the banns out for their marriage smiled and nodded to her as he summoned the organist to change the music to Mendelssohn's 'Wedding March' and there William stood in front of her, with his friend Jimmy Roberts by his side. His mother and father, both with tears in their eyes, looked up at her as Uncle Rob took her arm and she started the walk down the aisle to marry the man she had loved since the first day that she had seen him. She closed her eyes and held tight to William's hand as she said, 'I do' and nearly cried as he slipped the gold band of her wedding ring on her finger.

She was now Mrs William Winfield, for richer or poorer, in sickness or in health. Till death did them part.

Chapter 23

The Palace, Leeds, 1921

Mary looked at the photograph of her and William's wedding; it had been twenty-seven years to the day since they had married but it seemed a lifetime away. She picked up the silver-framed photograph and kissed it: every minute of the day she missed him, oh, how she missed him, sometimes wishing herself under the earth with him.

'Oh, William, I'll always love you. Why did you have to go and leave me?' Mary whispered and placed the photograph back on the table beside her. She closed her eyes and conjured William in her mind, his smile, his touch, his kisses that she missed so much. She had everything a woman could wish for except the man she loved by her side …

Life had been so good; the Palace had been profitable, so much so that William had planned to buy another hotel in Manchester. They had been blessed with a beautiful daughter they had named Eve, after Mary's mother, and a son called Toby and they had wanted for nothing. Then the war came, the war they'd said would end before Christmas and street after street of working-class Leeds' lads went off to fight for their country. The Leeds Pals, they were called, as one friend encouraged another friend to join them for excitement and for the love of their country. But the war didn't end at Christmas; instead, it went on and on and thousands of the young and innocent were slaughtered on the fields of Flanders and in the trenches that were filled with rats, feeding on the bodies of the slaughtered. She'd watched as William had read the newspaper every morning and grown more and more restless, feeling that he should do more than run a place of enjoyment and leisure for the higher classes when young men were dying on his behalf. Then the day came that she had dreaded. Even though he was of an age that he did not have to go and fight, William had gone out in Leeds and returned to tell her that he had enlisted and in a few weeks he would be joining the local lads fighting the Hun. She remembered kissing him and looking at him with both pride and heartbreak as she kissed him in his smart uniform on the busy railway station platform. Women were crying and sobbing, all fearing that it would be the last time they would hold their loved one in their arms.

Every time the post came she had looked straight away for letters from William and, when received, she read them with fervour. Then the letters stopped and she had feared the worse. She was right to do so, for the telegraph boy brought the bad news that he'd taken to so many homes in Leeds: William had been killed when his battalion went over the top on the battlefields of the Somme. Tears filled Mary's eyes as she remembered holding the telegram and nearly fainting as she looked at the words, so cold and clinical, telling her that life would never be the same for her and her children. She could have given up then; it would have been easy just to have sold the hotel and gone to live comfortably in the countryside around Leeds, but she knew that was not what William would have wanted her to do. Instead, she had stood her ground and taken over the running of the hotel, using it for many a function to raise funds for the valiant lads fighting for King and Country and it had been the making of her – she'd been accepted by the best of society and was appointed the first woman to sit on the Leeds Board of Trade. Now Mary looked around her, sighing; she'd come a long way, that was for sure, but she would have done a lot more if William had been by her side.

'Mother, are you all right?'

Mary felt a gentle hand on her shoulder and turned to look at her nineteen-year-old daughter, who had quietly walked into the apartment at the Palace that the two of them called home. It had taken eight years of marriage for Mary to conceive and Eve was the most precious thing in her life now William was no longer with her.

'Yes, yes, I'm all right, thank you, Eve. I was just thinking of your father because it would have been our wedding anniversary today. I miss him so much . . .' Mary sighed.

Eve walked around and, squatting down in front of her mother, hugged her. 'I know you do. I have such good memories of him and I miss him too. He was a wonderful father, used to tuck me into bed every night when I was small, no matter how busy he was, and take me out for a drive in that boneshaker of a car of his after Grandad had persuaded him to buy it. He'd have loved the ones that are on the roads now.'

'Oh, Lord, he wouldn't be fit to be on the road now, he'd go so fast. I can just see him and Toby with their heads under the bonnet, thinking themselves top mechanics, when neither would have had a clue about anything!' Mary said and laughed. 'How are things going downstairs? I suppose I'd better show my face and make sure everything runs smoothly.' Mary stood up next to Eve and kissed her gently on the cheek. She was a throwback to her grandmother, with blonde hair and blue eyes, and was tall and slender, the dress she was in emphasising her height. Gone now were the restricting corsets that Mary had worn at her age – straight, drop-waist dresses were all the fashion and women were starting to have more say in their lives.

'It's really busy and the jazz band was just setting up in the bar. Molly was instructing them on what to do and making sure they behaved before telling her girls to get the bar tidy and make sure they have all they need for the busy night ahead.'

'Good for Molly – she'll not take any rubbish from anyone; she's a good manageress. Now, do I need to powder my nose or do I look respectable enough for our customers?'

Mary glanced at herself in the mirror on the wall and looked intently at her features. Time had been kind to her; her hair was still dark and shiny, her skin free of wrinkles, she didn't show any worries that might slumber within.

'Mother, you *always* look beautiful, you know you do. Come on, take my arm and we'll walk down the stairs together. I love Saturday night because it's always busy, full of people making the most of their free time and enjoying life.' Eve smiled and linked her arm through her mother's as they walked along the landing from their apartment and stood at the top of the stairs. 'Listen, the band has started. The girls behind the bar will not be able to keep their feet still nor will most of the drinkers. I love watching them doing the Texas Tommy and the Turkey Trot!'

'I remember the first time I danced with your father. It was on the day we celebrated the birth of the Prince of Wales and soldiers paraded through the city and I knew then and there he was the man for me. I'm glad women are not as restricted as I was when I was growing up, but I do worry that perhaps things have gone too far.' Mary stepped down the newly decorated stairs and through the lobby, filled with people off the street of Leeds coming to listen to the music in the bar and drink the now-popular cocktails. 'I don't know if I'll get used to this décor, Eve, it's a bit plain for me, but I was told that art deco is all the rage with its sharp lines and straightforward images. It's completely different from what I grew up with.' Mary looked around the lobby and then at Eve.

'It's a new age, Mother; after the war and the flu pandemic, everyone knows that life is for living and has to be grasped *now*. The decoration is wonderful and goes so well in the bar. We can give New York and London a real run for their money – just look at the people flooding in. They know that you are progressive and that you manage the Palace better than any man.' Eve let go of her mother's arm as people nodded their heads and politely acknowledged the owner and her daughter.

Mary smiled. 'You and Toby are a good mixture of me and your father. After my day, I needn't worry, the Palace will be in good hands.' She looked across at her son who stood proud and smart in his Palace uniform, with her close friend Nancy, both seeing to guests' needs. 'Now, let's go and treat ourselves to a cocktail. Your father will be laughing somewhere in heaven – he introduced them to the Palace long before you were born but nobody showed any interest in them then. Now it is what we sell the most, in the most outlandish mixtures.'

'I know, and I must say, I enjoy them. I also enjoy looking at Richard when he makes them in the cocktail shaker and smiles at me with a twinkle in his eye.' Eve wrinkled her nose and smiled bashfully at her mother.

'Now, that's how it begins, so be careful about what you wish for, my darling. Although I know he's a good man with a good heart and he'll get my blessing to court you. And while money isn't everything, it does help and financially, you are your own woman, I've made sure of that!'

Mary walked down her well-trodden route into the bar, and every time she walked it she thought about how she had first come to work behind the bar, new to management, and how Faith Robinson had taken an instant dislike to her. Looking back, Faith was probably right to have taken a dislike to her. After all, she had been a threat to her and William. She watched now as Eve flirted with Richard the barman, Nancy's son, Eve making all the running. She was very much the new generation, dressed like all the rest of the young women in a shimmering shift dress with a headband around her sharply-cut, bobbed hair. They thought nothing of smoking a cheroot in a long holder while they danced around the dance floor. The world was changing and women would hopefully be as strong as any man. Perhaps, Mary thought, she had lived in the best age, when men were in charge – or so they thought. William's mother, Jill, had been the making of the Winfield empire, although the men in her life would not admit as much and now she herself was running the Palace. Eve came across with a filled cocktail glass in her hand and passed it to her mother.

'Here, Mother, try this cocktail. It's called The Last Word – equal parts gin, maraschino, Chartreuse and lime juice – and Richard says it's selling really fast.' Eve watched as her mother sipped the new drink slowly.

'Yes, I can see why!' Mary smiled. 'So cheers, and here's to us, the Gin Palace Girls, long may we rule!'

'I'll second that!' Mary's mother-in-law, Jill, put her hand on Mary's shoulder. 'Plus, I'll try one of those, they look really good.'

'Mother, you and Father have decided to join us – I'm so glad.' Mary turned and kissed Jill and Thomas on their cheeks. They had been her rocks when she had lost the love of her life. They were the closest family in Leeds and she was glad that they had managed, at their age, to join the celebrations.

'Did you think you could keep us two old codgers away? The Palace and gin will always be in our blood.' Jill looked at her husband and smiled. She sipped the drink that Eve had quickly got for her grandmother. 'Cheers, ladies! I am the original Gin Girl, but here's remembering Eve, your mother, dear Mary, and Nell. They would be so very proud of you all and this fabulous Gin Palace. Cheers, my dears.'

Cocktail Recipes

Known at the turn of the century as American Drinks
From *Mrs Beeton's Book of Household Management*

Gin and Tonic

Imperial India had made the dinking of gin fashionable with soldiers drinking quinine in a vital fight against tropical decease. Unfortunately, quinine on its own was bitter so in order to disguise this Indian tonic water had been invented and so there was a new craze of gin and tonic gripping the country by the more fashionable especially by the wives of serving officers.

Gin Cocktail

1 measure of gin
10 drops of candy syrup
10 drops of orange bitters
A small piece of lemon peel
Crushed ice

Half fill a tumbler with small pieces of ice, pour over it the gin, add the syrup and bitters, then cover and shake well. Strain into a small glass, place the small piece of lemon peel on the top.

Gin Rickey

1 measure of gin

1 dessertspoonful of lemon or lime juice
Soda water
Ice

Place a small piece of ice at the bottom of a champagne glass, strain over it the lemon juice, add the gin, fill up with soda water, and serve.

Pineapple Julep
1 Pineapple
1 bottle of sparkling Moselle
1 gill of gin
1 gill of raspberry syrup
½ gill of Maraschino
Juice of 2 oranges
1lb of crushed ice

Slice the pineapple thinly, and then cut into eight sections. Put all the liquids into a glass jug or bowl, add the ice and pineapple and serve.

Silver Fizz
1 measure of gin
The juice of ½ a lemon
The white of one egg
1 teaspoonful of icing sugar

A pinch of carbonate of soda
Crushed ice

Fill a tumbler ¾ full of crushed ice, pour over the gin and lemon juice, then add the egg white beaten to a white froth. Shake well, then strain into another tumbler containing the icing sugar, and carbonate of soda. Serve at once.

Sloe Gin Cocktail
1 measure of sloe gin
½ measure of dry gin
10 drops of orange bitters
Lemon peel
Crushed ice

Half fill a tumbler with crushed ice, pour over the gins and bitters. Shake well and strain into a small glass and top with lemon peel before serving.

Brain Duster
½ measure of vermouth
½ measure of absinthe
¼ teaspoon of sugar
Crushed ice
¼ teaspoon of carbonate of soda

Put the vermouth, absinthe, and sugar into a glass, add a few pieces of ice and shake well. Strain into a small glass and add the carbonate of soda and serve.

Manhattan
½ measure of vermouth
½ measure of whisky
10 drops of Angostura Bitters
6 drops of Curaçao
Crushed ice
Lemon peel
Put all the ingredients except the lemon peel into a cocktail shaker and shake. Strain into a tumbler and serve with a slice of lemon.

Martini Cocktail
½ measure of dry gin
½ measure of Vermouth
6 drops of candy syrup
12 drops of orange bitters
Lemon peel
Crushed ice

Half fill a tumbler with crushed ice, pour over it all the liquids, shake well and then strain into a glass. Serve with the lemon peel as ingredients.

Yankee Invigorator
¼ of a pint of strong clear coffee
½ measure of port
½ measure of brandy
1 egg
Sugar to taste
Ice

Break and beat the egg well, add the coffee, port, and brandy and sweeten to taste. Add the ice, shake well and then serve.

In the 1920s, nobody is safe from scandal . . .

Amy Harrington leads a privileged life out in London society. Her maid, Alice Jordan, lives in the poverty-ridden East End. But when a disgraced Amy is disowned by her parents and fiancé, Alice is the only person she can turn to . . .

Forced to give up her life of luxury, Amy lodges with Alice's friendly working class family. But while Amy hatches a plan to get revenge on her former love who caused her downfall, Alice finds herself swept into the glittering society her mistress has just lost. And when Amy meets Alice's handsome older brother Tom, they can only hope that love can conquer all . . .

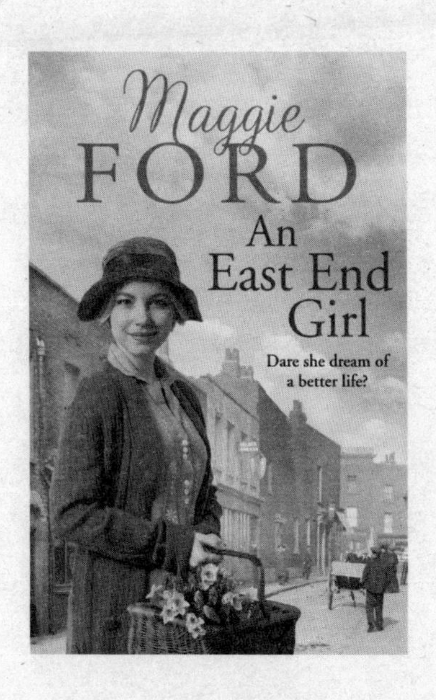

Will she ever be anything more than an East End girl?

Cissy Farmer longs to escape her life in London's Docklands where times are hard and money is tight. And when she meets the debonair Langley Makepeace, her dream seems within reach.

But the price of belonging in Langley's brittle, sophisticated world could be much higher than Cissy ever imagined. Torn between Langley and her gentle childhood sweetheart, Eddie Bennet, she is forced to gamble on her future chance of happiness, a decision that will change her life forever …

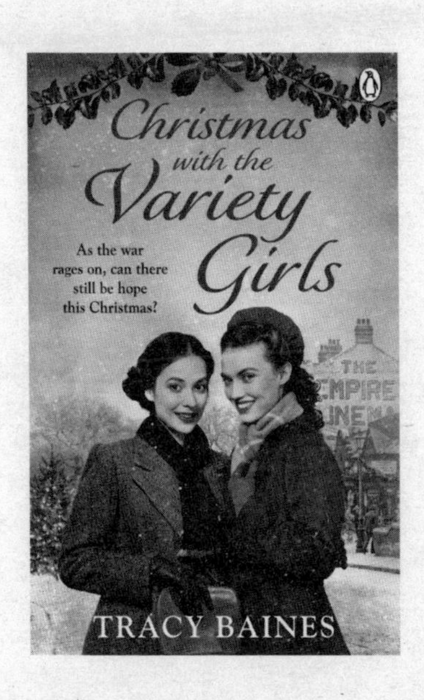

Will Christmas bring an unexpected reunion? . . .

Frances O'Leary has always dreamed of being a dancer. But after war is declared and the theatres begin to close, Frances and the variety girls must search for work elsewhere.

However, Frances is hiding a secret. As far as her best friend Jessie knows, Frances is a young aunt who adores her niece, Imogen – but what she doesn't know is that their relationship runs much deeper. Now, with the sweetheart who cruelly abandoned her returning to England, will her secret finally be revealed? . . .